NEVER
A BRIDESMAID

Visit us at www.boldstrokesbooks.com

By the Author

Stolen Kiss

Never a Bridesmaid

NEVER A BRIDESMAID

by

Spencer Greene

2024

ISBN 13: 978-1-63679-559-1

THIS TRADE PAPERBACK ORIGINAL IS PUBLISHED BY
BOLD STROKES BOOKS, INC.
P.O. BOX 249
VALLEY FALLS, NY 12185

FIRST EDITION: FEBRUARY 2024

CREDITS
EDITOR: CINDY CRESAP
PRODUCTION DESIGN: SUSAN RAMUNDO
COVER DESIGN BY INK SPIRAL DESIGN

Acknowledgments

I want to express my deepest gratitude to NP, for being the first reader, even when she'd rather be reading sci-fi. Your support has been integral.

Special thanks to Cindy Cresap, whose editing prowess fixed all my grammar and plot holes, and to Scrivener, for being the silent partner in this creative journey.

With sincere appreciation,
SG

Dedication

To NP, my most biased reader.

CHAPTER ONE

There is absolutely nothing you can say to get me to be a *bridesmaid* in Bernie's wedding."

"I am your mother, Jessica Monroe, and this is not a request." Jessica was shocked by her mom's command. The last thing she could've imagined was her picture-perfect younger sister wanting her in her wedding party. What had it been, two years since they'd done more than text?

"Mom, I hate weddings, I hate all of Bernie's friends, and really, does Bernie even want me to be a bridesmaid? I'm sure she's more concerned about her wedding pictures looking as *basic* as she is. Why would she want me ruining it?"

"I don't know if *basic* is good or bad, but I'm going to assume it's bad and ask that you stop picking on your sister." Jessica could hear the exasperation in her mom's voice. "She loves you very much and is adamant that you're in her bridal party."

Jessica rolled her eyes. She doubted very much if Bernie even knew her mom was making this phone call. Still, she sensed that she was losing footing with her mom. She didn't actually want to be mean about her sister—Jessica loved her sister, it's just that she happened to be the polar opposite of Jessica. Bernie was preppy and loved a good "Live, Laugh, Love" picture in her living room, while Jessica would rather burn that "Live, Laugh, Love" picture in effigy.

"Mom, listen. If you want me to show up for the wedding, I can do that. I'll sit on her side of the aisle. I'll even throw rice when the doves are released and she's whisked away on a horse-drawn carriage. But I am not hanging out with Bernie and the girls who tortured me in high school for more than is absolutely necessary!" Jessica was sure that would be the final clincher. Playing the high school bullying card usually got her mom to cave. Judy Monroe was a softy at the core of it. She just took a little reminding.

There was silence on the other end of the line, and Jessica wondered if the call might have been dropped.

"Hello? Mom, are you there?"

"I'm here." The prior irritation had disappeared from her mom's voice. "I know it was hard for you when you were younger and I'm sorry I wasn't always the mother you needed, especially when you were first coming out..."

Jessica could hear the emotion in her mom's voice, and she felt a pang of appreciation for her. "Mom, we've been through all of this before. You're amazing, and that was a long time ago."

"Honey, I know, but I'll never stop saying I wish I had been there in the way you needed."

Jessica couldn't help but soften at her mom's heartfelt words. Not to mention, the last thing she wanted was to go into all that.

"Not understanding what you were going through sooner is still one of my biggest regrets. But one of my other regrets"— Jessica could hear her mom's tone grow firmer—"is letting you and your sister grow so distant. When you were little, you two were so close! She worshipped you, and you were always so protective of her. I don't know why that changed."

Jessica barely remembered a time when she and her sister were close. It felt like they had always been from different planets.

"This wedding is important to your sister, and having you be a part of it is important to me. So. If you won't agree to this the easy way, we're going to have to do it the hard way."

Jessica loved her mom, and she also knew she didn't play when it came to getting what she wanted. The question was, what did her mom have on her? And could Jessica stick to her plan for self-preservation?

"You know that I'm the executor of your father's will, which means I have control over your trust."

Jessica's mouth went dry.

"I know you haven't needed that money so far, but I also know you've been planning to use it to set off on a new venture, is that correct?"

Jessica's mom knew that was correct. Jessica had been busting her ass for the last ten years as a journalist at the Daily Paper, a DC news website that was destroying her soul. She was constantly churning out puff pieces and clickbait and she was about done being used and abused by her misogynistic editor. She had shared with her mom a while back that she intended to use the trust money to open a bookstore in Dupont Circle. Her ultimate vision was for a bookstore-coffee shop-activist space, and everything was in motion for her to start the project in earnest in the next year.

Jessica's dad passed away seven years ago, and books were always something the two of them connected over. Her plan felt like a way to honor his legacy, and a way to move into a life she wanted versus a life she was surviving. Jessica's mom and dad divorced when she was fourteen, but they remained close friends and co-parents until his death. When he passed, he left a trust for Jessica and her sister that they couldn't access until they were at least twenty-five, but her mother was named as executor with a special little clause that allowed her to make the final decision about when they each had access. Jessica's mom knew all that she'd been going through at work, and she couldn't believe her mom was using that clause against her. It was basically extortion.

"Mom, no, you wouldn't."

"Jessica, I didn't want to, but this is important!"

"How is some stupid wedding important enough to upheave my whole life!" Jessica was fuming at this point.

"This isn't about a wedding. This is about your sister. This is about what your father would have wanted. He would've wanted his daughters to support each other. And I want that too. You need to support your sister in the things that matter to her, including her wedding. And if you do, I'll continue to support you in the things that matter to you."

Jessica was floored. Never before had her mom used her dad against her like this. Jessica's mom was generous and supportive, and she wouldn't do something like this carelessly. This was the nuclear option, so Jessica knew it was final. Which meant she needed to make a decision. In general, Jessica wasn't in the habit of asking for financial support from her family. She'd worked to stay financially independent since graduating college. But this trust was something that she did have plans for. She knew she needed to decide then and there what was more important to her: her bookstore and the future she envisioned for herself, or saving herself from a super-annoying couple of days playing bridesmaid?

What does a bridesmaid do anyways? It can't be more than a few days of, well, torture...

Jessica already knew what her answer was. It wasn't just the money, it was also the fact that her mom wanted this so much that she was going to these lengths. Deep down, Jessica didn't want to upset her mom. Yes, she wanted to stay a million miles away from anything having to do with weddings—not to mention all of Bernie's friends—but more than that, she wanted her mom to be okay. The last seven years had been hard on her, and Jessica's angstiness about her sister hadn't helped. The decision was made. Jessica would have to be a bridesmaid after all. She congratulated herself on her generosity.

"Okay, okay, Mom, I'll do it." Jessica heard a little exclamation of excitement on the other end of the line, and she could already feel her brattiness bubbling up. "But, Mom, this is it. No more lording the trust over me, okay? I'm doing this one excruciatingly painful thing and that's it."

"Understood!" Her mom's reply came back full of earnestness.

The gravity of Jessica's commitment started to settle in. She realized she didn't quite know what this "bridesmaid" thing was actually going to look like...

"So, what happens next? I don't have to plan anything, do I?" Already, the thought of figuring out what her obnoxiously heterosexual sister would like for pre-wedding *rituals* felt next to impossible. If she was expected to do anything like that, she was going to have to talk to her best friend, Bryce. Bryce was fluent in all things straight women. It was actually kind of weird that he was best friends with Jessica, who was nowhere near able to navigate straight girl world. If anything, he'd be a better selection for the bridal party. Maybe he could sub in somehow?

Bryce and Jessica became friends in college, where they bonded over a shared love of campy shows and Lady Gaga. They both loved each other deeply and never asked the other to be anything but who they were. It didn't hurt that they were both unapologetically gay and still lived in the same city.

"No, you don't have to plan anything," her mom said. "All of that will, of course, be handled by the maid of honor." It was honestly kind of remarkable how little Jessica knew about weddings. Of course, the maid of honor handled all the planning! Then it dawned on her who the maid of honor would be.

Oh no...

"Wait, Mom, please don't tell me...is Tanner Caldwell going to be the maid of honor?"

"Honey, of course she is! She's been your sister's best friend since the ninth grade."

Jessica thought she was upset before, but this new detail was thrusting her into nightmare territory. Of course Tanner would be the maid of honor. Jessica should have anticipated that. It wasn't like she hadn't considered that Tanner would be at the wedding, it just felt like in a big, two-hundred-person event, she could get through the whole thing without having to really see Tanner, let alone interact with her. But now, as her involvement was becoming more integral, she knew avoiding Tanner would be impossible.

Jessica tried to take a deep breath. Maybe it wouldn't be that bad—honestly, how much time could she possibly be required to spend with the bridal party?

"I thought you and Tanner were friendly. Or you were when you were younger?"

It was true, she and Tanner had been friendly when they were younger, but her mom wasn't privy to everything that happened when Jessica was coming out, by design. Some things were just too personal, especially when the person responsible was still very much in her family's life and one of her mom's favorite people.

"Not for a long time, Mom." Jessica hoped that would be enough to end that line of questioning. "Okay, so what all does this entail? I have to, what? Stand with Bernie during the ceremony? Is that it?"

Jessica's mom laughed at that. "Honey, have you never been to a wedding?"

"Not one that wasn't some pagan non-hierarchal commitment ceremony at an ayahuasca retreat."

"A what retreat?" Jessica's mom asked pointedly.

"Nothing, Mom." Another instance where she didn't need her mom knowing everything about her life. "I honestly kind of haven't."

"Well then, how do you know you don't like them?"

Jessica groaned. "Mom, trust me. I know."

Her mom was getting exasperated again. "Okay, well, I'm sure you'll have some responsibilities during the ceremony and the reception, not to mention the rehearsal dinner."

That didn't seem like too much. Most of that would be with the other two hundred guests.

"And then, of course, there's the bridesmaid luncheon and the dress fitting."

"Wait, what? Why does she need another lunch? Also, a dress fitting? I'm supposed to do what—weigh in on a stupid dress? Fawn on cue?"

"Jessica, this is all very standard."

Jessica was seething. This is one of the major reasons she hated weddings. So much compulsory heterosexual social conforming. This was going to eat her soul.

"Okay, Mom, enough! I mean, this has got to be it. I cannot commit to spending all my free time doing these ridiculous activities."

"Well, don't worry, it'll all be over in the next six months. The wedding is in March. You'll get plenty of space between the first few events."

Six months of her life, trapped in a regressive social calendar, and all with Tanner Caldwell, a person she'd hoped never to see again.

Jessica sighed. "Okay, when's the first thing?" She was already dreading the answer.

"Well, I'm not sure. You'll have to talk to your sister to get the specifics, but I believe Tanner is planning Bernie's bachelorette party in Asheville in two weeks."

"Two weeks! Bachelorette! Asheville!" Jessica couldn't decide what to be more upset about. No, actually, she did know. It was the Tanner Caldwell part. "Mom, please no. That's too soon. How about I skip this one thing and I do all the rest?"

"A deal's a deal, my love. Why don't I give you some time to process this."

Jessica was so mad she was seeing red. "Mom, I'm begging you. Not a bachelorette party. That's going to kill me."

"I love you, sweetie. Call your sister!"

The call ended. Jessica was left in a panicked daze. This call had not gone anything like she expected. She had been completely manipulated by her mother and wound up fully committed to participating in a bachelorette party in Asheville with her least favorite people in the world, organized by the actual worst person possible, Tanner Caldwell.

❖

Jessica didn't call her sister right away. She needed time to recover from her mom's indecent proposal. Instead, she tossed her phone aside, threw herself dramatically across her burgundy sheets, and prayed for the sweet relief of sleep. She was already socially exhausted from what she could only imagine would be the bachelorette party from hell.

Unfortunately, it was barely eight a.m. Her mom had a habit of calling her at the crack of dawn—and sleep did not come easily. Once it set in that she had no other options, she begrudgingly sat back up in bed, grabbed her computer, and started looking up "What do people do at a bachelorette party?" As she read through the results, she became more and more certain she wasn't going to survive Asheville. She closed her computer and collapsed back onto her bed again, newly worn out. Buried in her covers, she fell into a depression nap.

Despite the morning hour, Jessica's room was still nearly pitch-black from the blackout curtains covering the windows. Normally, her apartment was full of light, but since her mom called so early, she had yet to open the curtains. She lived on the third story of a hundred-year-old row house in Washington, DC. Each floor of the row house had been converted into apartments. Hers was a one-bedroom, and she was in love with it. It had original wood floors and crown molding, which added to her room's current vampire cave aesthetic. Her furniture was sparse and mostly from "Craigslist free" listings, but what she did have showcased a good eye for antiques.

Growing up, Jessica would have been considered a bit of an "emo kid," listening to sad rock music and hanging with her few similarly inclined friends at the mall. Now that she was in her late twenties, she'd dropped most of the loud makeup and safety pin shirts, but she still rarely wore anything but black. Her apartment, on the other hand, was full of color. The walls were covered in art, and when she did play music these days, it was significantly more upbeat. Jessica found that depressing music and decor may have been more of a childhood rebellion.

Now her emo roots had transitioned into other parts of her personality, like her fascination with the dark side of the world that she liked to focus on in her journalism. Most people wanted to be comforted by what they saw in the news, but Jessica wanted to make sure no one looked away from difficult truths. Her misogynistic editor, Tom, was less interested in what Jessica wanted to write and seemed to intentionally assign her puff pieces or just generally things that made her uncomfortable. She was currently being forced to work on a piece about a corrupt local official, but with a focus on his performative philanthropy work in the LGBTQ community. Jessica had been furious with the assignment and was totally over having so little creative control. She knew Tom was going to hate the article she was about to turn in. Which was another reason not to flake on the bachelorette party. Jessica would need the trust money if things fell through at her current job, which she knew they eventually would.

Jessica was awoken by a text message from Bryce.

Hey, I'm in your neighborhood. Want to get coffee?

It was the last day in September. Finally drawing her curtains aside, Jessica saw that the weather was beautiful, and although she'd been planning to waste her day inside writing or bingeing one of her favorite shows, she just couldn't say no. She knew this could be one of the last warm weekends for a while.

Joltz in 10?

Bryce was quick to like her message. After brushing her teeth, Jessica pulled on a pair of distressed black jeans and her black Smiths shirt. She grabbed her well-worn black motorcycle jacket at the door and darted into the stairwell. She did, however, forget to change out of her "house Crocs," so the look didn't quite come off as cool as she would have wished. She only realized at the door to the building, but decided it wasn't worth going back up two flights of stairs to change them. She wasn't really invested in this day anyway.

Joltz was a coffee shop at the end of her street that was owned by a local family. They served everything from smoothies to cappuccinos to pizza. None of it was particularly exceptional, but the place was close to her building, the service was amazing, and she loved Ahmed and Fatima, the owners.

Jessica stumbled up to the counter to put in her order. She assumed Bryce was already out back on the patio because he was most likely already at Joltz when he texted. He was a morning person and would have been working on his screenplay all morning, like he did almost every Saturday. Jessica greeted Ahmed and Fatima, who were both behind the counter, and ordered her first cappuccino of the day.

"Long night?" Fatima asked in that half-scolding way only a mother could pull off without offending. Jessica wished a long night was why she was so harried. It was impossible to explain an emotional hangover from a fifteen-minute phone call with her mom.

"Something like that," she said instead.

"You go out too much," Fatima continued. "You're too young to be looking this tired in the morning."

"Is that the secret to why you look so young, Mrs. Bahar?"

Fatima tutted playfully. She loved when Jessica was the tiniest bit flirty. "I don't know about that. I've been feeling old lately with these kids and their tactics." She pointed over to her two children, both around middle school age. They were sitting at a table together as they often were, with the pretense of doing homework. As usual, they had their phones out and presented the same lifeless, zoned out face.

"I hear that," Jessica replied. Twenty-seven was still young, but the distance between herself and those kids was becoming an endless chasm.

"Bryce is out back," Ahmed said. "I'll bring your coffee out when it's ready."

"Thank you, Mr. Bahar!" Jessica grabbed a banana from the counter and paid. When she got to the small, intimate patio, she saw Bryce typing furiously on his computer. He had the most hilarious determination face that Jessica just loved. He wore an outrageous pair of heart-shaped sunglasses and an honest-to-God pink boa. It was hard to imagine what kind of weather necessitated a boa, but as usual, he was pulling it off. As Jessica came closer, Bryce gave her a brief once-over and then looked up at her with contempt.

"Why on earth are you wearing Crocs, Jessica?" Jessica knew she wasn't going to get away with the shoe choice, but not even a hello?

"It was an accident!" she protested. "I left in a hurry."

"Jess, there is no level of emergency that would make this okay. Please leave and come back when you're dressed." Bryce went back to typing as if he hadn't just dismissed her. Jessica ignored him and sat down with a loud harumph. She was used to this kind of treatment. Being friends with a "fashionista" like Bryce came with its licks. Of course, he wouldn't really make her go home. Not from Joltz, anyway. Now if they were instead at some "scene" space, she would absolutely not get through the door. Especially since Bryce was usually the one deciding who came through the door. He was the organizer of most queer activities in the city, and especially in their shared neighborhood, Columbia Heights.

Ahmed placed the coffee in front of Jessica with a subtle glance toward her shoes. He didn't have a visible reaction, but that was only because he was kind, unlike Bryce. Jessica gave him a smile in thanks before he turned back toward the kitchen.

"So," Bryce began. "Why are you looking so awful? Late night?"

"What's with everyone? You're the second person in five minutes to comment on my appearance and my social life. Is this an intervention?"

"Aren't we testy this morning?" Bryce said, closing his laptop with interest. "What's up your butt today?"

"I did, yes, have a somewhat late night, but that's not why I'm tired."

Bryce looked her up and down. "Lisa, the bartender at QBar," he stated with determination.

Jessica's mouth fell open. "How do you do that? You weren't even there!"

Bryce took a sip of what had to be his seventeenth coffee, considering how long he'd been awake.

"I'm just clairvoyant like that. Come on, you know I'm witchy," he said as he raised his thick, manicured eyebrows. "Plus, I follow her on Instagram and she had a video of you singing 'Constant Craving' at two a.m. from the jukebox. Why do you always choose the saddest songs?"

Jessica was hit with embarrassment. She wasn't on social media so she never knew when her actions were being broadcasted or who was watching.

"Ughhh… I have got to tell that woman to stop posting about me," she groaned.

"Yeah, good luck with that. She's probably trying to get more lesbians in QBar and thinks advertising the town fuck boi would help get butts on the dance floor. Now the song choice, I can't explain."

"'Constant Craving' is a classic!" Jessica explained forcefully. "And I'm not a fuck-boi."

"Of course it's a classic. I'm not a pleb, I'm just saying, no one wants to cry all night. At least this one is better than the other night at karaoke when you sang the Cure. Seriously, Jess, please don't revert to the sad little goth girl you were in high school."

Jessica knew he wasn't serious, he just liked to tease her after he saw a photo of her with her mall rat friends from tenth grade. He had it up on his refrigerator just for posterity.

"Speaking of high school..." Jessica began.

"Anything that starts with speaking of high school can't be good," Bryce interjected. They both carried scars from their respective adolescent experiences. Bryce was a total nerd in high school and very much a late bloomer. It wasn't until he'd spent a few years in New York after growing up in Oklahoma that he was able to exorcise some of those demons.

"My sister. You know my sister, Bernie?"

"Yes, of course. Future contestant on the Real Housewives, Bernadine Monroe, iconic."

Jessica could never tell if some of the things Bryce said were compliments or not.

"Well, she's getting married and I'm going to have to be a bridesmaid in her wedding." Jessica paused for comment, but Bryce just looked at her impatiently.

"And...what's the issue?"

"The issue is, besides all the obvious wedding shit I hate, I'm going to have to spend the next six months going to a bunch of dumb events with my sister and all of her fembot friends. The very girls who treated me like shit in high school. And worst of all, her maid of honor is my absolute archnemesis, Tanner Caldwell."

Bryce started to laugh. "You have an archnemesis, Jess? Are you a superhero and didn't tell me?"

"Har-har," Jessica responded. "I promise you, she is totally worthy of the villain title."

Bryce's eyes turned kind. He could dish it out, but at the end of the day, he loved Jessica and he always made sure she knew he had her back.

"I'm sorry, Jess. What a nightmare. Can't you just not do it? I mean, you have to go to the wedding, obviously, it's your sister...but all the rest? Doesn't she know what you're like? I mean, I'd barely let you come to my wedding, let alone my bachelor party! Not that I would have a bachelor party if I was going to get married. Unless that was just code for an orgy, and then I guess you could be invited."

Jessica knew she would, of course, be at any wedding he had. She'd be the best woman. "I'm not coming to your pre-wedding orgy, Bryce. And the only reason I'm going to Bernie's stuff is because my mom is holding back the trust from my dad's estate unless I go to all of the pre-wedding rituals and act appropriately."

Bryce took another sip of his coffee. "Welp, I guess that's it for the bookstore." Bryce was deeply supportive of Jessica leaving her job, and he had spent many an afternoon in that very coffee shop helping with plans for her future business.

"It's honestly so unfair. And the first thing is a bachelorette party in Asheville in two weeks. Can you believe that? And my mom *just* told me! Bernie hasn't even asked me yet. And I just know that little turncoat Tanner is going to plan the most obnoxiously heterosexual bachelorette party in existence, which is just so....Ugh!"

Bryce looked at Jessica puzzled. "Well, yeah. They usually are pretty hetero. I mean that's kind of the point."

Jessica was already so annoyed with Tanner and she hadn't even seen her yet. "That's the thing. Tanner is gay. But that won't stop her from creating the most annoying compulsory straight bachelorette party in history. Bryce, she works for mommy+me, that weird Christian mommy site that basically tells women to ignore their postpartum depression and pray. I mean, what kind of lesbian does that?"

Bryce was eyeing Jessica suspiciously. "I mean, we aren't just a monolith, Jessica. Even lesbians have mommy issues. And Christian issues."

Jessica didn't like being called out for her stereotyping.

"If you just saw her, you'd know what I mean, Bryce. She looks exactly like what you'd imagine the most popular girl in high school would look like. Blond hair, perfectly symmetrical face, captain of the cheerleading team. Whatever kind of queer she is, I can't relate. We're from totally different planets and her whole thing makes it harder for the rest of us." Jessica knew she was sounding petulant now.

"So blond people can't be queer now? You seem a little more spiteful than usual, Jess. Are you sure this is just about some mommy blog and her hair color?" Bryce pursed his lips knowingly.

Jessica was obviously coming across completely transparent to Bryce. She couldn't decide if she wanted to tell him everything or just leave it there. But she realized that if she was going to tell anyone, Bryce would be a good person to try out.

"Okay, well, there is more to the story," she admitted. "We were co-editors of the school paper together. She was out and I wasn't. When I was figuring all that out, well, let's just say she showed her true colors."

Bryce seemed to lose some of his humor at that. "She's that girl? I remember that whole catastrophe. She sucks." His loyalty was as usual, starkly with her.

"It's honestly so much worse *that* she's gay. I mean the other girls were awful because that's their predisposition, but Tanner? She was the first out person I ever knew and she was just such an…incredible disappointment." Jessica didn't want to go into everything that happened again. Somehow it was still painful. "And then she's best friends with my sister. It's just a constant reminder."

The truth was, Jessica wasn't only thinking about her high school experience being gay. She was also remembering the years she spent afterward, when she was scared to be herself, scared to trust, thinking everyone would find her as inconsequential as she felt every day after…everything. Bryce remembered what she was like when he first met her, unconfident, closed off. She was so far from being that person.

Bryce reached across the table and held her hand. "I'm so sorry, friend."

Jessica let out a deep and soulful sigh. She would have to get a handle on her emotions if she was going to survive the next six months.

"It's fine. But you know what?" Jessica asked. "What I really need from you is help knowing how to handle all these random events I have to go to. Like, Bryce, what am I going to do if I have to deal with male strippers!" Jessica let some of the levity back in the conversation.

"How do you know it won't be female strippers?" Bryce joked.

"First of all, I don't want to have to deal with any strippers. But second, I am so certain Tanner is going to keep it to the standard *Magic Mike* level of queerness."

"You obviously didn't see that movie," Bryce said conspiratorially.

It was true that most super straight things were actually pretty gay. Take, for instance, cowboys. And *Top Gun*.

"Please help me." Jessica gave him her saddest, most pitiful eyes.

Bryce looked at her like a pageant girl he was sizing up for a ball gown. "I'll help get you sorority ready. And I can tell you now, you're going to have to lose the Crocs."

CHAPTER TWO

Looking over the span of DC's National Airport, Jessica couldn't help but wonder if there was anyone in the entire place more miserable than she was. The two weeks of "prep" she'd done for the Asheville bachelorette did not do much to ready her for the weekend. Then again, all she really did was sulk and catastrophize.

She did get in as much queer fun as possible, hoping she could build up a resistance before she was pummeled into a Bravo show. She went out a lot, she danced to Robyn, she enjoyed cappuccinos at Joltz with Bryce. And she also hooked up with not one, but two people at QBar. One hookup was with an out-of-towner who Jessica didn't learn much about, other than that they were hot and had a memorable Midwestern accent. The other was a repeat hookup with Lisa, the bartender at QBar. Lisa was very, very good-looking and cool, and easy to get along with. She and Jessica were mostly just friends, but every so often they would tip into bed together. It was a pretty symbiotic and low maintenance arrangement. Normally, Jessica would be feeling pretty good about herself, but sitting in the airport dreading the next forty-eight hours had already humbled her.

She began to look through the email she'd received from Tanner, her "indoctrination email" as she had begun calling it to Bryce. Skipping through all the pleasantries and unnecessary platitudes, she got to the list of things to come. Yes, there was the weekend itself, but there were also the next six months to think about.

1. Bachelorette Weekend in Asheville, October 12–13
2. Bridal Shower in Maryland (the Monroes' hometown), December 1
3. Dress Fitting in NYC (where Bernie lived and where the wedding would be), February 1
4. Bridesmaid Luncheon and Rehearsal Dinner in NYC, March 14
5. Wedding Day at the Bowery Hotel in NYC, March 15

The list was exhaustive, meaning as long as she attended all of these events, her mom would give her access to the trust and she could leave her awful job and open her bookstore. Something she was desperate to do. All the events sounded dumb, but the thing she was most nervous about was the bachelorette party. Just thinking about flying to another state and stranding herself for a weekend was increasing her anxiety by the minute. The other events were at least closer to DC, and therefore easy to escape, or in New York City, where she had places she could slip away to. Her ex, who she was tentatively still friends with, lived in New York City, so she'd spent a lot of time there over the years.

The whole "wedding" thing was obviously an issue. Jessica hated weddings and it was for many reasons. For one, she hated all of the rituals that felt archaic and misogynistic, like, the father walking the daughter down the aisle to "give her away." The tradition of who paid for what was also kind of an odd relic of a time when marriage was akin to selling women off to the highest bidder.

Then there was the commercialization, the incredibly unreasonable cost of a wedding for the people getting married as well as the people who attended. Jessica would have to buy a bridesmaid dress for the event, or at least that's what Bryce said when they analyzed the list together. So there was a very large chance she would be forced into some sort of pink gown or something that totally triggered her gender dysphoria that she would have to pay at least a hundred dollars for, and that was an aspirational number. Then there was just the straightness of it all. Gay marriage hadn't been legal for very long and the experience of knowing this giant club existed that only straight people could get into just rubbed Jessica the wrong way. Now that same-sex marriage was legal, it didn't suddenly undo all the damage that was done before.

And then there were just her personal feelings about love. Jessica didn't believe that a piece of paper meant anything about who you loved or how much you loved them. When she loved someone, that was something personal and something that couldn't be summed up in a few badly written vows or that needed to be recognized by God or the state. The whole thing felt like it took something special and made it ordinary. This last reason was the one she usually kept to herself. She didn't like to advertise her more romantic side, but deep down her romantic side was what had her so sensitive about marriage. She wanted connection, she wanted to fall in love, and she wanted that love to be cared for and not strapped with a bunch of social baggage and expectation.

Jessica sat outside her gate, awkwardly slouching in an incredibly uncomfortable narrow chair while trying to avoid touching the people on either side of her who were taking up both of her armrests. She had on her over-the-ear headphones and dark Wayfarer sunglasses that were, to be honest, completely unnecessary inside the airport. But they fit the energy she was giving off—a "don't talk to me" vibe that seemed to be working well enough so far.

Jessica was in the middle of debating if going to the snack counter for some Bugles and a water was worth sacrificing her seat, when she spotted something that made her stomach drop.

It was only the back of a blond head, but she would've known that head anywhere. It was the head she had looked at many days of high school, from that exact position. Tanner Caldwell in the front of the class asking all the questions, Jessica in the back hoping no one called on her. Tanner was unmistakable, even with her face fully out of view.

"Shit," Jessica whispered to herself. Of course they would be on the same plane. One of the most annoying turns of fate for Jessica was that Tanner actually lived in DC as well. It was an odd coincidence that had never really been an issue for Jessica. One time a few years ago, Jessica spotted Tanner at a Pride event downtown, but she had easily ducked out of the way and avoided the awkwardness of an encounter. Other than that, though, Jessica hadn't seen her around. DC was pretty big, but it was kind of odd to be two gay women and not run into each other. There were exactly two lesbian bars and Jessica had easily run into every single ex she'd ever had at one of the bars, but not Tanner.

Not that she was an ex or anything, Jessica thought to herself. Still, the chances of being on the same flight were, it turned out, pretty high, but somehow Jessica had not anticipated it. Now the question was, what would be more likely to keep herself unseen longer—going to get a snack or staying where she was? Staying put seemed safer. And since no amount of snack craving was worth the risk of being seen by Tanner, the decision was made. She would let herself get hangry slowly until she was forced to deal with Tanner at the Airbnb.

Jessica unconsciously switched songs to an old favorite from high school and mindlessly scrolled on her phone. But the truth was that now that she knew Tanner was close by, she couldn't help but steal a glance. At first, she couldn't really make out if Tanner had changed much. She still sat with that annoyingly perfect posture and her hair looked shiny and straight, just like it did when they were sixteen. Jessica continued pretending to ignore her, but when she got up to plug her phone into one of the standing chargers, she could finally see Tanner fully. She was wearing a tight plain white T-shirt, a jean jacket, black leggings, and flats. Although she had been gorgeous in high school, she had grown somehow even more beautiful. She was curvier than she was at sixteen, which made her all the more appealing. Jessica watched Tanner bend down to plug her own phone into an outlet and then toss her hair casually as she searched through her purse until she found a pair of adorably dorky horn-rimmed glasses. Jessica was annoyed that the glasses made her look, if possible, even hotter.

To be clear, Jessica despised Tanner. She disliked everything about her, especially how attractive she was. When they were younger, the fact that she was so beautiful was a torment, but in a completely different way. When Jessica would sit behind her in class, she had a hard time learning anything since she was too busy being distracted by a hair flip or a small smile from Tanner. It was a cliché, having a crush on the most popular girl in school. And then, when they had developed a friendship while working on the school paper, she learned more about the kind of person Tanner was, or pretended to be anyway, and her crush grew even stronger.

Jessica was grateful she was no longer the gawky high school kid she used to be, and that she no longer had to be the victim of that sort of unrequited infatuation. Not to mention, she finally learned exactly who Tanner really was, and if anything could squelch a crush, being outed by the most popular girl in school would do it. And the fact that Tanner was gay herself was just the cherry on top. Jessica could already feel herself getting worked up about it.

It was at that moment that Tanner scanned her space and almost immediately looked toward Jessica. Their eyes met for a moment, but Jessica looked away quickly, pretending she didn't notice or recognize the person she so obviously had been conspicuously staring at. Jessica pretended to occupy herself with her bags and her phone. Eventually, though, she couldn't help but look up again. Tanner was looking right at her. This time, Jessica wasn't so fast and Tanner raised her hand with a small wave. The gesture was tentative. Jessica gave Tanner a look of contempt, rolled her eyes, and went back to her phone. She wasn't going to give Tanner the satisfaction of thinking they were in any way on friendly terms.

The next time Jessica looked over, Tanner was decidedly not looking her way. She seemed to be completely focused on her phone and Jessica found herself relieved. Hopefully, that would nip any sort of reconciliation in the bud. There was no way to come back from what Tanner had done, and all Jessica wanted was to survive the wedding and collect the money for her bookstore. She didn't have to make nice with Tanner Caldwell, no matter how hot she looked in glasses.

❖

As luck would have it, though, things did get worse for Jessica. She was the last section to board due to her late ticket purchase. This meant she was forced to check her very small carry-on. Usually that would be a fairly normal setback, but Jessica was in no mood today for even minor hiccups. Begrudgingly, she passed her bag to the attendant, who responded to Jessica's obvious frustration with a bored look before dumping the bag on top of a pile of other luggage. Jessica winced and tried to remember if she'd brought anything breakable. She supposed her laptop had been through worse.

Her seat, of course, was at the back of the plane. This meant that not only would she be mere feet from the bathroom for the duration of the flight, she was also forced to pass Tanner as she walked down the aisle. Jessica tried to count her blessings. At least she wouldn't be sitting near Tanner and, thankfully, Tanner had seemed to get the memo about avoiding eye contact at all costs. As long as Tanner just stayed put for the next couple of hours, Jessica might be able to get through the flight and maybe even to the Airbnb without any further interaction.

Jessica's wish was almost granted until she found herself across from Tanner at the baggage claim. Tanner had positioned herself at the very front where the bags would first emerge, forcing Jessica to stand about a hundred feet down just to make sure she didn't spontaneously combust from proximity. She waited impatiently as the conveyor belt sluggishly came to life and bag after bag appeared. It seemed that everyone else's luggage came out first until Jessica and Tanner were two of the last few people left at the carousel. Eventually, nobody else was between them, just an expanse of empty space and a massive silence punctuated by the lumbering knocks of the worn-out carousel.

After what felt like an eternity, a new bag appeared on the belt and Tanner moved to get it. It was at that moment that Jessica noticed her small weekender tangled up in Tanner's giant luggage, the type of bag that you would take on a two-week vacation, not a weekend trip. To Jessica, the bag was an obvious sign that Tanner hadn't changed a bit since high school. She was still such a princess.

Jessica tried to hang back, but Tanner was untangling her bag with as much care and attention as someone removing a bag of garbage.

"Hey, watch it! That's my bag," Jessica couldn't help but call out. She moved toward their impossibly tangled up bags.

"Oh, sorry!" Tanner's voice was deep and soft. Jessica had almost forgotten how it sounded. Tanner looked up with what appeared to be shock, then seemed to realize it was Jessica who was approaching her. "Oh, it's you..." Her voice sounded odd. She seemed almost kinder once she noticed it was Jessica's bag.

"Yeah, well, you didn't have to bring such a big bag for one weekend. It's crushing my laptop."

Tanner's demeanor shifted. She seemed to bristle at the assertion. "I had to bring extra stuff for the bachelorette, and maybe don't put something so expensive and fragile into a bag this flimsy." She held the weekender up for Jessica to grab, having just gotten it untangled. Gone was the apologetic "talking to a bystander" Tanner, and in her place was the confident head cheerleader who had never done anything wrong in her life.

Jessica grabbed the bag, holding the same contemptuous look from earlier. "Yeah, whatever." She turned to walk out to the rideshare area. Jessica knew she had been rude, and although that wasn't her normal state, she did not feel guilty. Well, she did feel a little bad for thinking Tanner was a princess for her giant bag. It actually made sense that as the maid of honor, she might need to bring a few more things than everyone else. But still, she didn't have to throw Jessica's bag around like that. Or be so defensive, she thought defensively.

Sighing, Jessica opened the rideshare app on her phone and ordered a car, then rolled her eyes at the seven-minute wait. She'd never had to wait more than a couple of minutes in DC. Plus, she didn't want to open herself up to any more contact with Tanner, who would presumably need to be in the same general pickup area as Jessica. She crossed her arms over her chest and stood with her legs wide, the universal "don't fuck with me" body language. Maybe this would keep Tanner at a distance, at least until the car arrived.

Then she felt a tap on her shoulder. She turned to find Tanner right next to her, not trying at all to keep the unspoken agreement to avoid each other at all costs.

"Hey, so we're going to the same place. Do you think we should share a ride?" The question was so natural and Tanner asked it as if they hadn't just been in a standoff a few minutes ago. It would have been the most normal thing in the world to say yes, but Jessica was not feeling normal. She was feeling vengeful.

"Yeah, I'm good riding alone." Her tone was sharp. Tanner's eyes went wide and she seemed to be again taken aback by Jessica's contempt.

"Okay, well, I guess I'll just get a car and we can both pay double just to end up at the same place at the same time." Tanner's response was obviously sarcastic, but Jessica couldn't tell if she was trying to come across as lighthearted. Either way, she seemed to be waiting for a response.

"Yeah, I guess that's what we'll have to do." Jessica grabbed her phone and looked at it with finality, avoiding Tanner's eyes. Tanner must have gotten the message because she moved further down the pickup area. Jessica tried to relax the tension that had built in her shoulders. But then a notification popped up on her screen. The driver had canceled the ride and now a new car was fifteen minutes away.

Fuck.

At nearly the same moment, she saw a huge Escalade pull up in front of Tanner. The driver came out to help her with her giant bag and Tanner opened the door to the back seat. Then she paused, turning back toward Jessica.

"Are you sure?" she called again, with a kindness that felt completely out of place considering the very clear animosity emanating from Jessica.

"I'm good," Jessica shouted back. Tanner shrugged and got in the car. As it flew off, Jessica noticed the app had added five more minutes to her wait. Wasn't that so like Tanner, she got some three-minute wait while everyone else sat around for hours.

I bet her rideshare rating is higher than mine, Jessica thought with another eye roll. Jessica was a fantastic tipper and she was always polite, but nothing could compare to the incredible power Tanner had when she walked through the world with her sparkly smile and her shiny blond hair. *And her sultry, deep voice...*

Jessica shook her head. She needed to stop feeding into Tanner's hotness. Not to mention her tendency to compare herself to Tanner. Jessica was an adult, high school was over, and she could not fall into old habits. And anyway, she was not at the mercy of the rideshare gods. She could see quite clearly that the taxi queue had only a few people and there were plenty of cabs. She'd get there just as quickly as Tanner, even if she did have to pay a bit more for a taxi. But she decided it was a small price to avoid spending thirty-five minutes trapped in a car with her least favorite person in the world.

CHAPTER THREE

After a thirty-minute trip from the airport, Jessica's taxi turned up a steep, windy hill. The car slowed to a snail's pace as the incline began to get more and more steep. Jessica started to develop a strong, foreboding feeling in her gut as the driver began to cuss lightly and look around anxiously.

"I'm not sure the car is going to make it up this hill," he said nervously.

Jessica blanched. "This is the address," she assured him. "I can't imagine it would be unreachable by car?" But deep down, Jessica could tell she was out of her depth on the topography of Asheville. The Airbnb was titled the "Bird's Nest," which suddenly sounded a lot less cute than it had a few hours ago. And which implied they had quite a bit farther to ascend.

Jessica could feel the cab driver start to really push on the gas to get through a particularly vertical part of the hill, when suddenly they both heard the loud scraping sound of metal against concrete. It was clear by the sound that the car was being completely scraped up on the bottom as it continued to shriek in pain. The driver slammed on the brakes, pummeling Jessica into the front seat.

"Shit, my car is fucked up!" The driver was fully irate and banging his hands on the steering wheel.

"Umm, I can just get out here," Jessica said weakly. She paid the cab fare, resolving that double the price for the tip should be enough to compensate the damage, and the driver slowly reversed down the drive to the long screeching sound of the car continuing its collision with the ground. The scraping seemed to last forever.

Jessica felt unsteady from both the uncomfortable ending of her ride and the seemingly psychotic angle of the hill. Who built a house so far up a hill that it wasn't navigable by car? Shouldn't someone have warned her? Jessica checked the email from Tanner about the Airbnb. This time she noticed the explicit warning in all caps: ONLY ACCESSIBLE BY SUV. Figured. Jessica remembered Tanner's Escalade rideshare and was reminded of her own stubborn ineptitude.

She took her bag and draped it over herself, preparing for the trek up the rest of the hill. The house wasn't yet visible, hopefully due to the steepness and the trees rather than the actual distance she'd have to climb. She wasn't the biggest fan of heights, so even at the height she was at, her legs were getting wobbly. It seemed she had found new meaning for the phrase "walk of shame."

❖

When Jessica reached the summit of the hill, which should have really been considered a mountain, she dropped her bag and fell with her hands on her knees in an embarrassing display of her lack of fitness. Jessica did not think of herself as "out of shape," but fifteen minutes on a forty-five-degree incline had proven her wrong.

But as she came to her senses, she was able to look up to find the most charming log cabin—tree house?—she had ever seen. A curved wooden stairwell wound around several enormous trees to land at the entrance of a large wooden house with what looked like small pod-like rooms branching off. Multiple balconies were variously furnished with hammocks, small tables, and bird feeders. A large sign displayed the cabin's somewhat cheesy name as the "Bird's Nest." Even from Jessica's vantage point, she could see the back deck had an amazing view of the Blue Ridge Mountains and what looked like the corner of an enormous hot tub. If Jessica wasn't feeling so stubborn and critical—not to mention in a near meltdown after the climb—she would have liked the kitsch factor of the place.

Unfortunately, however, the house wasn't the only thing towering above her. Four women were also staring down from the wraparound porch, watching her struggle to catch her breath. Their faces were fixed in expressions of pity. Jessica could swear she heard somebody cluck with over-the-top sympathy.

"Jess!" one of them yelled out, while rushing to descend the winding wooden stairs. It was Bernie, full of energy as she jogged down to Jessica and wrapped her in a full on, way too tight hug. Jessica was too caught off guard, and off balance, to reciprocate with the same gusto. She found herself somewhat taken aback by the sheer ferocity of the embrace. Abruptly, Bernie let go and stepped back, seeming a little chagrined.

"You're here! Finally! Don't worry, we didn't start without you. Well, not much..." Bernie gave a sheepish grin.

Bernie was petite with a slim build, dark brown hair, and brown eyes. She was known for her toothy smile and charming personality by most everyone who met her. Jessica truly loved her sister; it just sometimes took seeing her to remember how much.

Based on her sister's warm greeting, Jessica found that she was relieved to see her sister was happy to see her. She hadn't realized it, but part of her thought maybe her mom had forced Bernie to invite her. And although Jessica hadn't wanted to come, she also didn't want to be some problem Bernie had to deal with all weekend.

Jessica forced her face into an inviting grin. "I'm here!" she said with as much enthusiasm as she could muster while taking in her little sister's bachelorette weekend getup.

Bernie's features were similar to Jessica's, but what was dark and sultry on Jessica came across as sweet and earnest on Bernie. Especially in her current ensemble. Bernie was wearing a hot pink wedding veil along with a matching pink shirt that said "Future Mrs. Gray." Jessica winced before reminding herself to be supportive.

Bernie grabbed Jessica's bag from the ground and directed her up the stairs and into the lion's den. Jessica ascended the stairs slowly, her calves already on fire. At the top of the landing, she was met with her bachelorette weekend housemates, all of whom were wearing matching shirts in that same hot pink color, but with the words "Girl Squad" across the chest instead. Jessica was faced with her future.

Alexandra Ramos was the first person to greet her. She had been Bernie's roommate from Boston University and the two became close enough that Alex had even accompanied Bernie to their father's funeral. That's where Jessica met Alex initially—obviously an inopportune place to get to know her—and they'd only crossed paths maybe one other odd weekend. Alex was striking and curvaceous, and usually flaunting an amazing cosmopolitan style that accented her looks and bold personality. Today, however, her typical stylishness was masked by the ridiculous pink shirt. Based on her expression, Jessica wondered if Alex might be even less into the kitschy bachelorette stuff than she was. Either way, Jessica was actually not too upset that Alex was there, as she wasn't the worst of Bernie's friends. It had seemed like Bernie upgraded a bit when she left home and got out of her high school crowd.

The next person to reluctantly say hello was none other than Kayla Kelly, somebody Jessica did know well. Kayla's blond hair was styled in an updo, the same one she used all of high school, kind of a sporty cheerleader hair thing. She wore a blank expression on her face that gave the impression of boredom or disinterest, something that was a classic attribute of Kayla. She really wasn't interested, at least not in Jessica. And the feeling was mutual. Kayla was one of the last people in the universe that Jessica ever wanted to hang with, second only to Tanner, of course.

There was something about having seen Tanner from below, like she was on a pedestal. It was such a perfect metaphor that it almost seemed choreographed. This was how Jessica had always felt around Tanner, below her. Jessica was glad they were now both on the porch, on the same level physically at least. Jessica took advantage of Tanner's hesitation and greeted her as though they hadn't just had a showdown at the Asheville Airport. For her part, Tanner seemed to just go along with it. Jessica couldn't decide if that was a kindness or if even here, a decade later, Tanner was pretending in public not to know her in every opportunity she could find.

Once the awkward hellos finally ended, Bernie interjected with another burst of enthusiasm. "Okay, Jess, as you can see, we all have girl squad shirts, so let's get you changed and let's get a mimosa in your hand! It's wine o'clock, ladies!"

Every one of those words felt like nails on a chalkboard. Jessica almost considered refusing, but seeing her sister's eager, hopeful face told her this would be one of many fights she was likely to lose this weekend. Instead, she smiled weakly, agreed, and entered the Bird's Nest. Where she became immediately disoriented by the chaotic layout of the space. The main room was spacious and comfortable, yet somehow cramped due to the large array of furniture that seemed to have been stuffed haphazardly inside. Squishy-looking sofas and armchairs were arranged in the living area along with a variety of side tables, lamps, and ottomans. To the right was a massive kitchen and dining area complete with an island, barstools, and a dining table situated beneath an almost elfin-looking chandelier. But the most unsettling part was the pod rooms that she'd seen from outside the house. They seemed to be connected to the main room solely by little rope bridges and backless staircases that were somehow both adorable and incredibly ominous. This was all a nightmare for anyone with fear of heights, and it put Jessica immediately into fight-or-flight mode.

Where the hell am I going to sleep? Jessica wasn't in the habit of talking to herself, but something about the interior of the house combined with the crew outside made her want to paint a volleyball and call it Wilson.

"Do you need to find your room?" Alex had come in behind her and was clearly offering her a kindness.

"Yeah, I think so. I have no idea where to go." Jessica smiled uncertainly at Alex. "I assume everyone called rooms?"

"Well, Bernie has her own room because she's the bride. I'm in the double bedroom with Kayla." Jessica could hear irritation in Alex's voice. "And I think you're with Tanner."

"What? Why am I with Tanner?"

Alex shrugged and lowered her voice. "Listen, I'm not really the biggest Kayla fan, so trust me, I'd trade if I could. But Tanner was very particular about everything."

Jessica rolled her eyes. "Okay, whatever. I mean, it's just two nights."

Alex gave her a curious look, but all she said was, "I'll show you where it is." She led the way up a short, curving staircase and then onto a rope bridge hallway that, upon further inspection, was obviously built to look much less stable than it actually was. Even so, Jessica found herself hugging the railing and inching across like a toddler.

"Man, you are not good with heights, are you?" Alex asked with a little tease in her voice.

"Who decided to rent a tree house!" Jessica responded, her legs shaking. Alex laughed good-naturedly.

Finally, Jessica made it across the bridge and into the bedroom, where she was met with the worst-case scenario. A single queen bed stood in the middle of the circular room. Was she supposed to share that with Tanner?

"What the fuck, no!" Jessica exclaimed petulantly.

Alex looked at her. "I mean, it's not that bad, right? Didn't you go to high school together?" She dropped her voice to a whisper. "And, like, you're both gay. Right?"

Jessica was taken aback. What was that supposed to mean? "You think that just because I'm gay, we're supposed to be okay sleeping together?"

"What? No, I just meant… Well, it was just…" Alex looked embarrassed and seemed reluctant to expand.

"Just say it," Jessica said. She already knew it was going to be offensive.

"Well, it's just Kayla was kind of weird about sleeping in the same room with anyone who was gay. I think Tanner didn't want to deal with it or make it Bernie's problem, but it's all super weird and, well, anyway, I just want to say for the record, I am not cosigning anything that girl says!"

"So you're telling me that Kayla won't sleep in the same room as a lesbian. What about Tanner, aren't they best friends?"

Alex shrugged. "Look, I don't know all the dynamics. I'm just here for Bernie and trying to keep the peace. I guess it's better you know. Again, I think Tanner is just managing it and I'm sure that if Bernie knew…"

"Whatever, I get it," Jessica said sharply. "I really don't care about Kayla or Tanner or how they've decided to manage their weird, homophobic friendship."

Jessica looked around one more time, asking herself if she was really going to let the "one bed trope" take her down this early.

"I'm sleeping on the couch." Jessica remembered seeing at least one couch in the main room that might be long enough to fit her. She would be just fine there. "Besides, this way I can avoid spending all weekend in heights exposure therapy freaking out and crawling across these bridges." She grinned at Alex in an attempt to release the tension that had built in the room.

Besides, this wasn't her first time dealing with this uncomfortable dynamic between Kayla, Tanner, and herself. She knew what it felt like to have Kayla Kelly, and then everybody else, treat her like some sort of pariah while somehow holding a completely different standard for Tanner. Alex's comment had brought her right back to how she'd felt in high school, having nothing and no one. She remembered wondering if there was something wrong with her, if it would have been different if she was prettier or more athletic or more *something*, maybe more like Tanner. This feeling took Jessica years to overcome, and one of the most important factors was staying away from people like Kayla. Unfortunately, she could see that this was going to be extra difficult since they were trapped in a treehouse together for the next few days.

Alex returned the smile and went over to the bed to grab the bright pink shirt and a little care package that had been left for Jessica. Alex tossed everything to Jessica, who caught it easily and inspected the care package with trepidation. It looked like some combination of Etsy monogrammed junk, an assortment of penis straws, and a head band with springs on top that led to a large assortment of, you guessed it, penises again, with the words "Same Penis Forever" written across it.

Jessica sighed heavily and Alex gave another laugh. The two of them moved back (slowly) through the tree house halls. When they reached the living room area, Jessica put her stuff down on a couch, staking her claim.

Alex looked at her a bit dubiously. "I'm not sure I get why you would choose this clearly uncomfortable couch over that Tempur-Pedic mattress, but whatever! There should be three bathrooms, I think, so feel free to use whatever one you want."

With that, Alex turned back toward the front porch, but then she stopped. "Maybe I shouldn't have mentioned that stuff with Kayla to you, or like said something or something…" Alex looked a bit ashamed as she stumbled over the words.

Jessica could see the confusion for Alex. The fact that Tanner wasn't addressing it herself, as a gay person, kind of made it hard for Alex to know what to do. The whole thing felt like something Jessica didn't want to touch with a ten-foot pole.

"It seems like Tanner could have said something to Kayla if she'd wanted to."

Alex looked relieved. It felt like she might've been genuinely concerned that Jessica might be upset. What Alex didn't know was that Jessica had a hundred things to be upset about, and Alex not getting involved with those two was not even making the list.

Alex seemed to shake it off and spoke with a different energy. "Whatever, I'm here 'cause I love Bernie and I'm ready to have some fun. I just finished my nursing certification exam, so I'm ready to get fucked up!"

Alex's smile was mischievous, and Jessica was starting to think this woman might be more okay, especially considering the company.

"Let me just get changed and I'll meet you out there." Jessica unfolded the shirt and held it against herself, trying to imagine it on her. Alex looked at her and let out a maniacal laugh.

Jessica couldn't help but laugh too. "What?"

"Honestly, the main reason I came in was because I wanted to see your face when you saw yourself in that shirt for the first time."

Jessica laughed as she rolled up the shirt in her hands to put it over the shirt she was wearing. "Maybe grab the fire extinguisher in case I'm engulfed in flames?" She pulled it on and walked over to a mirror. It was just as she thought. She looked like she was in drag.

Alex took a quick photo with her phone. Jessica turned, hoping her face showed her feelings of betrayal. "How could you?!"

"See you out there!" Alex said with a sashay as she left.

Jessica looked back at herself in the mirror. Her skin tone was the absolute worst combination with hot pink, something she only learned in this moment. She got her phone out and took a picture as well. Bryce deserved a pick-me-up.

❖

The rest of the afternoon went exactly as expected. Jessica hung out on the porch with everyone else, doing everything in her power to spend as much time as possible next to Bernie and, surprisingly, Alex, who ended up being a pretty easy person to talk to. Kayla, of course, was exactly who she had always been. At one point, she told everyone how much her husband made for a living.

Bernie was sweet and wonderful as usual, but she was a bit scared to call out Kayla when she was being rude or monopolizing. This seemed to be a relic of high school that Bernie hadn't quite overcome. Alex, on the other hand, had no such qualms about interrupting Kayla. There was clearly some tension building there. Alex was interesting and funny, and she seemed to bring out a better side of Bernie.

Tanner, however, was an enigma. She appeared to busy herself with passing out paper copies of the itinerary, topping off everyone's drinks, and keeping everything on schedule. But she was strangely quiet otherwise. Jessica couldn't remember a time in high school when Tanner had been this reserved. She wasn't exactly the center of attention all the time, at least not of her own accord, but she'd always had an easy charisma in social situations and was far from a wallflower. With the five of them, though, she seemed almost to fade into the background.

Jessica was relieved about it in one sense—she didn't want to be phony with Tanner in front of her sister—but something about her changed vibe disquieted Jessica.

Alex's earlier comments about the sleeping arrangements made Jessica a little more tuned into Kayla's and Tanner's body language. She decided that they seemed to be distant. Maybe things really had changed since high school, It wasn't as though Jessica would have heard. All she knew was that they were all still friends with Bernie, and close enough to be in her bridal party. If there was a rift, it couldn't have been too bad.

And anyway, she wasn't there to diagnose the internal dynamics of the "Girl Squad." She was there to assuage her mom, and to support Bernie. With that in mind, Jessica tried her hardest to participate in the conversations around her. She was pretty sure she wouldn't be able to keep up the near-pleasant, nonjudgmental facade she was currently showcasing for the entire weekend, so she might as well try as hard as she could when she had the energy. She figured that she'd be drained in a few hours and would turn into the snarky little brat she knew she was about everything "wedding." At least the mimosas were helping, and she was a little charmed by the cabin, now that she didn't have to test her fear of heights.

As the sun began to set, and they had filled themselves up on the tacos Tanner had strategically ordered at just the right moment, timing them perfectly for their next stop, a karaoke bar, they all went to their respective rooms to get ready.

Tanner didn't say anything about the room adjustment, and Jessica didn't press it. She still couldn't believe Tanner had agreed to the original arrangement in the first place. But her new "room" did have its own set of drawbacks. Chief among them was its location in the middle of the main thoroughfare, with everybody passing through to get to the shower, to see what everyone else was wearing, to get another drink. It was lucky Jessica wasn't an especially modest person, because privacy was going to be hard to come by. She halfheartedly tried to shift the couch into a more secluded position, but it was heavier than it looked and she gave up almost immediately.

By the time everyone was ready to go, they were about thirty minutes off schedule, which Jessica thought was pretty good considering. But of course, it turned out that Tanner had expected this all along. It seemed that the itinerary was designed for manipulation rather than accuracy. Jessica decided the whole thing was annoying.

Chapter Four

Jessica had the privilege of being the only person in the Uber who had to crawl out from the very back of the SUV. It was impossible to be graceful. She could feel the Girl Squad's eyes on her as she wrestled with the tab that was supposed to collapse the middle row, before giving up and attempting a slow kind of army roll over the seat back. When she finally made it out of the car and onto the ground outside the karaoke bar, Jessica heard Kayla mutter "took you long enough."

If Kayla hadn't already started toward the bar, Jessica might have thrown something back, but maybe it was better that she didn't get the chance. Her borrowed time as near-pleasant Jessica was running out. At least Bernie, Tanner, and Alex had waited to make sure she was in one piece, but Jessica almost wished they hadn't—the whole production wasn't exactly her most graceful. And after an afternoon of mimosas and avoiding two out of four people on an intimate vacation, Jessica was past tipsy.

"Sooo, want to go inside?" Jessica said, trying not to sound as embarrassed as she was. Yes, she told herself, it's perfectly normal to struggle to get out of a car, but Jessica was just not feeling good about any level of embarrassment in front of Tanner or Kayla.

Tanner gave them a little intro to the place as they walked toward the entrance. "Okay, so this is the Mic Drop. It's a new thing in downtown Asheville. We've got a private room for the whole night. Everyone has to sing at least one song and our bride-to-be gets to duet whenever she wants or veto any song you choose."

"Yeah, we know how karaoke works, Tanner," Kayla said with the exact amount of irritation that she usually seemed to reserve especially for Jessica. "Anyway, why are we doing something so lame? We should be out at a club or something!"

Jessica could see her sister look between Tanner and Kayla anxiously.

"It's going to be fun," Tanner replied with that characteristic confidence. "I promise," she added just for Bernie.

Bernie gave a little whoop of excitement. "Come on, ladies, you know I can't miss an opportunity to sing. Let's do this! Girl Squad on three!"

Everyone but Jessica immediately put their hands in and repeated the refrain in a cheer.

Did they all practice this before she arrived?

❖

The group was led into an incredibly spacious and glitzy karaoke room. The focal point of the room was a sunken middle area that had several black leather couches, a large screen, and ample audio equipment. There were neon signs with an assortment of random words that were loosely associated with karaoke, like "sing" or "drinks." In the higher level encircling the middle area was a small bar with a private bartender. The room was dark, but there was an assortment of strobe lights, a disco ball, and a spotlight on the microphone at the front.

Jessica didn't want to admit it, but she kind of loved the place. She liked that it was private and intimate but was also clearly designed to inspire playfulness and fun. Of all the bachelorette party options that cycled through her mind, the possibilities for how this night could go, this was kind of cool. She kept this to herself as she plopped herself down on one of the couches. The other women seemed a little awkward. Alex didn't seem like someone who would love a place that kitschy and Kayla was holding herself like she thought she might get tetanus from the couches, but Bernie looked absolutely thrilled.

"Tan, this is so perfect! Now I get to hold you all hostage while I sing my sixth-grade chorus audition song, 'My Heart Will Go On.'" Bernie wrapped Tanner in one of her classic Bernie hugs. Tanner looked perfectly content to be embraced by her. "That was the plan. If you decide this is a Bernie Monroe private concert, that's what it'll be!" Tanner was looking at Bernie with nothing but support and unconditional love. Jessica looked away, suddenly feeling a prickly feeling on her skin.

They each got a drink and the songs began. Bernie was true to her word and started them off with a Celine Dion song followed by another Celine Dion song, and then Alex took over just to protect her ears from what was turning into Bernie massacring the French language as she cycled through Celine Dion's discography. Alex brought the group back with her very smooth rendition of "Back to Black."

"Alex, why are you always so cool!" Bernie said, hugging Alex with such uncool affection. Alex laughed but tutted. "Bernie, that song is cool no matter who sings it!"

"Okay, maybe, but you knew to choose it. Sooo, Alex!" Bernie added, teasing her.

Alex rolled her eyes.

Kayla watched with a sour face. "So, what's next, Tanner? This isn't even PG13, it's PG. Is this what the whole weekend is going to be, like, a middle school sleepover?" Kayla threw back another glass of champagne.

Before Tanner could answer, Alex responded. "Lay off, Kayla. We're here for Bernie and Bernie likes to sing. Stop being so critical."

Kayla looked at Alex with what could only be described as a rapidly growing contempt. "Bernie is just being nice! She'd much rather be at a club, right, Bernie?"

Bernie was again looking between them. "Ummm, I'm happy doing anything as long as we all get to be together."

Jessica highly doubted that Bernie didn't have a preference. It did seem like karaoke was perfect for Bernie, but who knew? Maybe she was looking for more of a quintessential bachelorette experience.

Jessica noticed that Tanner wasn't stepping in to defend herself or her plans for the night. It was odd considering how much work obviously went into everything, not to mention the demonstrated competence she had for planning. Kayla could dish it out, but she had absolutely no ability to organize anything. She should have been grateful. It was annoying that Jessica found herself automatically on Tanner's side.

Tanner side-stepped the whole conversation and announced that Bernie would be performing a duet with Alex. The decision broke the tension for a bit, at least getting Alex and Kayla separated. Who would have thought they would be the ones least able to get along? Jessica was sure it would be her at least. Once everything was set up and the two of them started singing "That's What Friends Are For," Jessica noticed Tanner excuse herself, probably to use the restroom. Jessica was left with Kayla watching the two college roommates profess their undying friendship love. Kayla was clearly uncomfortable. To say she was jealous was obvious, but it was sort of shocking on an adult woman at her friend's bachelorette. *I mean, Bernie naturally would have other friends after high school, right?*

Jessica was relieved not to have to make chitchat anymore, since Kayla didn't even try. She could watch undisturbed as everyone consecutively subjected themselves to this private humiliation. It was kind of perfect.

When Tanner did return, Jessica couldn't help but steal a look at her. She wasn't as quiet as she had been at the bar, but still she was a little reserved. She would laugh with everyone, but she seemed to be just a little rigid. Maybe that just came with maid of honor duties. But it wasn't only Jessica who was looking. Jessica could feel Tanner's eyes on her as well. When they accidentally caught each other's eyes, they both looked away chaotically. What was it, irritation? Maybe Tanner was responsible for social cohesion and Jessica was a social terrorist just waiting to act.

Kayla continued to be mildly surly and uninterested, but as the group began to get more boisterous, she seemed to start to give in. She did a pretty boring rendition of "Blurred Lines" that reminded Jessica why she hated that song. It was catchy, but deeply offensive. Having Kayla sing it helped Jessica forget the catchy part.

As time went on, it became more and more clear that she and Tanner were the only people who had not performed. Jessica was sure that she was one more Bernie song away from being discovered, so she decided to volunteer. She picked something she thought would hit with everyone, choosing "Dreams" by Fleetwood Mac. Jessica's logic was that everyone loved it and Bernie was not likely to veto it.

"I accept!" Bernie exclaimed with her bridal staff, which must have been a part of her Etsy gift package.

Jessica stood under the spotlight and suddenly everyone was quiet. It felt like that was not the vibe when everyone else sang, but maybe she was just being paranoid. To be clear, Jessica was not a good singer. She wasn't blessed with any sort of tone awareness, but she did love music and she loved that song, so she sang with as much gusto as she had. She had decided before beginning that this would be her last burst of energy for the night. When the song ended, Bernie was wolf-whistling and Alex gave a standing ovation. Kayla barely clapped, but the person Jessica noticed most was Tanner. During the performance, Jessica could feel the intensity of Tanner's stare. She was trying to find a focal point, a place to look while she sang, but she kept finding Tanner's eyes. Something about being on display made her unable to avoid them. And for the first time since arriving at the airport, Tanner wasn't looking away either. So when the song ended, Tanner's clapping felt intimate and Jessica just wanted to go back to her seat, the farthest place from Tanner she could find, and stop whatever weird vibe was lingering between them.

The truth was, it wasn't just Jessica's hatred for Tanner that bothered Jessica. It was the fact that she used to like her. Jessica had wanted so badly for Tanner to notice her when she was a teen and then when they became friends, it all made it so much worse when Tanner hurt her the way she did. Now, with her guard down and after the vulnerability of doing something she wasn't good at in a performance, she did not like the feeling of reverting back to her high school self.

Jessica sat with gusto. The plan was to harden herself again, get her walls back up, but then Bernie made her next decree with her bachelorette staff.

"Tanner, you're next, and you and I both know you are just sandbagging us all to make this more interesting. I'm picking the song."

Tanner's blush was noticeable, even in the neon lighting, but she acquiesced quickly. It was all very faux gracious and humble—so very "Tanner." Tanner stood at the mic looking innocent. Jessica sighed audibly, clearly exasperated. Tanner must have heard it because she seemed to shrink into herself. This was not the first time that night she seemed off. Jessica had really never seen her lose stride this way, even when they were younger.

The song began with a crashing thunderstorm. Celine Dion's "It's All Coming Back" began with all its unmistakable corniness. Obviously, this was what Bernie would choose. Jessica hadn't realized her sister's obsession ran this deep. It felt a bit old for someone in their late twenties, but then she remembered why her sister loved it so much. Yes, it was her choir audition pick, but that was only because her dad had helped her select the music. He was a proud French Canadian and he felt that Celine was a national treasure, that and making sure they never bad-mouthed Tim Hortons.

Thinking about Bernie and her love for Celine Dion reminded Jessica how much his death must have affected her. They hadn't really talked about it and Jessica wasn't quite sure why. Thinking of her dad made Tanner's song that much more poignant. Not to mention, of Celine Dion's discography, this song was Jessica's favorite. A guilty pleasure that she really only listened to on the most discreet headphones, but that filled her with the campy pleasure of a show tune.

But it wasn't just the song. Tanner was...an amazing singer. She had complete control of her voice and the song was not an easy one. But it was more than that. Karaoke was not just about having a good voice. Jessica knew lots of people with great voices who were terrible at karaoke. It took a certain amount of humility, stage presence, and total acceptance of inevitable debasement of the entire experience. Tanner was fun, she was animated. She even made her voice sound bad at just the right moments, sacrificing form for a flamboyant hand gesture or a soulful look. It was perfection.

Jessica would have given anything to be immune to Tanner's ineffable charm, but she wasn't. She laughed on cue, and she clapped when she got to the loud part. She was spineless.

So Tanner was good at karaoke. Jessica could give her that and still hate her. When Tanner finished, she bowed deeply and then rose, looking around at everyone until she landed on Jessica. They locked eyes, and Jessica couldn't help but balk at how effortlessly beautiful Tanner was. It was honestly obnoxious.

Tanner came to sit back down as Bernie went up for her next song. Jessica noticed that as soon as the attention was on someone else, it seemed like Tanner relaxed. It might have appeared like she enjoyed being up there, but it was pretty clear from her now-deflated state that performance was work for Tanner. Again, Jessica had to school herself on not analyzing the enemy. All of these nice seductive sweet qualities were just the lure that pulled you in. Jessica had already experienced the trap. Never again.

Bernie had finally moved on to another Canadian, Avril Lavigne's "Sk8er Boi" when there was a knock on the door.

Tanner got up, clearly not surprised by the knock. "Wonder who that could be?" she asked in obvious faux surprise. She opened the door and two burly firemen in fire hats came in. One had an honest to God axe and the other a hose that led to nowhere.

"Oh no..." Jessica said uselessly as all three of the others started screaming. Honestly, Jessica thought, why an axe? That could not be a safe prop, it was literally a weapon. The music changed to "Pony" by Ginuwine. Jessica knew what was coming and found herself leaving the conversation pit as quickly as she could, hoping to sneak out if possible.

"We heard there was a fire, but looking around it seems like it's just that you ladies are just a little too...hot!" One fireman ripped off his Velcroed poncho material fireman's jacket, showing off his ripped abs and red suspenders. Something told Jessica the hat was staying on. The line was corny, but what could she expect, this was how it went.

"Where is the future Mrs. Gray?" the other fireman asked, ripping his jacket off as well. Bernie whooped at the top of her lungs. She was clearly down for whatever these men had planned for her.

Suffice it to say, it was worse than Jessica could have imagined. They put Bernie on a chair in the middle of the room and gave her what could only be described as a very intense and provocative lap dance. The worst part wasn't the naked men, that Jessica could take or leave, it was the way they sort of manhandled Bernie and the other bridesmaids. Their G-strings were wildly close to Bernie's face, and at one point during Alex's turn, they lifted her and turned her upside down. Jessica had to ask herself who was actually being objectified here.

Jessica at no time gave any consent to be involved. She and Tanner were the only two who didn't participate. Of everyone, Kayla was most in her element. At one point, Jessica wasn't sure if her lap dance would ever end, she was clearly getting her life. After what she decided was an appropriate amount of time, Jessica snuck out of the room and the bar. She needed to get a break from all of the dick energy. It was all just a bit too much inside. A little fresh air would do her good.

❖

Jessica spent about fifteen minutes on a bench outside the karaoke bar just watching the crowd on Lexington Avenue. It was after midnight, and she was considering whether she could sneak back to the Airbnb without being noticed when one of the dancers came out. He was wearing some of his clothes for a change and had his fireman hat under his arm. He gave her a little wave indicating if he could come over to her bench. She thought what the hell and beckoned him over. He pulled out a cigarette.

"Do you have a light? I left it in my other pants."

She did, so she lit his cigarette for him. Jessica had quit a few years ago, but she still had the habit of carrying a lighter.

"Thanks. I'm Bryan by the way," he added, sitting back and stretching out. Jessica imagined he had a lot of long nights in his line of work.

"I'm Jessica." She decided he seemed pretty welcoming. "So, do you do a lot of bachelorette parties?" Jessica was strangely curious now that she noticed he was just a guy and not only a beefcake in cosplay.

"Yeah, basically all bachelorettes or birthday parties. I also do go-go a few nights a week at a local gay bar. Asheville's not a bad city for this sort of thing. A lot of bachelorette or bachelor weekends."

Jessica was surprised to hear he worked at a gay bar. The lap dances felt real in a way that had her assuming they were both extremely heterosexual. "Oh, cool. So, are you gay and you do this for the money?" She regretted the question as soon as it came out.

He took another drag and responded unaffected by the personal question. "I'm straight, but I don't really care who my clients are. It's a job. Keith, the other guy, he's gay. I think he might prefer things like this just so that he can have a bit of separation in his life, but you'd have to ask him."

The casualness of his response was a nice reminder that things weren't always so rigid. Who was she to assume anything about someone? Of course, stripping was a job. How much could it matter who the client was?

"I noticed you and the chick who hired us weren't so into it. Do you have any notes?" Bryan asked playfully. Jessica could tell he knew he was good at what he did. He must have just wanted to make conversation.

"No notes!" Jessica responded supportively. "Just not my bag of chips, if you know what I mean." She tried to communicate what she meant with a knowing glance.

"Ah, yeah that makes sense. When Keith called me about this job he said the other woman was a friend from his DC days. Seems like if two out of five of y'all aren't into men, we could have brought a different gendered person for the job."

Jessica shrugged. "I'm not the one planning the events. Might be a better question for the person who hired you."

At that moment, Keith, the other dancer, and Tanner came outside. He was carrying his bag and was redressed in all of his firefighter gear. Tanner gave him an envelope with what must have been his payment or his tip. She also gave him a huge hug and held him longer than any mere acquaintance. When they pulled apart, she said, "Thank you for making this so perfect. Say hi to Sam for me. I wish I could have come visited with you both."

"It's so okay, my love," he responded affectionately. "I'll be up to visit for the high heel race in a few weeks. Don't think I won't be calling you to reserve your futon. Do you think your friends had a good time?"

Tanner was looking at him with tenderness. "You were perfect. Thank you! It was so good, I almost got in there!"

Keith looked at her skeptically. "It would be a cold day in hell, but you let me know if you ever want to experiment, with a lap dance that is!" he said with a wink.

"I think that's my cue," Bryan said to Jessica. "Thanks for the light."

Keith and Tanner turned toward the two of them on the bench. It was clear from Tanner's expression that she hadn't noticed Jessica eavesdropping.

"See ya, thanks for the chat!" she responded. Keith gave her a good-bye wave and the dancers headed off. Tanner and Jessica were left in awkward silence.

Jessica was not sure what to do next. She wasn't going to be able to slip out under Tanner's nose, but she wasn't eager to go back inside. She settled on waiting for Tanner to head back in since it was her party, but Tanner didn't move. She was lingering and the silence was hanging awkwardly. Jessica stayed where she was uncertainly. She was about to give in and go back inside herself when Tanner spoke.

"Keith used to live in DC. His boyfriend Sam used to work with me."

"I didn't ask," Jessica shot back. Tanner seemed struck by Jessica's words.

"Okay sorry, I was just trying to make conversation."

Things got awkward and quiet again.

"Does this whole weekend have to be like this between us?" The question was oddly soft. Again, Jessica was surprised Tanner wasn't fighting back or storming off. She seemed to be taking the high ground. Well, Jessica wasn't going to let Tanner be the bigger person.

"I don't know why you would want to make conversation..."

Tanner didn't respond.

Jessica knew she couldn't be less inviting, but she couldn't stop herself. "So you know Keith and his boyfriend from your fucked up, homophobic Christian website?" The question was intentionally bitchy, but it was most likely the truth.

Tanner turned away, avoiding eye contact. Jessica had her answer. "Never mind, I thought we could be civil, but I'll just leave you alone." Tanner didn't seem angry, she seemed almost sad. She began to walk away from Jessica and back toward the bar.

"Listen, Tanner..." Jessica's tone began to soften against her will, and Tanner paused and looked back at her. She couldn't maintain her state of anger without Tanner participating. "I don't know what you want from me. This is obviously not fun for either of us. I don't really know you and you don't really know me. Maybe we can just get through this weekend and try to be there for Bernie."

Tanner's sadness was more apparent now. She looked more crushed than anything else. "I just thought... I mean, we aren't so different. I think we can agree this isn't either of our scenes."

"I don't know anything about you. This seems very much your scene. You're the one planning this whole weekend and you literally put penis straws in my gift basket."

Tanner chuckled at that. "You can't think that was for my benefit?"

"I don't know...you literally chanted 'girl squad' like a cult member like a second ago." The charge wasn't quite fair and Jessica knew it. The weekend was for Bernie and if not for the frustration Jessica was feeling, she would have admired Tanner's playfulness, not to mention her extreme competence and attention to detail.

"Of course I don't want to drink out of a penis straw or hire male strippers. It's my job as the maid of honor to make sure Bernie has a good time and if you knew Bernie, you would know that she is just a little bit of a cliché. I'm not disappointing her on her bachelorette weekend just because you're a wet blanket!"

The judgment stung. The jab about knowing Bernie hit a little too close to home for Jessica. "I know Bernie," she insisted. "I just have limits and I would—" At that moment, the front door opened and a very drunk Bernie came stumbling out.

"There you both are!" She grabbed Tanner and Jessica and pulled them into a very uncomfortable group hug. Jessica was careful to keep some space between herself and Tanner like same-sided magnets.

"Tanner, I love my party! The karaoke was perfect! And then strippers? All I can say is I hope that isn't my last lap dance ever. I'm going to have to tell Chris he has something to live up to!" The image of Bernie's Wall Street fratty-looking fiancé giving a lap dance was now lasered into Jessica's brain.

Tanner laughed. "I'm sure he'll appreciate hearing the details, but let's save that phone call till tomorrow morning, okay, Bern?"

Bernie smiled indulgently. "You're such a good friend, Tan, always looking out." Bernie hadn't let go of Jessica and pulled her closer when she spoke far too loudly for their proximity. "I'm so happy you came, Jess. I thought you wouldn't." She clearly meant it affectionately, but Jessica couldn't help but feel guilty. "I wish we did stuff more, you know? It doesn't have to be karaoke. Just…stuff." The drunken babble was completely heart melting for Jessica, even after her conversation only minutes ago with Tanner. Before she could think of something to say, Tanner took control.

"Okay, drunky, let's head home. We're going to have so much more time with Jess this weekend."

The remark stung. Not because it was mean or anything. It was partially the guilt, but also the way she said "Jess." Clearly a slip from a time when they were familiar with each other, familiar enough to use a nickname. The whole conversation was starting to hurt in every which way.

"Can you stay with her while I get the others?" Tanner asked Jessica with a gentleness she didn't deserve. Jessica nodded and Tanner headed back inside. Jessica sat down on the bench and Bernie sat with her, laying her head on her shoulder and almost immediately starting to doze off. The feeling was nice. Jessica couldn't help but sense she had missed her sister these last years and this silent moment with her was making that more and more difficult to ignore.

Chapter Five

The conversation with Tanner didn't sit well with Jessica. There was something about Tanner's demeanor that made it hard to hold on to her feelings of hatred. Jessica could feel herself questioning her own reality. Was Tanner really that bad? Yes, being outed was awful and having it happen from someone she cared about was devastating, but they were so young at the time. This was the issue, this questioning. Jessica knew what happened when they were teenagers and she knew Tanner deserved her aversion, but people grow up. People change. It wasn't easy staying mad at the sixteen-year-old version of someone.

But there were also so many reminders of how much hurt she still had from when they were kids. She wasn't a very popular person in high school, but nothing prepared her for the isolation and loneliness she felt after everything happened. When she really thought about it, it wasn't like she was bullied, exactly, it was more like an all-consuming paranoia she felt about what people knew about her and whether or not she could trust anyone, especially after she had put all her trust in Tanner.

There was something so uniquely painful about having everyone else know something so private, something so personal, something she wasn't ready to talk about. It felt like she was naked in front of everyone every day at school. And it wasn't just having them know, it was the way she reacted to being outed. When Kayla confronted her, she lied. And afterward, anytime someone asked or it ever came up, she denied it. It wasn't until she was so depressed that her parents were getting concerned that she was basically forced to open up. And even after that, it wasn't until college, and after making friends like Bryce, that she was even able to feel like her sexual orientation was something that she could feel okay with, and ultimately proud of.

It was hard for Jessica to know what was real at this point. So much of the events of her childhood were hard to be objective about. She only knew her own perspective, and her own perspective took into consideration everything that came on the heels of being outed. The time she didn't go to prom because she felt like no one wanted her there. Was that real, or was that just something she imagined? The way her mom reacted to learning she was gay, the disappointment that was so evident on her face. Of course, that wasn't Tanner's fault, but it was all tangled up together into one big storm cloud of angst. Her mind was bouncing all over the place.

They all went back to the Airbnb, and mercifully for Jessica, everyone was ready for bed. The last thing Jessica wanted was everyone hanging out in the common space, aka her makeshift bedroom, forcing her to stay awake as well. They all went to their respective rooms and Jessica got her toiletry bag and searched for the closest empty bathroom. When she finished, she turned off the light and entered the dark hallway. In near blindness, she crashed into someone, dumping some of her toiletries onto the ground.

"I'm so sorry. I wasn't..." Tanner said as she helped pick things up off the floor.

"It's okay," Jessica replied automatically, picking up things as well. When she finished, she stood up, taking in Tanner in her sleep clothes. She had on a very out of character Rocky Horror Picture Show shirt and those very cute horn-rimmed glasses Jessica saw at the airport. Jessica confirmed her original assessment—the glasses made Tanner look, if possible, more stunning.

They stood there awkwardly. Jessica tried to move one way, but Tanner did the same. This happened no less than three times before they both laughed. The release felt good. Jessica wasn't trying to be friendly, but the physical awareness of the situation was impossible not to laugh at. Tanner finally reached out to hold Jessica in place as she moved past her. The gesture was clearly meant to be funny, but the contact felt intense. They both continued to stand there not moving, but it was Jessica's turn to help the situation.

"Okay, good night," she said. For the first time, Jessica could hear that her own voice had lost its defensiveness. The interaction felt normal, not like a conversation with her least favorite person in the universe.

"Good night," Tanner responded with a smile. This was also the first smile Jessica had seen from Tanner. It warmed her in a way she couldn't control.

Jessica scampered to her couch flustered and conflicted. She got into her makeshift bed and couldn't help but feel her body vibrating with energy. Nothing was going the way she planned, at least not when it came to Tanner.

She lay there for a while, ruminating on the last twenty-four hours. She couldn't help but question herself. Why was she holding on to so much anger? She didn't have to like Tanner, but couldn't she be indifferent? It was taking a surprising amount of energy to maintain her hatred. Especially when she thought about their last interaction outside the bathroom or the conversation outside the karaoke place.

But it wasn't just Tanner's kindness toward Jessica in spite of her lack of reciprocation, it was other things. It was the way Tanner was so attentive to Bernie. In high school, it made Jessica feel jealous to see the way her sister almost preferred Tanner to her, but seeing them together now, she was appreciative of the love that Tanner showed Bernie. She could see that there was a loyalty there. And it was also the overall competence and efficiency that Tanner brought to the weekend. Jessica was a sucker for anyone who was proficient or organized. Maybe it was because her home had always been so disorganized. Her parents were always late, her things were always going missing. She loved people who had a handle on situations. It calmed her frazzled mind.

Jessica could accept that Tanner had a lot of wonderful qualities, but she reminded herself that none of those things canceled out the very real damage Tanner had done when they were younger. It had affected her entire life, maybe more than she would even admit. But it wasn't just what happened, Tanner had other bad qualities.

Didn't she?

Jessica tried to remember. *What about her job? Yeah, what was that about?* Jessica sat up and reached for her computer from the nearby coffee table. She knew that Tanner worked for mommy+me.com, a Christian mommy website. She had never really looked into it because knowing that much told her she wasn't interested, but now that she had time and she was considering easing some of her contempt, she thought it might be good to know what exactly the site was about.

She typed in the URL and perused the site. The articles on the main page were fairly run-of-the-mill, mostly about community events and attachment parenting. She clicked on the weekly advice column that she assumed had to be Tanner. The column was called A Mother's Calling. She recognized the name from her sister mentioning it.

Title: Trusting Yourself When Motherhood Gets Tough
Dear moms,
Being a parent is an amazing journey, but it can also be challenging. There are days when we feel like we've got

everything under control, and there are days when we feel like we're barely keeping our heads above water. It's normal to feel overwhelmed or discouraged at times, but it's important to remember that you have the strength and resilience to handle whatever comes your way.

Here are a few things I've learned about trusting yourself when motherhood gets tough:

1. Lean on your support system.
2. Take care of yourself.
3. Trust your instincts.
4. Celebrate the small victories.

So if you're a mom who's feeling overwhelmed or discouraged, remember that you can always turn to A Mother's Calling for help and guidance. God loves you and cares about every detail of your life, including your role as a parent. And you're not alone—you have a community here to support and encourage you.

Blessings,

A Mother's Calling

Jessica read the blog entry and was pretty confused by it. Tanner definitely didn't have kids. *What the fuck was that?* She also didn't remember Tanner being religious when they were friends in high school. Actually, she could remember a particularly controversial school newspaper article involving abortion that Tanner wrote that led to some of the more religious students in school protesting. All of this did not add up.

She decided to google the site itself. A bunch of articles came up from well-known media sites calling out mommy+me as every kind of "phobic." Jessica scrolled through an article that referenced columns on the site titled "Religious discrimination and how same-sex marriage has hurt the American family" and "How to support your husband in the ways God intended." The article went on to call out the site's leadership as well as a history of working with far-right advertisers.

She considered reading more mommy+me articles, but decided she didn't want the clicks screwing with her advertising algorithm. Jessica wasn't religious, but she wasn't exactly anti-religious. She did, however, have very little exposure to this type of thing. I mean, it seemed clear that Tanner was…in the closet at work? Faking a persona? Or was her real-life self the fake one? The whole thing gave her a stomachache. It really didn't make any sense. A person, living this level of hypocrisy. It was one thing to have a fake persona in order to write a mommy blog, maybe that could help some people, but the site itself was clearly a dog whistle for homophobes and Christian fundamentalists who would definitely not be cool with having a lesbian as a columnist.

All of this really pissed Jessica off. After everything she had been through, she couldn't imagine being a part of something so fundamentally opposed to what she believed in. But then again, she really didn't know Tanner. Tanner came out when she was young, but maybe it wasn't that hard for her. It couldn't have been; she continued to be the most popular girl at school. Maybe she felt being gay wasn't a big deal. Jessica snapped her computer shut and turned herself around, shifting into position to go to sleep.

No, she wouldn't be forgiving Tanner anytime soon. She might not be the person she was when they were sixteen, but whoever Tanner was now, she wasn't someone Jessica wanted to know.

❖

Jessica was awakened by the very loud and annoying high-pitched whirring sound of the coffee grinder. The noise was incredibly persistent, and Jessica could feel it reverberating in her head. All of this brought each and every mimosa from yesterday to the forefront of her regrets. She took her pillow and smashed it over head, hoping to drown out the sound, to no avail. The grinding stopped, but then came the clanking of pans and the beeping of multiple different appliances. Jessica gave out a huff of frustration. The couch was, of course, a better option than the shared bedroom with Tanner, but at what cost! Who in their right mind needed to be up this early? Jessica shifted to peer over the back of the couch and see who the morning offender was. Of course, it was Tanner. Jessica looked at her phone, 11:40 a.m.

Okay, so it wasn't that early.

Jessica threw herself back onto the couch with an even louder growl.

"Shit, I'm sorry. Did I wake you?" Tanner's voice came from the kitchen.

"Obviously!" Jessica responded. Jessica was not a morning person, and this was the exact way she would treat anyone who woke her up. Well, it didn't help that it was Tanner.

"Sorry, I just have to start a few things for later." The response from Tanner was so even-keeled that Jessica realized her change in sleeping locations was not Tanner's problem. The kitchen was a public space and she needed to get over herself.

"No, it's okay!" Jessica shouted back, sounding like it definitely wasn't okay. "The kitchen is a public space." Jessica sat up in earnest this time but pulled her blankets close around her. The mountains were not particularly warm, and she could feel a nip in the air. "It's pretty late. Is no one else awake?"

"Not yet." Tanner began to move around the kitchen again, opening the fridge, pouring things, cutting them. "I think everyone is going to be on recovery mode today."

Jessica nodded and then yawned, stretching her arms as she contemplated if it would be weird to ask Tanner if she could use the bedroom to continue sleeping. Then she noticed Tanner looking at her. When she spotted Jessica catching her, she went back to her tasks.

Jessica decided not to give in to her base desire for more sleep and instead resolved to do the right thing and ask Tanner if she needed help. Jessica got up off the couch and pulled on some sweatpants. She had on an old intramural sports shirt from GW that she'd cut the sleeves off of and shivered slightly under the thin material. She grabbed the lambswool crewneck sweater she stole from her New York City ex before their breakup last fall. It was too big, but that's what made it amazing. She hadn't gotten an "I want my clothes back" text, so a year later, it seemed like she was home-free on keeping the sweater.

She shuffled into the kitchen area and leaned against the island. "Can I help with something?"

Tanner seemed a little flustered as she replied, "No, it's fine, I have it under control." She clearly did, but she had the coffee going, eggs cracked, and multiple pans with some sort of breakfast casserole being assembled, which seemed like a lot to Jessica.

"I'm sure you have it handled, but we should all pitch in. I mean this is Bernie's bachelorette, not the Ritz."

"Okay, umm…" Tanner looked around, clearly uncomfortable giving up control over one of her many food stations.

"How about I finish the coffee and then whisk the eggs?" Jessica said.

Tanner looked at her almost as if sizing her up.

"You will be here supervising the whole time, I promise."

"Okay," she replied reluctantly, and Jessica moved over to the coffee station and started loading the French press and filling up the kettle. They worked together well. Jessica finished her jobs and then took over chopping an onion. The silence was less weird than Jessica would have anticipated. Once they got the oven loaded and they each had a cup of coffee, finding something to say felt more imminent.

Tanner broke first. "So, we both live in DC."

Was that supposed to be a question? Jessica was still salty from learning about Tanner's day job the night before.

Tanner went on. "Kind of interesting that we ended up in the same city."

"I mean, not really. We both grew up in a suburb in Maryland, it's basically our hometown." Jessica's responses were obviously making everything more awkward, but she couldn't help it, she didn't want to chitchat. But between the sounds of the kitchen and the fact that she didn't have her own room, she was a little stuck.

Tanner tried again. "It doesn't feel like where we grew up to me. I don't really run into anyone from home."

Jessica felt the same way, even if it didn't seem that way from what she said previously. She loved DC. It was completely different from where she grew up, something she appreciated immensely. Not only did she never run into anyone from high school, but she was able to reinvent herself almost immediately. Going to GW for undergrad and grad school meant that she had a completely new life and it had been that way for a while.

Jessica decided she would throw Tanner a bone. "You would think we would run into each other. There are only two lesbian bars in DC."

Tanner took a sip from her coffee and seemed to want to say something.

"What? You don't go out? Or?"

"I've seen you around a few times." She paused again. "Over the years."

This was surprising to Jessica. She remembered spotting Tanner one time at that Pride where she dodged out, quite sure Tanner hadn't seen her, but multiple times? The weirdest part for Jessica was just the idea of Tanner being around and her not noticing. That felt incredibly improbable.

"Where'd you see me?"

Tanner shrugged. "I don't know, it's just a few times. Once at a Mitski concert, another time at Phasefest." Then she hesitated again. "Actually, last week, I didn't *see* you, see you, but I do follow QBar on Instagram. So I mean, it's kind of like running into you to see you pop up like that."

Lisa and her stupid Instagram video.

"Oh no, was it the one where I was singing?" Jessica was mortified.

Tanner laughed. "It was. I imagine it was good rehearsal for last night."

Jessica couldn't help but laugh too. "It's weird. How come I haven't seen you even though we've been in the same rooms? A few times at least, anyway."

"Maybe you just didn't notice me."

"Not possible." Did she say that out loud or in her head? From the blushing look on Tanner's face, she'd definitely said it out loud. "I mean, you know, just 'cause I know you from before. …And whatever…you know what I mean."

Jessica felt like she had slipped again, back into the honey trap. She needed to remind herself that Tanner was not a good person, not then and not now—A Mother's Calling? What was that?—and no matter how inviting she was being in this moment, she didn't have a spine. Tanner was not somebody to trust.

Jessica decided the best move was to end this conversation. She cleared her throat and excused herself, saying she wanted to use the bathroom and start getting ready for the day. Tanner seemed to switch gears as well, going back to setup mode for when everyone else woke up. In fact, Jessica was surprised that none of them had appeared in the common room yet since it was past twelve at this point. She hadn't expected to get so much alone time with Tanner.

When Jessica got to the bathroom, she closed the door firmly behind her, relieved to get some much-needed privacy. Maybe that's all the fluttering feeling in her stomach was, a disruption in her usual morning alone-time. But a glance in the mirror showed her face was flushed pink…had she been flustered? Irritated, she chided herself on letting Tanner, well, get to her anyway. Indifference, she chided herself. She needed to work on being indifferent.

❖

Somehow, Jessica found herself keeled over again, hands on her knees, catching her breath and sure she was going to pass out. If she wasn't fully inundated with bachelorette kitsch, she was in physical turmoil. First the hill, then the heights, and now this post-brunch hike that she didn't realize was optional (which was actually written in italics on the itinerary itself, next-level Type A from Tanner). Now she was on a trail somewhere in the Blue Ridge Mountains, being fully left behind by Bernie, Alex, and Tanner. Kayla had stayed behind, very much still recovering from yesterday. Jessica pictured Kayla laid out in a hammock at the Bird's Nest and felt a surge of jealousy. That could have been her, had she participated at all in the coordinating conversation that morning instead of texting with Bryce and checking QBar's Instagram, hoping to live vicariously through her friends.

The hike would have been difficult on a normal day, but with the very persistent hangover pounding in her head, Jessica was pretty sure it might be the most arduous physical experience of her life. Alex was some sort of cross-fit athlete, so she was easily not breaking a sweat. Bernie had somehow woken up hangover-free, something the gods must have blessed her with in honor of her wedding, and who knew why Tanner wasn't struggling. Maybe Jessica was the only one who wasn't a gym rat. Or maybe the others had some kind of mountain goat gene hidden in their DNA somewhere.

With effort, Jessica stood back up and began "hiking" again, slowly. It wasn't that she was totally out of shape—she walked everywhere in DC and went on the occasional run with Bryce—it was the topography. These were MOUNTAINS! Scaling terrain like this required a totally different set of muscles than walking around a relatively flat city like DC. Not to mention the added psychological turmoil of heights. But Jessica soon learned that as long as she focused on looking *out* rather than down, the landscape was manageable, at least on a mental health level.

Maybe a bit better than manageable. Once she got her breath under control and worked back up from her snail's pace to a more reasonable speed, Jessica had to admire the scenery. The towering trees stretched as far as she could see, and the mountain scape lived up to its name, their salute was a deep, hazy blue that seemed to change with the movement of the sun. The air filling Jessica's lungs felt crisp and clean, and the scent of pine was all around her. Despite everything, it was hard to stay surly in a setting like that. When Jessica reached the next peak, she found Bernie, Alex, and Tanner lying on some rocks on an overlook.

"Finally!" Alex exclaimed, clearly calling Jessica out.

"I'm not used to this!" Jessica responded, feeling angsty. "Y'all can leave me. I don't mind finishing it out on my own." A solo hike would have been preferable anyways.

It was Bernie who spoke up. "Jess, we are doing this together even if it means we end up at a crawl." The announcement was obviously meant to be kind and supportive, but it was mostly embarrassing. If it was just the physical exertion, Jessica could have steeled herself and picked up her clip, but the craggy overlook was a lot. She was again dealing with the ever-present sudden cliff's edge that kept sending her into a low-key panic attack.

The group had a short water break, allowing Jessica time to give herself an internal pep talk, and then they set off again at a much slower pace that seemed designed to keep the group together. With the lower level of exertion, it was easier for them to chat. Until now, Jessica had gotten through the weekend pretty easily without ruffling any feathers. She marveled at the accomplishment—she was basically a model of supportive sister.

But then the conversation turned, of course, to wedding-related topics. Alex was asking Bernie about all of her choices so far, flowers, venues, photographers, all the things that apparently came with wedding planning. Bernie seemed to have some of it figured out, but mostly she just sounded overwhelmed.

Jessica should have kept her thoughts to herself, but something about her deprivation of needs and her pounding headache made it hard for her to keep her mask on.

"Well, I know if I ever get married," Alex said, "I'd want to do a destination wedding. Why not get a trip out of it!"

"Totally," Bernie replied. "I wish we could. It's just Chris has a big family and it seemed easier to have it in New York, somewhere they could all get to easily."

"Or you could just go on a trip," Jessica interjected.

"What's that?" Alex responded.

"I mean, you could just go on a trip. You don't have to get married. Seems more economical than forcing all of your friends and families to spend thousands of dollars on travel and clothes." And out came the wedding monster.

It was clear from Alex's face that she wasn't really getting it. "Yeah, I was just saying if I had to have a wedding…"

"But you don't *have to* have a wedding. Like no one is making anyone here get married or have some big wedding. Think about all the other ways you could use your money." Jessica threw out the response without thinking. Only after saying it did she realize the implications for Bernie, who was literally planning her wedding. Jessica immediately regretted her snappy retort. She looked up with remorse, seeking Bernie's face, but found Tanner's instead.

Tanner's eyes flashed. "Just because getting married isn't important to you doesn't mean it isn't important to some people. There are so few rituals in this life. What's wrong with being with the people you love and recognizing a new stage in life?"

Bernie seemed to perk up a bit after Tanner spoke. Jessica hadn't meant to make Bernie feel bad, she just had some hang-ups about marriage. Not to mention, just ten years ago, people like Jessica and Tanner couldn't have even gotten married! What right did Tanner have to defend an institution like that?

"Okay sure," Jessica responded. "It's definitely okay that weddings are important to some people. It's just, does all of this stuff have to be the default? I mean like taking your husband's last name. I live my whole life with my name, then suddenly I have to give it up for some random man I met two and a half years ago?"

"Or woman!" Alex said from the side.

"Or woman, you're right. It's not just the misogynistic stuff, it's the erasing of yourself or the erasing of someone else just because of this societal convention."

"Are you taking Chris's name?" Alex asked Bernie, slightly redirecting from Jessica's rant, but still failing to ease the tension.

"I don't know yet..." Bernie's response seemed cautious. Maybe she was less uncertain before Jessica started proliferating.

Tanner again took up for her. "Some people are more traditional. You have an image in your head of the dress, the ceremony, all of that. Who's to say what's right or wrong."

Jessica tsked loudly, making it clear how she felt about Tanner's response.

By this point, the group had stopped walking and Tanner turned to face Jessica. "What? What's your issue with that?"

"I just think that's very on brand for you," Jessica responded antagonistically.

"I didn't say I was into traditional for myself, I'm just saying what's the big deal."

Jessica gave an exaggerated eye roll. Tanner flushed red while Bernie and Alex shuffled their feet awkwardly in the background.

"I'm seriously not very traditional."

"I think A Mother's Calling says about all there is to say about how traditional you are."

Tanner seemed frazzled by the segue.

"I'm not really following," Alex added.

"She's saying that because of where I work, I can't possibly have my own personal beliefs or values."

"Interesting you mention beliefs and values since those are literally the things you write about. So yeah, I do think it's pretty difficult for me to take you seriously right now."

"Shhh!" Bernie said urgently. Tanner had been about to respond, as evidenced by her increasingly red face and combative stance, but everyone seemed to register from Bernie's timing and intense hand gestures that something was happening. Bernie pointed to the side and not twenty feet away was some sort of large predatory cat, frozen in place and staring at the four of them, seeming just as shocked as they were.

"Oh my God!" Alex whisper-yelled with very clear panic in her voice.

"What do we do!" Bernie hissed, eyes wide.

Jessica was completely frozen. She was already at an eight on her anxiety level from the heights, but this rocketed her well past ten as she stared straight in the eyes of what looked like a mountain lion. Not to mention, Jessica was closest to the animal and most likely to be in last place if they all decided to make a run for it, which was exactly what Jessica was about to do until she felt a hand on her arm.

"Don't run," Tanner said clearly to everyone, but most pointedly to Jessica. Her volume was loud but not panicked. "Put your arms out, make yourself big, and make noise."

The group was slow to react to Tanner's words, but they started lifting their arms and babbling incoherently. Alex seemed to be reciting the words of a Taylor Swift song. Tanner's grip on Jessica's arm was strong and confident, almost protective.

"Okay, start walking, but don't turn your back or avert your eyes too much."

Everyone started walking, but before they did, Tanner put herself in front of Jessica, taking on the most vulnerable position. The move was so shocking to Jessica that she almost forgot she needed to move.

"Jess, follow your sister. You're going to be fine." Tanner's tone was strong, and Jessica was somehow sure that Tanner knew what she was doing.

The group moved slowly and kept their arms up in the air, trying to make themselves look bigger.

"Keep talking to each other, even if it's just random words. You want it to know you're a human. It'll be less likely to attack."

"Are you sure we aren't supposed to make ourselves small or something, the fetal position? I read that somewhere." Alex's voice sounded as shaky as Jessica felt.

Bernie responded at a louder than normal volume but with a calm in her voice. "I think that's bears. Or at least a type of bear."

"Just keep walking and talking," Tanner said, trailing behind them just a bit, very much between Jessica and the mountain lion.

"We aren't that far from the end of the loop, so just a little farther I think," Bernie added, getting her confidence back with Tanner to rely on. Once they passed a particularly sharp curve, the mountain lion fell out of view.

"Are we good?" Jessica asked Tanner, feeling at that moment that she was the authority on all things mountain lion.

"I don't know. It could be following, so we should keep making noise—and don't run—but most likely it moved on." The words weren't especially comforting, so they continued the next ten minutes having loud incoherent conversations. Jessica felt her heart beating all the way in her ears.

Finally, they came to the end of the trail and their car was within view. As soon as they got to the parking lot, their "walk" could barely be called that and ended in a fierce dash to get in and lock the doors. Once they were all in and they were sure no mountain lion was approaching, they all let out frantic sighs or screams that culminated in laughter. There was so much pressure built up that the release felt intoxicating. Alex turned around from the driver's seat to look at Tanner, who was in the back with Jessica.

"Tanner, you're a life saver! How did you do that!" Her enthusiasm and relief were palpable. Jessica could tell Alex wanted to envelop Tanner with appreciation. "Oh my God, yes, Tanner, you are so ridiculously amazing!" Bernie added. "We almost died!"

Jessica couldn't figure out how to use her voice. "I just hike a lot, so I knew what to do." Tanner's humility seemed genuine to Jessica. Or maybe Jessica was incapable of her usual suspicion in this moment.

They all took turns thanking Tanner and reenacting every moment of the last twenty minutes. The mountain lion went from four feet long to ten, and Tanner's heroics turned into her throwing herself in front of Jessica and the rest of the group like a superhero.

Jessica was still frozen. She couldn't even get out a thank you. All she could think about was the place on her arm where Tanner had held her, strong and capable. It felt almost bruised from her grasp, but that wasn't what bothered Jessica.

CHAPTER SIX

The group ended up going out for sandwiches in the nearby town. There was an energy between the four of them, perhaps just the adrenaline from a near-death experience. Jessica didn't know how close they had come to being mauled by an animal, but the fear was enough for her to feel a sense of closeness to the group. Bernie texted Kayla to see if she wanted to join for lunch, but she didn't reply, to Jessica's relief. Stomachs full and blood pressure back to normal, they headed back to the Airbnb and enjoyed a well-timed siesta.

The thing about the itinerary was that it was perfect. At first, Jessica might have thought having no plans for the evening was a mistake, but in reality, it took pressure off of everyone and allowed the group to enjoy the sprawling accommodations and view. They all lounged around on the front and back porches with magazines or books, taking in the amazing scenery. Alex and Tanner took two Adirondack chairs in the back, while Jessica got some alone time with Bernie in the hot tub. Kayla said she had some phone calls home to make, but Jessica spotted her watching TV when she went to the bathroom. It was sort of amazing how someone could choose the Real Housewives over the exquisite mountains and relaxed socializing. But this was all good for Jessica since she had yet to have any sort of conflict, or interaction for that matter, with Kayla. And the more time passed, the fewer opportunities there would be for unpleasantness.

At first, Jessica felt a little awkward hanging out with Bernie in the hot tub. It wasn't that Jessica had any sort of animosity toward her sister, she just wasn't used to being around her. She decided she should see it as an opportunity for them to reconnect—it would be good to learn more about Bernie's life these days, especially about this guy she was marrying.

Jessica jumped right in. "So, Bern, what is Chris like?"

Bernie lit up at the question. "He's amazing, Jess. He's kind and handsome, I—I think you would like him."

Bernie had a history of dating guys who, to put it mildly, totally sucked. It wasn't just that they were shitty or dull, it was much worse. The last guy Bernie dated was actually outwardly cruel to her. Jessica met him at a birthday dinner for their mom and couldn't believe the way he micromanaged everything Bernie said and repeatedly put her down. And all the boyfriends before that were just some variation of that guy in different degrees going all the way back to high school, where Bernie dated the first version, Kyle Clarkson. Jessica remembered thinking he was the biggest idiot in the school who basically jerked Bernie around for three years only for Bernie to discover that he had been cheating on her the whole time. Bernie was trusting, and sometimes trusting people get hurt the most.

"I guess I'll be meeting him soon!" Jessica tried to put some needed excitement in her voice. She was starting to feel guilty. She knew from her mom that Bernie and Chris had been together for two and a half years. That was a pretty long time not to meet a sibling's partner. "I'm sorry I haven't been around that much," Jessica said.

"It's okay!" Bernie's response came out fast, almost as if she didn't want Jessica to feel guilty for even a second. That only made it worse. "I know you have a whole life going on and I'm just happy you're here."

Jessica wasn't sure if Bernie was just saying that. She still wasn't certain if her mom was making Bernie include her in the wedding, but the words sounded genuine. Jessica wanted to lighten the mood, so she brought up what she learned on the hike.

"So...you're considering becoming Bernadine... What's his last name again?"

"Gray."

"Gray, that's quite a name." Then she did some quick math. "Wait, your fiancé is named Chris Gray? Like Christian Grey from *Fifty Shades of Grey*?" The concept was hilarious to Jessica. Bernie turned fifty shades of blushed. "Well, his mom named him before the books came out, obviously!"

"That's so funny! Poor thing, how does he survive that?"

Bernie laughed as well. "Well, I think it hasn't hurt with women, but I think he gets a lot of ribbing at work. Everyone is always gifting him floggers or things like that. You know, he works on Wall Street, so the crowd can get a little fratty."

"That sounds like my nightmare." The fratty Wall Street crowd didn't sound promising and neither did his literary reference namesake, but Jessica really couldn't hold that against him. Bernie said he was kind, an underrated quality, and she would have some time this weekend to do some recon. Maybe Alex would have a take.

"How do you like DC?" After a small lull, it seemed like Bernie was eager to keep the conversation going. She looked at Jessica with such interest.

"It's cool. I hate my job, but you know, I like the city."

"Mom says you have a cool apartment and a bit of a scene there."

Jessica rolled her eyes. "Mom makes everything so cringe!"

Bernie laughed. "She does, but she means well."

It was true that they both got along with their mom. Why was it they couldn't really make it happen between them? And when Jessica thought about it, it wasn't just after their dad died seven years ago. This distance was before all that, going back to high school even.

"Maybe I could visit sometime?" Bernie's question held trepidation that Jessica hadn't expected. It never even occurred to her that Bernie might want to visit.

"For sure, you are totally welcome! You and Christian Grey." She couldn't help but say his name with a teasing tone.

"It's Chris," she corrected her. "And I was thinking maybe I'd come alone? Get some sister time?"

"Sorry, I'll keep the teasing to a minimum." Jessica was surprised by how easily the conversation flowed. Yes, Bernie was always kind, but something about her with her friends around had made Jessica forget that they could get along. Even the idea that Bernie wanted to come visit and stay with her solo was surprising. "And yeah, I'd like that," Jessica said, deciding she really would.

They went on chatting for a bit, but they were both starting to get pruney and with the sun going down, they were both feeling ready for a glass of wine. The group was scheduled for serve-yourself pasta in about an hour, courtesy of a caterer Tanner had diligently worked into the itinerary, and Jessica was finally able to hydrate and relax enough for a glass.

She decided the polite thing to do would be to offer to the others as well, so she wrapped herself in a towel and set out toward the back lawn where Alex and Tanner were to see if they wanted a glass. Because of trees and the other greenery, she was somehow able to sneak up behind them unheard, catching some of their conversation when she overheard her name and stopped.

"…yeah, Jessica seemed pretty irritated with you on the trail." Jessica could hear Alex's voice and froze.

"Yeah, she doesn't like me very much."

"I bet she liked you a little more after you saved all of us from that mountain lion."

"I doubt it." Jessica heard a sadness in Tanner's voice.

They both went quiet. Jessica was about to sneak away when she heard Alex say, "She is pretty hot though, you have to admit that at least."

Jessica was shocked and flattered. She did not expect that from Alex, and she wouldn't admit it, but she was even more fixated on Tanner's response.

"I didn't know you were into women?" Tanner said.

"I have eyes!" Alex said playfully. "I mean she has that whole dark brooding androgynous thing going. I'm pretty straight, but I might make an exception for her." It was clearly a joke, but still deeply flattering to Jessica. "Come on, is she not your type or something?"

The pause was endless.

"She's definitely my type," Tanner finally said with exasperated sigh.

Jessica couldn't believe what she was hearing. Did Tanner just admit that Jessica was her type? This was almost too much for her to process. She knew she should stop listening, but she couldn't. She had to hear more.

"I knew it! I thought I saw you checking her out at the karaoke bar."

"I was not!"

"Come on, why not? I mean, you're gay, she's gay, what's the problem?"

"Listen, just because I admitted she's hot doesn't mean I'm interested. Besides, did you forget the part where she hates me?"

"Yeah, why is that? I mean, you two seem like pretty cool people. Not to mention, you live in the same city, you both have Bernie."

Hearing that Tanner was attracted to her had Jessica's heart beating out of her chest. But she was also extremely curious about what Tanner's take on their dynamic was.

"It's kind of a long story, but I think things were just kind of confusing when we were in high school. And I...well, I made some mistakes."

Jessica thought that was a pretty diplomatic way of talking about outing the only other gay girl that she knew in the school.

"Have you ever thought about talking to her about it?" Alex asked.

"I think it's pretty clear she doesn't want anything to do with me."

"I don't know about that," Alex said in a teasing tone. "You weren't the only one I saw checking someone out."

Jessica heard what sounded like a guffaw. "Stop! I wasn't checking her out and neither was she."

"Whatever, you two can do whatever little staring game you're playing in peace. I'll just mind my own business."

Jessica was about as embarrassed as she could possibly be, so she decided this would be a good moment to sneak away. It wasn't worth hearing any more about how transparent her involuntary attraction to Tanner was. She was able to slink back up the deck and in the door where she was alone in the main room, her sleeping room.

What had she just heard? Tanner thought she was hot? Alex picked up on something between them? This was not good. She was right back in high school, acting like a puppy dog, waiting for Tanner to give her a compliment or a look, anything to let her know she wasn't invisible. Jessica did not want to fall into this again. Not to mention, Tanner's version of events, no matter how vague, proved that she remembered what happened. On some level, just knowing that gave Jessica a deep feeling of relief. Knowing this older version of Tanner had her second-guessing her memory of events when she was younger, but it seemed that Tanner knew what she did and also knew she didn't have much of a chance in hell of fixing things between them. What she didn't know was how her actions affected Jessica. Tanner would have to have been in her life, been the friend she'd pretended to be to know how consequential her actions were. Jessica tried hard to remind herself to stay true to that in the coming days.

❖

"You bitches ready?" Kayla shouted through the house as the Uber pulled up.

What was supposed to be a "low-key night in" had become the complete opposite. Somehow, they had all agreed to go to a "club" as the only way to get Kayla to stop complaining and to stop calling them all losers. It was pretty sad that they all caved, but it was their last night and Tanner did have a long contingency list of "night life options" for just this exact brand of peer pressure.

The dinner earlier was awkward, not that anyone noticed. Jessica's head was full of conflicting things. Overhearing Tanner's thoughts and feelings wasn't an easy thing to forget, and as the night went on she could find herself remembering Tanner's words and experiencing an involuntary swoop in her stomach and a very visible and debilitating blush.

As they piled into the car, on their way to Eclipse Lounge, the most popular and most likely to be annoying club in Asheville, Jessica found herself distracted. She didn't even think to complain about the destination or what she could only imagine would be an absolutely awful straight club with bad music, bad drinks, and all-around bad vibes. They all piled into an extra-large SUV, coordinated by Tanner and obviously equipped to handle the steep hill. Jessica found herself seated next to Tanner in the very back. Her awareness of Tanner had always been present, but since she overheard her attraction to her, it seemed her awareness had become more pronounced. The very back seats were smaller and more cramped. Her jean-clad leg was pressed against Tanner's bare leg as she was in a pretty short and revealing red dress. The look was sultry, and Jessica was sure she would be a distraction for everyone in the club, including herself. The place where their legs touched was all she could think about. It made it hard to hear the conversation, which was mostly a relief because Kayla was telling some story about Bernie and Tanner in high school that included the prom and some sort of cheerleading ritual, all of which Jessica was in no way interested in. She remembered all the stupid things the popular kids used to do and she was never going to be someone who would go to prom. Not to mention, by that point she had been outed and the idea of going to some formal dance where all the people who bullied her grinding on each other and crowning each other in ridiculous fake ceremonies was not something that would have interested her. Tanner was prom queen of her year and Bernie the year after so that told her all she needed to know.

When they arrived at the club Tanner got out of the car first pulling Jessica out of her reverie. The club was big and glitzy with a thumping electronic beat already reaching them on the street. Jessica was going considerably slower on the drinking, so the music was a little loud for her at that point. Kayla, however, was already at a ten and seemed to be the hype girl for the excursion since it seemed like everyone was a little lukewarm on the activity.

"Wooooooo, finally, we get to dance!" Kayla was clearly one-track-minded.

Bernie and Alex seemed to be able to get a little more excited, but Tanner was back to her stand-offish quiet self. At this point, Jessica was starting to think that was what she was like all the time. They went in and had their purses checked and their IDs. Jessica didn't have a purse so she zipped right in and got a preview. The club was large and full of people. The music was loud and the strobe lights were flashing so hard that Jessica was mostly concentrating on adjusting her balance to the intensity of the situation. It was almost like getting her sea legs. Jessica couldn't help but notice how many people there were. That was the thing about straight places, they could be so big because there were so many of them. If she went to a queer bar, even in a big city, it was usually a pretty small place with an even smaller dance floor, especially if it wasn't a gay guy bar. This bar wasn't even the only club in downtown Asheville. There were at least three more on the list. It was overwhelming to imagine frequenting places like that ever.

Everyone came in and received a wristband that led to a little VIP lounge area to the right of the DJ stand.

"How did we get this?" Alex asked the group.

"I called earlier to get us access to the VIP area just so we wouldn't have to fight for seating," Tanner responded. Even when the group changed their plans, the ever competent Tanner found a way to make the experience as seamless as possible. One of the security people led them to the roped-off area where they had a few lounge chairs reserved and a bottle of champagne on ice.

"The champagne comes with the VIP area," the bouncer explained. They all sat down except for Kayla. She was ready to dance. She put her purse on the lounger, but then went straight out to the dance floor. The song was some techno remix of a Drake song, and Jessica was unable to imagine going out there with Kayla, even though on some level, she did want to dance. Alex, Bernie, and Tanner were attempting to talk, but the volume of the music had most of what was being said come down to short spurts of observation and nods. Jessica was very much over champagne so she let the others enjoy as she watched the dance floor anthropologically. Two guys from the adjoining couches in the VIP area came over and offered to buy them, but more specifically Alex, a drink. They seemed like two rather standard guys, and Bernie and Alex seemed to enjoy the attention. Tanner smiled kindly, but she slowly seemed to back out of the exchange and sit back on her lounge chair.

Jessica had nothing to say, and it seemed neither did Tanner, but they took turns watching the dance floor and accidentally exchanging looks. As the guys' group started to integrate a little more with their own, Jessica noticed Tanner move a bit closer to her more isolated edge of the couch, perhaps so she didn't get caught in the very obvious flirting going on between Bernie, Alex, and the guys. Jessica sipped her complimentary bottled water.

"I'm going to go to the main bar to get a drink!" Jessica yelled over to Bernie. She wasn't sure if Bernie heard, but she thumbs-upped her and continued her conversation. Bernie might not have heard, but Tanner did.

"Can I come with? I can't have any of this champagne after last night."

Jessica shrugged but waited a little bit for Tanner to get her things together. Yes, she had softened to Tanner already.

They moved toward the main bar to the right of the DJ stand very close to their section and were immediately bombarded with bodies pushing their way to the front. Jessica found herself staying close to Tanner just out of pure survival. Again, this was not how it was at the places she frequented. There was almost always a pretty safe circle of space and no men passing her in the back or putting their hand on the small of her back when they passed her. She was getting more and more irate as each touch or jab or nudge happened. They both got to the bar at about the same time, but the bartender seemed to zero in almost immediately on Tanner.

"What can I get you, beautiful?" he asked, moving quickly but still finding a way to be creepy.

"What do you want?" Tanner shouted.

Jessica thought fast. "A lager."

"Two lagers," Tanner repeated. The man got them fast, swiped her card, and then moved on to the next person.

"Thanks," Jessica said. They worked their way out of the crowd and just as they got to the fringes, a man bumped into Jessica spilling his entire rum and Coke down her shirt. He was fully unaware she was there and barely acknowledged what he had done as Jessica held her shirt out to dry.

"Hey, what the fuck, man?" Tanner yelled at the oblivious man. He definitely heard her and looked around almost as if seeing them both for the first time.

"Sorry, lady," he said, clearly for Tanner's sake.

Tanner rolled her eyes and reached out for Jessica's hand.

"Come on!" She pulled Jessica through the crowed to a door that led to a heated patio. The music was still playing but at a considerably lower decibel, and they had a lot more space to maneuver. They went to the patio's edge and paused. Jessica was pretty wet from his drink, but worse than the wetness was the smell of rum that would be on her for the rest of the night.

Jessica could tell that Tanner was just as relieved as she was to get some air and some space from all the people.

"Thanks for telling that guy off…and for the drink."

"You're welcome."

"And for saving me from getting mauled by a mountain lion," Jessica added, knowing that was something she still needed to acknowledge.

"I don't know if he was going to maul us. He was probably more scared of us than we were of him."

"He didn't look very scared to me."

Tanner seemed uncomfortable with the praise.

"You're welcome."

The silence between them came back.

"You know…" Tanner began. "Never mind." The words were said as if she was holding something back.

"What?"

"No, it's okay. Maybe it's better not to get into it."

"No, what?" But Jessica was afraid of the answer, but she couldn't not know. She hoped it wasn't some big conversation about the past, like Alex had suggested.

To her relief, Tanner said, "I'm not really that into marriage either. I agree with you about the money and traditions and all that. Not to mention just the history of it as a woman, as a queer person, just for the record."

Jessica let go of the breath she was holding. Oh yeah, their argument from the hike. That was a relief.

"That's really surprising to me."

"Because of my job?"

"Yes, mainly, but for other reasons too."

"Okay, what other reasons? Because I'm not more 'alternative looking' or because I attend corporate-sponsored pride parades? Don't try to tell me you don't."

"I don't work for an anti-LGBTQ Christian propaganda site!" Jessica didn't like the corporate pride dig because Tanner was right. She was building her impression off of some pretty aesthetic assumptions. But the site! How could Tanner do something like that? "And don't tell me it's just a 'job.' I'm sure that's what the Nazis said!"

"Why are Nazis everyone's go-to example whenever they want to make a point?"

"Are you saying it isn't a fucked up site?"

Tanner seemed to consider Jessica's question. "I think the site has many problems and it's done many things I don't agree with, yes."

"So why do you work there?" The question was burning in Jessica. It didn't make any sense. "And a mommy blog? I feel like I would have heard if you had some kids I don't know about."

"If you must know, I don't exactly choose the job or the column. A Mother's Calling was a blog that my college mentor ran, and she was wonderful. She got sick and she couldn't keep up so I took over to help out."

This was not what Jessica expected. She was helping someone out. Jessica couldn't decide if that changed things.

"So you pretend to have a kid? That's seriously so weird, Tanner." The kid thing didn't factor into her explanation.

"I guess it could seem that way, but I helped raise my sister's daughter, Gracie, since she was a single mother, and it just felt like a small detail at the time."

Jessica considered all that Tanner had said. Her explanation definitely showed things in a different light, even the fake kid considering she did have a kid in her life and the blog seemed to be more of a persona than anything. Jessica could accept a lot of that if she stretched, but the site itself? It was borderline a Breitbart subsidiary.

"Okay, sure, but how could you possibly work for a site that was so anti-queer. I mean that should be hard for anyone, but as a queer person?"

Tanner took a sip of her beer. "I don't know if things are so black-and-white for me."

Tanner was infuriating.

"How could anything be more black-and-white than not working for an organization that teaches people to hate themselves or tells people they need to not act on their homosexuality? I read a few articles, I know what its politics are."

Tanner seemed to consider. "You work at the Daily Paper right?"

"Yeah, so?"

"So I imagine your readers mostly live in DC and New York and are pretty similar politically, at least on certain issues... right?"

"I mean depends how far left you go."

"Well, for instance, on LGBTQ+ issues, it's not like you are converting many people. It's a bubble, right? Everyone has a Coexist sticker on their Subaru."

"Kind of an oversimplification, but okay. What's your point?"

"My point is when I took over the column, I knew who I would be reaching. I would be reaching mothers, most likely conservative mothers who don't have space to talk about what they're going through or things like postpartum or gender roles. These mothers raise kids many of whom turn out to be LGBTQ+ and through this column I can start to move the conversation to empathy and acceptance. It's not easy to thread the needle, but I always talk about acceptance and kindness. And when a mother writes in talking about being scared her kid might be gay, I'm the person receiving that letter and not someone else, someone who might give very different advice. When I think about impact, this is where I make the most impact."

The logic was interesting, and the passion that Tanner expressed was compelling, but Jessica just couldn't help but be critical. The utilitarian argument was kind of a slippery slope.

"That's sort of a dangerous morality don't you think? I mean you are bringing more readers to the site, and even if your column is what you say it is, what's the column below it or above it?"

Tanner seemed to consider Jessica's point.

"I'm not a perfect person. This job isn't where I wanted to end up, but life has been a complicated road for me and this is where I landed. I make a difference in my way, and for now that's enough. You can have your opinion of me if you want. I'm sure there is a lot you can judge about me, but that is the answer to your question."

The declaration had a finality to it. Jessica was reluctant to pry any further. Tanner had been pretty open for someone who knew Jessica was most likely going to hate anything she had to say. But when Jessica searched herself, she knew she didn't have the same ire that she had when she first read the column. She could see some mitigating factors. It wasn't something she could do, but weren't there ways she compromised every day at the Daily Paper? She didn't fully relate, but the idea that Tanner was some sort of monster who was a turncoat alt-right queer person was no longer on the table. This again threw Jessica off her stride.

"Maybe we should agree to disagree on this," she said, since she needed more time to consider her feelings.

Tanner seemed fine with the armistice. "Do you want to go inside?"

"Not particularly. I prefer you to a gaggle of horny club people," Jessica responded, not thinking about the implication of her words. A couple of days ago, she would have felt more than happy to have Tanner experience the snideness of her words, but it didn't feel the same now. Maybe it was the mountain lion or the conversation about her job, but Jessica regretted what she said.

"Maybe I should go inside," Tanner said, deflated.

"Hey, listen, I…you don't have to. I shouldn't have said that." Jessica decided then and there to take a step to ease their awkwardness. "It seems like we have a lot more time between now and the wedding that we'll be spending together and I really don't want to be an asshole to you the whole time, so how about a truce, or a fresh start? I don't really know you anymore." *Or maybe ever at all.* "So let's just be cordial. What do you think?"

"I would really like that." Tanner sighed in what sounded like relief, and then Jessica saw the first genuine smile from Tanner the whole weekend. It was contagious. Jessica felt a weight lift as well. "Okay, maybe we should go back inside, just to make sure Bernie doesn't go home with some rando and ruin her Fifty Shades-themed wedding."

"Bernie would never allow a Fifty Shades-themed…" Tanner caught herself. "That was a joke."

"Yeah, that was a joke," Jessica said pointedly. They both laughed, less because it was funny and more because there was so much relief felt from having the tension between them release a bit.

"Okay," Tanner said, comically pepping herself up. "Let's go back in. I do have to warn you, I'm a pretty good dancer and if they play even one Rihanna song, I have to go out on the dance floor."

"Oh, well, that makes two of us… I must dance when Rihanna plays."

When they both reentered the club, all of the "girl squad" were on the dance floor sans guys, and both Tanner and Jessica joined them.

"Where'd your admirers go?" Jessica asked Alex over the music, as Alex moved to the music.

"We got bored and confessed that most of us were married, about to be, or gay. They moved on after that."

Jessica danced along with everyone and couldn't help but feel she was actually having some fun. She watched Tanner through the strobe lights, and she had to admit, if only to herself, that Tanner was a good dancer. But maybe the word wasn't "good." She was a ridiculously sexy dancer, and try as Jessica might, she just couldn't keep her eyes off of her.

❖

"Okay, promise me I'll see you in Boston in December!" Alex said, hugging Tanner good-bye.

"I'm sad you can't make the bridal shower, but don't worry, I'll fill you in at the next wedding thing. You are for sure going to be at the dress fitting in New York, right?"

"Wouldn't miss it!"

Jessica was packed and sitting on her bed/couch in what was consistently the most populated room in the house. Hearing about the bridal shower and the dress fitting was really setting in how much time she was going to have to dedicate to this wedding in the coming months.

She wished she could ride with Alex, but Alex wasn't heading to the airport just yet. She was visiting with a friend in Asheville for one more night. Kayla had left earlier that morning, something Jessica was very aware of since her clanging and loud stepping woke her up at five a.m. Bernie left shortly after, but she, quite sweetly, scheduled in some time having coffee solo with Jessica. It was all very cute, and Jessica was surprised to realize that she was looking forward to Bernie potentially visiting.

The only person left was Tanner, who had specifically tried to be the last person to leave in order to handle all the final requirements for leaving the Airbnb. Coincidentally, it seemed Jessica and Tanner were both on the same flight out, something they were finally able to discuss without Jessica adding some snarky comment or agreeing to pay sixty dollars for an extra Uber.

This time, they agreed to ride together. If that wasn't progress Jessica didn't know what was.

❖

The ride was mostly in comfortable silence, something Jessica could not imagine being possible a few days ago. The night before had been a turning point for her and Tanner and she was left with a new feeling, almost something healing. She looked over at Tanner, as they wove through some of those hills that had made it impossible for her to get to the house via car. Tanner looked relaxed, perhaps for the first time over the course of the entire trip. Tanner had her sunglasses on and what looked like the most comfortable cardigan sweater.

When Jessica saw Tanner at the airport, she remembered thinking she was still a preppy cheerleader nightmare, but now, after spending some time together, she could see that Tanner was different. She looked like more of an adult than any of the other women from the bachelorette, including Jessica. She had a poise and a quiet presence that hadn't been there when they were kids. And of course, she was beautiful. Beautiful in a way she hadn't been before.

There was also something withholding, something jaded about her demeanor. This wasn't the bright young person that Jessica was friends with, or the cold unfeeling person who had hurt her so badly. This person was someone new. This person was someone she was just starting to get to know. But the thing about Tanner was that all of the versions of her were interesting to Jessica, whether she liked to admit it or not. Even hating Tanner was a form of obsession. Seeing this new side of Tanner wasn't helping.

"I was thinking," Jessica said. "For the bridal shower in Maryland, maybe we could carpool."

Tanner didn't respond right away. It was clear she was not expecting the question. Well, not so much question, it was more a statement. Not that Jessica wasn't overwhelmed with the weird feeling that Tanner might say no. It was honestly so disorienting to suddenly be on the other foot with Tanner.

"Yeah, I ummm...that works for me."

"Do you have a car?" Jessica was not equipped with any form of transportation that wasn't some form of public transportation.

"I was going to borrow my roommate's car, so I can just, maybe pick you up?"

"Okay, great. I live in Columbia Heights. How about you?"

"Dupont. Your place is basically on the way."

"Yeah, it's kind of weird that we live so close." Jessica said it without thinking.

"Yeah, I know. I imagine we go to the same Trader Joe's." The joke was a mercy.

"Ah, that's why I haven't run into you. I'm more of a Safeway person."

"Well, that explains it."

Talking about DC and imagining being in the same neighborhood had already started to feel weird to Jessica. She was almost letting Tanner into her world, something she imagined would feel painful. But it didn't feel painful; it felt the opposite.

"So now that the weekend's over, how do you feel about bachelorette parties?" Jessica asked, again surprised to find she wanted to continue talking to Tanner. It barely mattered what they chose to talk about.

"Well..." Tanner considered. "Since this was my first bachelorette party ever, and I planned the whole thing, I think it was mostly a success."

"This was your first! You seemed like such a vet, with the party favors and the strippers, not to mention that impeccable schedule work you did. You would think you got paid to do this sort of thing." Jessica could see the blush on Tanner's face.

"Well, like I told you before this really isn't my thing. I wouldn't do this for anyone other than Bernie." Tanner expressed that same seriousness that seemed to always come out whenever Tanner talked about Bernie.

"Besides, you would be surprised by what comes up when you google 'what is normal for a straight bachelorette party.'"

"Did you really?" Jessica asked, laughing.

"Exact Google search."

"Well, as far as I can tell, you checked every box," Jessica said, hoping to assuage any nerves she might have about whether it was a success. "I know for sure that Bernie had an amazing time. She couldn't stop talking about it this morning."

"Thanks for saying that. How about you? Did you have at least the smallest, tiniest little smidge of fun?"

Jessica considered. "Fun isn't quite the word I'd use to describe my first and last bachelorette party ever."

Tanner laughed. "Your last, you think?"

"I know." She knew if it weren't for her mom, she would decline any future invitations, not that anyone she knew would have something like that, or more accurately invite her.

"But..." Jessica added, "as far as ridiculous misogynistic rituals that completely miss the point of love or partnership, this was okay."

Tanner seemed to take this response as a kindness, but Jessica couldn't help but notice in the reflection of the Uber window, Tanner was smiling as she looked out the window.

CHAPTER SEVEN

It was late November and about a week until the bridal shower. Jessica was looking at her Instagram when she noticed a friend request from Tanner Caldwell. She had been sitting at her office at the Daily Paper, very much not working on the latest article that was sucking her soul out of her body, when the request stopped her in her tracks. It wasn't that she hadn't thought about Tanner in the month between the bachelorette and this friend request. It was actually the opposite. She had thought about Tanner often, a little too often. At first, it was an odd dream, which made some sense after spending time together. It wasn't uncommon for people who were around most often to show up in Jessica's dreams, along with her fifth-grade karate teacher. But then, she kept thinking she saw Tanner in the street. It was happening a lot. Basically, any blond head from behind or a flash of someone's profile made her do a double take. Yesterday, she saw a runner outside her house, and her stomach almost dropped out of her body as she stared down this very confused innocent bystander. It never turned out to be Tanner, which was a relief, but clearly, Jessica's mind had become infected. And just knowing they lived close to each other had her feeling paranoid.

She looked at the request and investigated the profile picture. She wasn't sure yet if she wanted to accept, but she did want to at least see if she could get a glimpse of Tanner's life through the photo. Unfortunately, her profile photo wasn't of her face. It was a zoomed-in picture of She-Ra from the new, very queer Netflix series. It was, if possible, even more annoying to have a cartoon that Jessica fully loved be thrust in her face. It was just something else they had in common. These little details were so unexpected, but then again, Jessica could fill a library with all the things she didn't know about Tanner. This was just another thing to add to the list. Tanner didn't have much else publicly visible; her profile was set to private, so Jessica would have to accept the request to see more. She was still a little too conflicted to make that decision just yet.

Jessica decided to go back to the article she was assigned—"A beloved local Walgreens is being closed down." Not only was the idea that a Walgreens was "beloved" a stretch, but it was also just turning into a CVS. It was clearly a slow news week. But even that still wasn't enough to convince her editor to let her work on the article she actually wanted to write. That one was about the growing effects of climate change on lower income housing areas in DC based on the city's decision to spend less on green space.

Jessica mindlessly typed away, but the Walgreens article was so asinine that she was able to simultaneously consider the friend request.

An Instagram friend request didn't mean she and Tanner were friends. It was just something that people did after spending time together, wasn't it? Alex had friended her after a week. Kayla hadn't, but that wasn't a surprise. But it wasn't just the request, it was how long Tanner had waited. They hadn't texted at all since leaving the bachelorette. Did they still have a plan for the bridal shower? Were they still carpooling? Maybe this was Tanner's way of putting out feelers. Or maybe she just forgot about Jessica and she came up as a possible friend in her algorithm.

What did it matter? Jessica was already getting herself in a funk about it.

Her phone rang. She picked it up, desperate to get out of her head.

"Jessica, come to my office." Not a request, no "please" or "when you have a moment." No, just a typical summons from Tom, Jessica's asshole boss.

She started to reply, only to realize he had already ended the call.

Jessica took a deep breath, a mediative moment to calm her system.

Keep calm, just get through, she said to herself on the out breath.

Jessica walked especially slowly as she made her way through the small but clichéd newsroom. It was full of cubicles. At a different time, there might have been the sound of people running around and phone calls, something reminiscent of the Woodward and Bernstein and Deep Throat eras, but today it was mostly just people quietly typing, or looking at their phones with headphones on. It was all quite a bit less sexy than she imagined when she first envisioned a career in journalism.

Jessica arrived outside a closed door labeled "Tom Wilson, Editor in Chief." She knocked loudly.

"Yeah?" she heard through the door, as if Tom hadn't just called her over a moment ago.

She came in to find Tom standing with a golf club in his hand in his unnecessarily spacious room, putting a ball into one of those office putting mats. Couldn't he even pretend he was working?

Jessica wouldn't have minded so much if he wasn't such a douche.

"How's the article going?" he asked in that way he had of not really caring about the answer.

"Just about finished," she replied. She learned early that he didn't want details.

"I've got a few things coming up this week, so I'm going to have to give you a few more assignments to beef up the weekend papers."

To be clear, it wasn't a paper, even with the word in the name. It was actually just an online media site, and a couple of articles with a twenty-four-hour turnaround wasn't a small request, it was a totally life-crushing request. It was already Friday, and she was hoping to blow off some steam after work. She had made plans with Bryce, and just based on Tom's not-request request, she was sure she'd be working late and getting up early to finish by tomorrow's noon deadline.

"How many do you need and on what?"

Tom gestured with his club toward a document on his desk. She had to cross the room to retrieve it. There were four articles on his list.

1. What your political party has to do with your astrological sign
2. A day in the life of Bow Bow, the zoo panda baby
3. Which Real Housewife Joe Biden STANS
4. Weather and climate: what's the difference?

It was all complete bullshit. Even just reading the list filled Jessica with a fiery rage. She took another deep breath, focused on what she wanted, and then just asked.

"Hey, Tom, if you need to fill some space, I have a climate change article I've been working on, talking about the effects on lower income—"

Tom immediately interrupted. "These subjects came straight from the R&D team for max SEO. Just do the list and get it to Anthony by noon tomorrow. I'm going to be on the golf course, so he'll be doing copy."

"What if I just sub one of them for my article, or for something more substantial? I mean, the climate versus weather piece could almost be something."

2223343333

Tom paused his incessant putting and considered her. "How about something about the lesbians in DC?" he said.

Jessica learned long ago that when Tom made a suggestion about writing about "lesbians," he didn't mean write about the queer community or their needs or issues. He meant write something salacious that made people want to click. Something that he could put with a picture of two busty femme women making out in a river of beer.

"How about I write something about the scarcity of queer women's spaces, or—"

"How about, five ways bi girls are hotter or, I don't know, reasons women seem to be 'going gay' more these days."

Both ideas were deeply offensive and just plain annoying. Jessica in no way wanted to contribute to the eroticization of bisexuality for the male gaze or perpetuate the idea that somehow queerness was a fad that's spreading. And of course Tom would ask her to write about lesbians, that's all he could ever think of when he looked at her. She couldn't help but feel his eyes linger way too long on her breasts, something he somehow had never learned to curb and something she really couldn't prove to HR, not that she had tried. Besides, she'd be leaving soon and then she would be her own boss.

"I think I'll just stick with the four on the list you gave me," Jessica said, struggling to mask her extreme disappointment.

"Suit yourself." Tom went back to his putting. "You would think you'd want to talk about your people. You know TDP is pro-LGBT," he added, almost as an inoculation against his litany of microaggressions.

Jessica didn't respond to the LGBT explanation, but she was able to get out of his office pretty quickly since she clearly had a huge workload on her plate. She walked back to her desk feeling the weight of the four more articles of trash weighing heavily on her. She was going to have to call Bryce and reschedule. Hopefully, her whole weekend wouldn't get eaten by this BS, since it was the last weekend she had to herself before the shower. She wanted to talk over her plan for the weekend and get some advice from Bryce about Tanner's friend request. At least she had a few hours left ahead of her where she would be so irritated with her job that she wouldn't be able to think about Tanner. At least, that's what she hoped.

❖

Jessica was able to finish all of the articles by Saturday, but she got them in a little late and really cut it tight. The deputy editor was irritated and let her know with his non-reply reply to her submission, but she didn't care. She was finally free. As soon as she turned everything in, she was on her way to QBar to meet up with Bryce, who was working with Lisa to organize a tea dance for the following Sunday, another reason Jessica was deeply disappointed to be going to her sister's bridal shower. She loved a daytime party, and this was going to be the first of a monthly party series Bryce was helping with. Instead, she was going to have to be dealing with wedding things again, but this time worse because she would be in her hometown. On one hand, it was nice not to be flying to some other state and stranding herself like last time. This time she would have the ability to get back to DC pretty easily. On the other hand, being in her hometown was not something she particularly enjoyed.

Still, she was happy that she was going to be able visit with her mom. And with everything she went through with the trip to Asheville, she wasn't too upset to see the bachelorette crew, with the exception of Kayla. Even so, she was a long way from finished with her wedding obligations and she was well aware.

But she didn't have to deal with any of it right now. At the moment, she was opening the door to QBar and finally feeling the relief she was so unable to find when she was at work. There was just something about being in a queer space that made everything okay.

Being surrounded by straight people all day, every day at work wore on her. She tried to remind herself that even though work was bad, her life now was still so much better than when she was younger. She had been thinking a lot more lately about high school and all she went through. These thoughts were coming up more and more. Something about the bachelorette weekend had her recalling all those feelings again, all those awkward days of hiding who she was and how it felt when no one understood. She didn't have those feelings anymore, she thought as she looked across the bar and saw Bryce and Lisa sitting at a high-top together, working on a clipboard. Lisa looked up first.

"Look what the cat dragged in," she said playfully.

As usual, Lisa looked fantastic. The sleeves of her tight-fitting white tee were rolled up, showing off toned biceps and a series of bold and playful tattoos covering one arm. Tumbles of auburn hair were pulling free from a short, messy braid that gave her a perfectly undone look without seeming sloppy. Her eyes were bright and mischievous as she laughed lightly at her bad joke.

The fact that Lisa and Jessica sometimes slept together had never been an issue in their friendship. It was just something that happened. If that sort of dynamic didn't work between them, Jessica would have chosen their friendship over everything. Lisa was one of her best friends and one of very few people who had become family to her. It was important for Jessica to establish a chosen family when she first moved to DC, especially after how isolated she felt during high school. But it had taken on an even larger importance when her father passed away and as her relationship with Bernie continued to be distant. It was hard to build a life without some feeling of family.

"Well, well, well," Bryce began. "If it isn't Jessica, the most unavailable person in DC. What happened last night? Did you blow me off with a fake work excuse to do something clandestine and dirty?"

Jessica joined them at the table with a loud harumph. "I think you know I would have told you if it was anything fun. I've been glued to my computer for like sixteen hours straight. Please tell me about your life outside of astrology and the Real Housewives."

Bryce and Lisa looked at each other with confusion.

"I don't know what that is referring to," Bryce began, "but I take any criticism of astrology or Real Housewives as a homophobic slur!"

Jessica realized that her articles on their own were kind of canon gay culture, but in the form she was given as an assignment, not so much.

"It's a long story, but suffice to say, please do not read the Daily Paper tomorrow. I'll be mortified as a writer and as a person."

"That shouldn't be too hard," Lisa said as a jab. They were all close enough that Jessica knew how they felt about her workplace. If they had ever been the types of people who read the Daily Paper, they weren't anymore after hearing stories about Tom. It was weird having her friends support her by not reading the paper she worked for. They did, however, read her articles. They just promised never to bring them up to her.

Bryce slid a clipboard over to Jessica. "Take a look. It's the plan for next Sunday. We're going to have a dance floor, a vodka sweet tea drink, some heat lamps set up so that all the little introvert queers can hang out at tables outside. You know, the ones who like to sit in their little groups and stare at each other."

Jessica looked at the list and was already boiling with jealousy. "Ugh, this is giving me so much FOMO!"

"What? Why?" Lisa began. "Aren't you coming?"

Jessica put her hands on her head. "I wish! I have to go to Maryland for my sister's 'bridal shower,' or whatever." She made air quotes with her fingers.

Bryce looked at her with his trademark snark. "You have got to start googling these things. I can't be constantly explaining standard straight culture to you."

Jessica eye-rolled in response. "I did Google it. I still don't get it. Why does anyone need a bridal shower on top of everything else?"

"Who knows," Lisa said. "But you know it's not just the straights who do it. When the Ashleys got married last fall," she said, referring to a known local lesbian couple with the same name, "they had a bridal shower, two separate bachelorette parties, one wedding in England for Ashley T.'s family and another in Memphis for Ashley M. That is two different destination weddings, and I heard they were both pretty miffed about people missing things. Thank God I wasn't invited."

Ashley T. was Lisa's ex, and they'd had rules about not inviting exes, something Jessica heard about and immediately scoffed at. One of the things Jessica appreciated about being queer was the way community was often stronger than a breakup. At least in most cases, exes were friendly, or at least tolerant of one another.

"I guess we're just as susceptible to the propaganda of the wedding industrial complex," Jessica said with disdain.

"You both need to stop being so jaded," Bryce said. "What's so wrong with people wanting to celebrate their love? And then throw elaborate, economically impulsive parties, and then force all that debt on others?"

The last part was for Jessica's benefit, but deep down, Jessica knew Bryce was a romantic who loved a good same-sex wedding.

Jessica saw her phone light up. She reached for it, dreading who it might be. There was a ninety percent chance it was work. But instead, she saw an unexpected name. Her stomach did a little flip. The name Tanner Caldwell flashed across the screen. Even after weeks without seeing or hearing from Tanner, the name still messed with her.

Lisa zeroed in on the change in Jessica's demeanor. "Who's that?" she asked in a teasing tone that very clearly indicated there was something interesting happening.

Jessica pulled her phone out of the sightline of her friends. "Nothing!" She knew her response was weird, to say the least.

Bryce was clearly catching on to some sort of vibe Jessica was giving off. "That sounded vague and guarded."

Jessica was already feeling deeply self-conscious about hiding a text from a person she didn't care about, didn't talk to, and didn't know why would be reaching out to her. She decided to just explain.

"It's just somebody from the bachelorette weekend. I don't know why she's texting."

Lisa looked at her skeptically. "That is a perfectly normal response and I would be fully uninterested if I didn't just watch the way you lit up when you looked at your phone. Your body language seemed very, very interested in this random woman from a bachelorette weekend."

"Was it her?" Bryce asked, ruining any kind of privacy Jessica wanted to have.

"If you must know, yes. But I don't think I reacted any type of way. I think I was just surprised to see her texting me." Jessica sipped her drink and the group went silent.

"So?" Bryce asked with hurrying hands. "Are you going to see what she said?"

Jessica looked at her phone. She didn't have preview on, so she couldn't really see anything. She harrumphed again loudly and then looked.

Hey, it's Tanner. Was just wondering, are you still down to carpool this weekend?

The text was perfectly ordinary, but just reading it brought a blush to Jessica's cheeks. She hadn't been sure if Tanner was going to reach out, and she was debating sending a similar text earlier that day.

"She's just asking about carpooling to the shower."

This seemed to be a bit less salacious than they expected so they proceeded to ignore her as they worked out the plans for their tea dance. Jessica leaned back and let them have some time. It also gave her some time to think about a response text.

Yeah, I'm still down to carpool. Still okay to drive?

The reply came quickly.

Yes, I can pick you up if that still works?

This was pretty convenient, since not only did Jessica not have a car, but she also did not have a concrete plan for getting to the shower if Tanner hadn't texted. She was considering as a backup plan, taking a one-hour Metro ride and then catching a forty-five-minute bus ride, all of which would have been absolutely awful.

That would be great, sending my address.

She shared her contact.

Jessica couldn't help but feel like she was being rude or weird. She added a *"thanks"* just for good measure.

Tanner responded with a *"np,"* the shortest most neutral acronym response humanly possible. From an onlooker's perspective, the conversation would seem completely benign and borderline boring. But Jessica was totally derailed by the texts and just the idea of making plans with Tanner, even if they were only logistical plans. She still wasn't acclimated to the idea of Tanner and her being friendly. It might never stop being jarring.

She rejoined the conversation with Bryce and Lisa, but the feeling of FOMO that she'd had earlier had begun to dissipate. For some reason, the weekend in Maryland wasn't feeling quite so awful anymore. And even though the text conversation with Tanner had ended and there wasn't any strong indication that a follow-up would come, she couldn't help but check her phone more often than usual, with a strange anticipation that she wasn't yet willing to look too closely at.

❖

It was the Friday before Sunday's bridal shower and Jessica was having a fairly pleasant phone conversation with her sister. Ever since the bachelorette weekend, Bernie and Jessica had been texting, and somehow texting had become a weekly call. Jessica had never had that kind of a relationship with her sister. Now, after experiencing how easy it was to connect with Bernie, she couldn't understand why their relationship had been so frayed for so long.

They had discussed the bachelorette weekend in detail and because of the frequency of their calls, they were on the level of knowing some of the people in each other's lives and the day-to-day. One thing they hadn't talked about was Tanner. Bernie knew Tanner and Jessica used to be friendly when they were in high school, just by virtue of them all going to the same school and their shared role as co-editors of the school paper. She also knew that Jessica had been outed, which Jessica assumed was how Bernie learned she was gay, since she'd never broached the subject of her sexuality with Bernie.

And Bernie not only knew that Jessica blamed Tanner, she also knew why. A few months after everything happened, Jessica blew up on Bernie and let her know exactly what she thought of her friends, especially Tanner. Bernie didn't defend them, but she also didn't offer comfort or an apology. It seemed like the whole thing was just something she didn't want to deal with. This didn't help their relationship. And then when their dad died, there was just too much between them. Jessica couldn't offer comfort to her sister because Bernie had become a stranger. And as far as getting comfort from Bernie, well, the past had already proved that wasn't likely to happen. All of it was yet another scar from what Tanner did.

Perhaps if Jessica had been able to have some sort of control over who knew about her sexuality and when, she and her sister could have had a more normal relationship. But the emotional chaos that she went through that year and the years after had made it impossible for Jessica to focus on resolving her relationship with her sister. She felt the same about what she went through with her parents, especially her mom. If she had been more in control of her story, maybe her mom's disappointment or discomfort wouldn't have ripped her up so deeply. Maybe if she had had a friend, a sister as an ally, anyone who could understand, she wouldn't have sunken so low. But that wasn't what happened.

And Jessica was still careful when talking to Bernie, and it was clear that Bernie was being careful as well. The fact that Bernie had discussed the weekend, discussed her life, and even discussed her complicated relationship with Kayla, but never once brought up Tanner's name, made it all feel kind of intentional.

"So I'm carpooling with Tanner to Maryland on Sunday," Jessica blurted out.

"I heard. Tanner told me. I'm happy you two are getting along." This was a slightly telling remark. So she did know they were talking.

"I don't know if I would go so far as to say that," Jessica hedged.

Bernie seemed to fumble her response. "Well, I just mean, I guess I was hoping you two could... I mean, you used to be pretty close."

I guess we're doing this. "I don't think there's much of a chance of us being friends again," Jessica said. "But I think we're going to be able to be cordial." Cordial seemed like a pretty huge shift from loathing.

"You know, she's different than she was when we were young. I mean, she's been through a lot since high school. She took on a lot when her sister got pregnant and didn't have anyone to help. I think putting college off and having to stay in Maryland to help raise Gracie made her grow up a lot faster than the rest of us. I bet if you were open, you'd like her."

Jessica didn't want to get into everything that happened in high school, but she wasn't loving the way Bernie seemed to focus on this new and amazing version of Tanner. It minimized the damage done from when they were younger, even if it was inadvertent. Jessica was going to have to be very frank with her sister.

"Do you understand what she did to me when we were in school?" The question was cutting.

Bernie was silent on the other end.

"She outed me. Do you understand what that feels like?" Jessica was struggling to keep her emotions under control. "I was just starting to understand my sexuality, and before I could even begin to feel comfortable, the entire school knew. And just because Tanner had the easiest time as a queer person in our school doesn't mean the rest of us did. I know you saw some of it, but you don't know all that I went through those years. What she did is unforgivable." The last word hung in the air.

"I'm so sorry that happened," Bernie said in a voice so small Jessica could barely hear her. But she didn't say, "I'm so sorry SHE did that to you." It was the amorphous happening in a vacuum comment that did nothing to calm Jessica.

"You understand that Tanner is the reason everyone found out, right? How could I ever be friends with her after that?"

"How do you know she was the one who told everyone?" Bernie was clearly not speaking with the comfortable tone they had developed over the past weeks. They were back to being strangers.

"I know because she was the only person I told." Jessica let out a derisive laugh. "And that's what sucked the most. I told her because I trusted her and because..." Jessica didn't want to explain how she felt about Tanner at the time. Because the truth was, yes, Tanner was a friend in a sense, but they weren't especially close. The real reason Jessica told Tanner was because deep down she had hoped that maybe if she told Tanner, she could get closer to telling her that she *liked her* liked her. All of it felt juvenile and ridiculous now and so Jessica tried to keep the conversation out of that territory.

"Because we were friends. So no. I'm not suddenly going to forget about what she did the last time I trusted her."

It was clear from the awkwardness of the call that Bernie had figured out that talking about Tanner wasn't going to get them anywhere.

"Whatever." Jessica tried to get their dynamic back. "It doesn't matter anymore. I'm really not trying to stir all this up. Like I said, I can be cordial. Despite what it might sound like from this conversation, I'm really not angry anymore. I've moved on."

Bernie seemed to get her feet under her finally. "I'm sorry I pushed you on that. I really wouldn't want to say or do anything to upset you. I've really liked talking to you." The sentiment was sweet, and it brought Jessica completely around. Bernie wasn't responsible for Tanner's behavior when they were kids.

"I've really liked us talking too." Jessica could feel Bernie's smile on the other end of the phone.

CHAPTER EIGHT

Jessica was brushing her teeth when she heard her phone ding with the text message letting her know Tanner was outside, waiting to drive her to the shower. She spit out toothpaste and responded with a *"Be right there."*

She was packed, mostly, but she always had a hard time with the essentials that she needed: keys, phone, sunglasses, Chapstick, all of which were always in different and unrelated locations. She fumbled around and finally got herself out the door.

Tanner was waiting outside in a very surprising red Camaro. The vintage car was kind of a mismatch for Tanner. Jessica remembered that she said she was borrowing her roommate's car, which made a bit more sense. But it was also an annoyance, considering she was a sucker for women who drove muscle cars. She didn't need another thing to get her all tied up about Tanner.

Tanner was double-parked in front of Jessica's house. She got out to help with her bag. It was weirdly sweet and chivalrous. Jessica refused the help and got her stuff arranged in the trunk on her own. They both got in the car and Jessica was better able to take in Tanner without all the awkwardness of being in the street dodging cars and figuring out how to greet each other.

Tanner was wearing a great vintage jean jacket and her, now typical, horn-rimmed glasses. The denim, the Camaro, and the glasses were all giving Tanner an effortlessly cool vibe.

Something that she didn't need on top of everything, since she was already painfully gorgeous.

Jessica watched as Tanner adjusted her seat, the radio, basically if there was something she could frantically fiddle with she did it. If Jessica didn't know better, she would think Tanner was nervous. Jessica realized they hadn't even greeted each other. They'd just gone straight into being weird car trip robots.

"Hi," Jessica said, trying to reset the situation and start things off more normally.

Tanner seemed to get the memo, because she stopped her fidgeting and gave Jessica her full attention. "Hi!"

"Thanks for picking me up. I'm really not sure how I was going to get there, so this is a huge help." The thank you was oddly formal, but Jessica had to say something. It would be rude if she didn't express some sort of gratitude about the ride.

"It's not a problem." Tanner put the car in drive. "Like I said, I live really close, so this was basically on the way."

She lived close, but Jessica knew it wasn't "on the way" exactly. It was at least minorly inconvenient. Tanner pulled into the street with a lot more confidence than Jessica expected, especially after picking up on Tanner's nervousness.

"This is a cool car."

"Isn't it?" Tanner responded. "My roommate is into cars so I get to seem cooler than I am."

Jessica noticed that the car was a stick shift, another thing that was deeply sexy.

"It's actually pretty shocking he lets me borrow it. He's had many years to vet my driving abilities."

"I don't know many people who know how to drive a stick shift anymore. I definitely can't, so don't think I can get us back if you need a break."

Tanner smiled. "I don't think you've been vetted so I'm not sure Neal would be too happy if I let you drive."

Jessica was actually thinking it was pretty nice to be driven around. She wasn't used to being the person who wasn't in control. Having Tanner drive her so expertly, knowing she couldn't even if she needed to, was in itself an act of trust. They got off of the congested side streets and onto one of the main arteries to the highway in record time with none of the usual stress that Jessica felt when she navigated DC by car.

Jessica was debating whether or not to make small talk when Tanner made the decision for them.

"So, what have you been up to since the bachelorette? I haven't seen you in any QBar Instagram stories lately."

This made Jessica smile. "Yeah, well, I had a talk with Lisa, the bartender who took that video after the last one, so I'm not sure you'll be able to keep tabs on me anymore."

"I wasn't keeping tabs!" Tanner exclaimed, mock offended. "No queer person in DC would have forgotten your version of 'Constant Craving.' Not that it was especially easy to decipher."

Jessica found herself giving a light shove to Tanner. It was oddly familiar to be tactile with Tanner, but also unexpected.

"So," Jessica began, knowing her next question might break their armistice. "How's work going?" She tried as hard as possible to keep the question neutral. For instance, she didn't make any barbs about the site or even mention it. She was just calling it "work."

Tanner glanced over, clearly checking if there was another part to the question. "It's okay." She paused a moment. "Well, mostly."

"Mostly doesn't sound too good."

"I'm considering whether to say this after I did such good work defending my job to you last time."

"I don't know if it was THAT good of a job." Jessica's tone was teasing.

"Okay, more reason not to elaborate!"

Jessica genuinely wanted to know, so she decided to get serious. "We all have complaints about work. I won't get on any soap boxes, I promise. I'll just listen."

Tanner seemed to soften. "I told you that I base a lot of what I do off my niece Gracie. She's doing fine but she's getting older, so my sister has been needing me around less and less. You can't imagine how hard it is writing material without Gracie. And then..." She hesitated again. "I did...kind of think about some of the things you said. I still stand by what I said about impact, but it takes a lot out of me."

"What do you mean?" This was interesting. Tanner thought about some of the things Jessica said?

"Well, I don't just have to write the articles. I also have to respond to commenters, and I have to attend meetings on site values, and it all just wears. Finding a way to meet someone where they're at on their views about homophobia or gender is just not always easy. I had to respond to this mother the other day who was asking about a good conversion program for her eight-year-old who was experiencing gender dysphoria and I wrote this whole thing out about how those programs are on par with child abuse and discussing parent groups and books she can read to help her understand more, but when it was over, I was just so depressed. I mean, conversion therapy is perfectly legal in her state, so really there wasn't much I could do to prevent her from just googling a program and I don't know..."

Jessica thought Tanner seemed exhausted just talking about it. "That sounds awful." Jessica had also thought about what Tanner had said about impact. She decided she couldn't do that kind of work, but it was possible that it was harder than she was making it out to be. Just hearing about it now in the car ride was really setting in how much effort Tanner was putting in, and that in itself was commendable. "Have you considered leaving?"

"More and more lately."

"Where would you go, another Christian site like that?"

Tanner gave her a withering look.

"What? Why is that a weird question? That's what your history is in."

"My history is in journalism. I took the job because of my mentor and because…because I needed something with some flexible hours for finishing school and Gracie. But now that she's older, I don't really need the same schedule."

"Well, take it from someone working in journalism—it's not as fun as I thought it was going to be." Jessica slouched in her chair as she thought about her asshole boss.

"No? You don't have secret meetings with Deep Throat in parking garages?"

Jessica laughed. "Not at all! Mainly I sit around regurgitating click-bait trashy articles for my fucked up editor who is constantly treating me like the subject matter expert on all things identity politics. It's so frustrating!"

"I thought you liked that sort of thing," Tanner said.

"Why would I like being reduced to my sexuality or my gender? I got into journalism to explore and investigate things that people need to know about. Not ten celebrities you didn't know were bisexual."

Tanner seemed to be considering what she was saying. "I've read some of your stuff."

Jessica groaned in embarrassment. "Please don't tell me that!"

Tanner laughed. "It wasn't bad! I mean, I don't know about your ten celebrity bisexual articles, but I have always loved the way you write no matter what you're writing about."

The compliment threw Jessica off. She didn't know what to say. Should she be thanking Tanner? She thought it better to ignore the compliment. "I'm sure you had to check up on my integrity after I called you out so hard at the bachelorette."

Tanner seemed to go back to her previous fidgety state. "Yes, I read some of your articles after the bachelorette, but I'd read some of your other stuff over the years."

Jessica was again caught off guard. "See, you are keeping tabs!" Jessica was trying not to show how much that remark interested her. Tanner was in full blush at that point.

"Okay maybe I was keeping some tabs, on your writing anyway. But even if I didn't, Bernie and your mom email your stuff around at least once a month. I'm part of the listserv at this point."

This was news to Jessica. Her mom's emails weren't surprising, but Bernie? Jessica wanted to change the focus. "Enough about me." It was weird how easy it was to chat now that Jessica wasn't constantly trying not to bite off Tanner's head. "If you could do anything else, what would you do?" The question lingered in the air.

"Honestly?"

"Honestly."

"It's kind of embarrassing."

"Nothing could be more embarrassing than mommy+me."

Tanner rolled her eyes. "Well, if I could do anything, I would still write, but I would want to write fiction."

"Like a novel?" The answer was unexpected.

"Yeah, like crime novels. I've been working on a series in my off time for a few years, but I've just never had the courage to send it to a publisher or an agent or anything. I'm probably never going to do anything with it, but that's my answer. I'd want to be a crime novelist."

Jessica could see the self-consciousness in Tanner's demeanor. This was a risk for Tanner, telling Jessica. Thinking back on when they were in high school and they both worked on the paper, the response began to be less surprising.

"You know, I always liked your writing too. Not just on the paper, which was great, but your submission to the Baltimore

Youth Short Fiction contest. You had that magical realism story about the haunted house in Baltimore. I remember thinking when I read it that I was so jealous of you. I could never have written something that creative."

This time it seemed like Tanner was the one taken off guard. "I can't believe you remember that. I didn't even think anyone outside of the competition read it."

Jessica tried to act cool about it. "Yeah, well, I had a subscription to their magazine, not to mention I had to know what I was up against when we were both running for editor. After I read it, I stepped up my game."

Talking about their time on the paper was dangerous territory considering their armistice.

"You made me better too," Tanner said. "I honestly have never tried as hard as when we were co-editors. That's another thing that sucks about writing for mommy+me. You work in a silo, there's no team to bounce ideas off of."

Jessica couldn't help but smile thinking about some of their afterschool paper meetings. She used to be so in awe of Tanner and how all of her ideas seemed so quick and smart. She could make new construction on campus into a hard-hitting piece on the corruption of the school boards. The administration even wanted to shut the paper down a few times. Jessica considered bringing all that up, but the closer they were getting to memory lane, the closer they were getting to the reason they stopped being friends.

"So, what about you?" Tanner asked. "Are you going to stay at the Daily Paper long-term?"

Jessica didn't know how much to divulge about her deal with her mom. She didn't really mind people knowing generally, but because of her growing relationship with Bernie she didn't want to advertise that she was being bribed to do wedding things for Bernie.

"I inherited some money from my father, and I have a plan to open a bookstore slash activist space. I'm still not sure when or how, but that's the plan." Even saying it out loud made it feel closer to happening.

"That sounds like something he would have liked." Tanner's words hit heavy. Of course Tanner knew her father when he was alive, she was over all the time hanging with Bernie. Tanner was the kind of friend who came on family trips and slept over once every few weeks. It was odd to have this person who was starting to feel like a whole new person know someone so significant. No one in Jessica's current life had ever met her father.

"I think he would have liked it too." A memory came back of Tanner at her father's funeral. Things were a lot fresher when she was twenty and she basically stayed as far away from Tanner as humanly possible, but she did have a picture in her head of Tanner holding Bernie at the gravesite. Jessica wasn't able to be there for her sister as much as she wished she'd been just because of what she was also going through, but with time, she could see how comforting it was knowing Tanner was able to be there for Bernie.

"Maybe when I get the guts to try to get my book published, your bookstore can sell it."

Jessica welcomed being able to move off of the subject of her dad. "I'm sure I would have to. It'll be a best-seller."

Tanner smiled but she didn't respond. The car turned silent, but a comfortable silence. They had both gone a long way into a very vulnerable conversation, and Jessica got a sense that they both needed a break. Eventually, Tanner turned the music up and they stayed that way till they reached Jessica's mom's house in Maryland. The ride was quiet, but Jessica's mind was not. She found herself again trying to figure out how to deal with the swirling conflicting feelings she was starting to have about Tanner Caldwell.

❖

Jessica thought a bachelorette party was cringe, but she had no idea there was a whole other level to this. Jessica had been starting to come around to the concept of a bachelorette party. It at least had a purpose. You got to celebrate with your friends, reminisce on the single life, push some boundaries. Although it was basically a modern accommodation to address the inherent sexism of the bachelor party, which was originally a singular event reserved for men. All of this was very annoying, but at least Jessica had survived the weekend.

A bridal shower was a completely different thing. She had never been to one, but after some googling and discussing with Bryce, it seemed to be almost like a baby shower, but for a wedding? Some sort of bride-centered party with well-wishes and games and presents. Again, this was on top of the wedding gifts and all the other dinners and things. But here she was, fulfilling her agreement. And this one she definitely couldn't skip, not since it was literally at her childhood house and her mom would be present.

One thing that Jessica learned on the ride over was that Tanner was not organizing this event. Kayla had taken point, mainly because she lived in Frederick, which was something Tanner expressed some relief about. It seemed the planning had been taking a lot out of her on top of everything.

When they both came to the door, Tanner went to ring the doorbell, but Jessica stopped her.

"Yo, I live here. We can just walk in." Jessica walked through the familiar foyer and went into the closest room she was likely to find her mom.

"Mom!" she called, circling the corner. She found her mom carrying a tray in the kitchen looking extremely stressed out. She repeated, "Hey, Mom!" Her mom turned and seemed to notice her for the first time.

"Jess, you're here! Come give me a kiss."

Jessica did not like that her mom was on her feet. This was Bernie's and, by delegation, Kayla's thing. Why was her mom frantically working in the kitchen?

"Before I do, can I help? Can I at least grab that tray?"

"You're a lifesaver," she said, hastily handing the tray to Jessica. This was also pretty indicative that she was being exploited. Her mom almost never said yes when asked if she needed some help. Where was Kayla or Bernie?

Jessica gave her mom a kiss with a tray in her hand and moved out of the way so she could see Tanner.

"Tanner, you're here too? Come give me a kiss as well." Tanner went over and Jessica's mom placed a practiced kiss on her cheek.

"Hi, Judy!" Tanner was on a first-name basis. "Can I help as well? I have hands."

Jessica's mom was clearly relieved to have Tanner helping, based on her reaction, significantly more so than Jessica it turned out. She began giving them instructions while she took what looked like a much-needed seat at the island. Once they were each at their stations, Jessica tried to get some information on what was going on. She and Tanner were a little early, but there really shouldn't have been this much stress on her mom.

"Where's Kayla?"

Her mom gave her a weary stare. "That girl!" The assertion was notable just on the fact that Jessica's mom rarely had something negative to say about someone. She always assumed the best in people. So if she was saying that, Kayla must have done something really annoying.

"What happened?" Tanner added.

"Kayla asked to use my house for the shower, which I was of course happy to do, but she also said she would be here to set things up. It starts in an hour, and I have decorations in boxes, I have food I've put together just in case, and I really don't know what's going to happen. No emails, no calls. I tried to get in touch with her all week and she was very evasive or disorganized."

"What! How could this happen? Did you tell Bernie?" Jessica had stopped prepping and was getting more and more angry.

"I didn't want to bother Bernie. She came in early this morning from a business trip in California and she seemed just ragged, and then a red-eye flight? I just thought I'd do the best I could." Jessica's mom sounded tired, and taking her in, Jessica felt like her mom looked older than when she saw her a month ago. Jessica was seeing red. She could tell already that she was too focused on what she wanted to do to Kayla and not what she needed to do to help her mom. Luckily, Tanner was also listening to the conversation.

Tanner had her phone to her ear, and they could both see that she was calling someone. Her face said it all: she was mad. The call rang for a while and then seemed to go voice mail.

"Kayla, it's Tanner. I'm sitting here in Mrs. Monroe's kitchen an hour before the party. Where are you!" Jessica estimated she was about a decibel below a yell. "Get yourself together and get over here. You need to organize the shower, not dump everything on Mrs. Monroe and run off. If you aren't here in fifteen minutes, you might as well stay home." She hung up and moved toward Jessica's mom.

"Where are the boxes?" Her tone was significantly softer when talking to Jessica's mom, but there was still a manager's energy to it. She showed her where the boxes were in the family room, with Jessica close behind.

"I cleaned and got everything organized the way I thought it should be as far as seating, but I didn't want to step on anyone's toes with the decorations." All of this had been dumped on her and Jessica couldn't believe what a selfish brat Kayla was, except, of course, she could believe it.

"Where's Bernie now?" Jessica asked.

"She was taking Chris around town to see some of her favorite spots, but I think she was planning to be back in half an hour."

"Okay," Tanner said definitively. "Jessica, will you help me?" It was less a question and more marching orders.

"Whatever you need," Jessica said without thinking about it.

Tanner was already in the boxes passing things out. "Don't worry, Judy, go sit down and rest a bit. We'll take it from here."

So now Jessica wasn't just attending a bridal shower, she was organizing one. Somehow, she wasn't mad about it.

❖

They got things together in record time. The decorations were atrocious. There was a monochromatic purple theme. But not an attractive purple, more of a grape color, something that did nothing to pull the space together. Jessica and Tanner got the whole place decorated and were able to get enough going to give Jessica's mom a much-needed break. She tapped back in to assist with the cooking once she had some time to get ready and once some of her stress was reduced when she saw all the crepe paper and table centerpieces set up. Jessica wasn't exactly proud of the result—things looked truly awful and slapped together—but she was proud of what she and Tanner made of it.

She was putting some final touches on a banner that said, "Love is in the air...and so is glitter!" by the tables in the backyard. The sign was, of course, covered in glitter, so Jessica was subsequently also covered in glitter. Tanner had come out to tell her they were done when she pointed out the glitter that was all over her head, face, shoulders, you name it. She tried to brush it off, but as glitter could be, she was surely never going to get it off.

Tanner was watching with amusement until she finally stopped Jessica from her frantic rubbing. "Stop, I'll help." She wiped it off in a much more strategic and pointed way, getting Jessica's shoulders and a couple of final flakes from her hair. Jessica was so annoyed by the glitter that she wasn't registering their proximity. They had not been this close in a very long time. It seemed Tanner hadn't noticed either since she was picking glitter out of her hair with a concentration that kept her fully focused. Jessica was able to better see what Tanner's eyes looked like up close. They were hazel and shimmering. She had applied a red lipstick sometime between when they were both inside decorating and now. It was bold and fully pulled Jessica's attention.

"You have a speckle on your cheek," Jessica said, chuckling and automatically rubbing it away. It was at that point that Tanner seemed to register where they both were. Jessica had not pulled her eyes from Tanner's lips. Something about working together, something about helping her family with Tanner had her forgetting all that was between them.

Jessica found herself stepping closer, and there wasn't much closer to go. Jessica could see Tanner's eyes widen and hear her breath catch. Just then, Bernie came out through the sliding glass door.

"Tanner!" she shouted. Jessica and Tanner stepped back. Bernie turned the corner accompanied by a guy with slicked back hair and a suit who could have been straight out of an advertisement for a yuppie.

Jessica couldn't quite process what had just happened. She wasn't about to kiss Tanner, was she? Because that was just so fully insane that she couldn't even process it. Not only was it the middle of the day at her mom's house, while they were in a very stressful situation, but she was also trying very very hard to be normal with Tanner, not to fall back into some sort of prehistoric crush.

"Jess, you're here too!" Bernie seemed not to pick up on any weird vibes in the air. Even though Tanner was very pointedly not looking at Jessica.

"I'm going to check on your mom," Tanner said after hugging both Bernie and Chris. She escaped so fast Jessica couldn't be sure what she was feeling. Was she running away because of Jessica? Maybe that moment had creeped her out or something?

"Jess, I want you to meet Chris. Chris, this is my sister, Jess."

Chris approached and gave Jessica a warm hug.

"Jessica, it's so amazing to finally meet you! Your sister has told me so much about you." His smile was warm and all of his Wall Street sleaze melted away. He was extremely open and already not what he seemed.

"Thanks, I've been wanting to meet you too." It seemed like Jessica was pulling off normal.

"You know, I've been wanting to meet you for a while. My work brings me to DC a lot and I was considering reaching out and trying to meet up on my own, but I didn't want to have our intro happen without Bernie the first time."

Jessica thought that was pretty considerate of him to be so socially conscious and to be interested in meeting her one-on-one. Jessica didn't want to like him off the bat, just knowing Bernie's track record, but she couldn't help it.

"You should text me next time you're in town." At least that way she could see for herself if he was hiding some sort of sociopathology.

"That would be amazing, I hear you live in Columbia Heights. My favorite Ethiopian restaurant is there."

Jessica loved Ethiopian and the fact that Chris knew DC neighborhoods at all made it clear he was someone who had actually hung around in DC.

"Okay, enough. Don't already be making dinner plans!" Bernie said. "I want to have my solo trip with my sister first!"

She said it possessively. Something Jessica hadn't heard from her in a long time.

"Don't worry, Bern, you get priority." They were already starting to feel like a family. Something that she hadn't even thought since their dad's death.

They were interrupted by the woman of the day, Kayla, who was dressed in a Lilly Pulitzer sheath dress looking like she spent about four hours getting ready.

"Bern! I'm so so sorry. The sitter was late and Bruce was asleep. I had the hardest time getting him to get dressed and picking up the cake and the food."

"What food?" Jessica asked, already seething.

"I got some food ordered from Terry's down the street. Otherwise, what were we going to eat and drink? Bruce is behind me with the wine and beer."

So there was some sort of plan, she just somehow had not thought to tell her mom. And she was very late.

"So you know, Kayla, my mom spent the whole day cooking and preparing because she had no idea you were bringing all this stuff!"

Kayla had an irritated face "Well, I told her when I organized this I would do everything. Why would she do that?"

"Maybe because you didn't answer her phone calls or her emails!" Kayla seemed either clueless or careless. Jessica knew she was two seconds from letting Kayla know exactly what a selfish asshole she was, but she decided instead to walk away. She needed a cold drink and she needed not to ruin her sister's shower.

"I'm heading inside. Nice to meet you, Chris."

He held his hand on his heart and said effusively. "So nice to meet you. Let's talk later about our date in DC." Jessica was again charmed by him doubling down.

She walked through the backyard and into the kitchen where her mother was dealing with Bruce, who was looking for counter space for all the food and drinks among all the food and drinks that were already there. He ended up moving into the other room and using up the living room table in what was becoming the sloppiest looking party ever. Jessica had given up and it seemed her mom had too, because she was already heading for the stairs to get some alone time upstairs.

People were beginning to cycle in. Jessica recognized some of them from high school or from the neighborhood, but there were some new people who must be either Bernie's new friends or from Chris's side. Alex wasn't coming because of a work conflict, so Jessica didn't have anyone else she knew or, it was more accurate to say, anyone she liked. It was already a pretty uncomfortable experience running into people from her high school, but if they were Bernie's, Kayla's, and Tanner's friends, they were definitely not Jessica's friends.

Jessica hadn't seen Tanner since their moment outside. She couldn't help it, she found herself looking for her. Was she hiding from Jessica?

Jessica moved through the rooms. Sometimes people would chat with her, but much of the time she was basically ignored, which was fine by her. She had a few conversations that were okay, including with some of Chris's friends who lived in the area. Even so, the environment had Jessica's spikes up.

Her mom still hadn't come downstairs, and Jessica was going to check on her and at least bring her a glass of wine, when she saw Tanner. She was chatting with a particularly loathsome guy from their high school who was clearly doing all the talking. Jessica considered stepping in to rescue her, but she wasn't sure if she was ready to address what happened outside. She was struggling with what to do when she noticed Chris come up and interrupt. Jessica could tell even from a distance that he was running interference. He said something and then Tanner and Chris walked away to the other side of the room. She then noticed Tanner and Chris looking back almost conspiratorially and Jessica was sure of what she saw. Another gold star for Chris.

Jessica could see Tanner scanning the room until her gaze landed on Jessica. Was she specifically looking for Jessica to hang with her or to avoid her? She looked away quickly and Jessica was again struggling to know how she felt about what happened outside. There was also just the obviously complicated things happening between them. Jessica had decided to start over with Tanner, or at least have a semblance of a clean slate, but she didn't expect that to mean that she was going to start acting on her attraction.

And that was the thing. Jessica was attracted to Tanner. She had always been attracted to Tanner and that was not an easy thing to turn off. The clean slate was not helping her to deal with the pull she inevitably felt. She decided she wasn't ready to talk to Tanner so she would keep her distance, no matter how awkward she looked quietly lurking around the party with no one to talk to.

Chapter Nine

The party went on with everyone mingling. Eventually, Kayla clanked her mom's nice wine glass with a spoon, bringing everyone to attention for some "bridal shower games." Then they were all forced to play "wedding trivia," which was absolutely abhorrent and basically a competition of who knew the most Emily Post factoids. Jessica stayed in the periphery in order to both not have to talk to her bullies and also because she could not have possibly answered one of those questions if her life depended on it.

Jessica avoided Tanner by keeping to the back of the room, but then noticed that Tanner must have been avoiding her too, because she never came over to Jessica's side of the room. The group had moved on to some sort of game where another one of Bernie's friends, someone Jessica didn't know, was playing famous love songs and the room was guessing their name or artist or something. There wasn't a very clear point system, and everyone was just basically shouting and getting annoyed. Jessica couldn't help but think that if Tanner had planned this, it would have all been one thousand times better. The thought was ridiculous. What did Jessica care how this all went down. Bernie seemed happy either way. She was sitting with Chris, laughing at everyone's guesses, interspersed with looking dreamily at Chris who was as often, or more often, doing the same thing.

Jessica took that opportunity to slip away and go back outside to get out of the crowd for a moment. She slowly came around to where she had shared her almost kiss with Tanner and noticed that Kayla was outside having a cigarette and chatting loudly with Whitney Tan, a very annoying person from their high school. Jessica turned to go since she felt they hadn't seen her when she heard her name.

"I don't even know why Jessica would come, honestly. Bernie doesn't even like her." Jessica could hear the annoying vocal fry, so distinctly Kayla.

"That's weird, I mean they are sisters."

"Yeah, I don't know. They haven't talked in a long time." Jessica knew from her conversations with Bernie that she wasn't super close with Kayla anymore. Having her in the wedding was more to avoid drama. "Bernie would never say it, but I think the homosexual thing freaks her out." The revelation was obviously insane. There was no way Bernie cared about that, but still, just hearing Kayla talk about her like this was bringing back a lot of old feelings that were not sitting well.

"That can't be true." Whitney responded. "Her best friend's Tanner."

"Yeah, but Tanner is girly. I think she's fine with it as long as she's not flaunting it. I mean you've seen Tanner, you can barely tell. But Jessica, she's constantly dressing like a man or shooting weird flirty looks at us. You should have seen her at the bachelorette weekend!" Jessica shouldn't have been surprised, but this lesbian predator trope was the exact same type of thing that had circulated around her high school.

"I know what you mean. I feel like she was lurking around just now checking everyone out," Whitney added. So much for any chance of anyone improving since high school.

"Well, I'm just happy I don't have to spend any more nights sleeping in the same house as lesbians. The bachelorette was enough."

"What about Tanner, isn't she your friend? She's working at your dad's site isn't she? How does that even work, I mean, Tanner's lifestyle isn't all that Christian."

"We aren't that close anymore, plus my dad isn't a fan either. I thought getting her connected with a community that was more focused on faith would get her back on His path, but at this point she's just a lost cause."

Jessica had heard enough. She walked back into the house and decided to steal away to her childhood bedroom. She took the private moment to think. So Kayla was a monster, that was no surprise. Whitney, the girl from high school, had been basically exactly the same as she was when they were young. Jessica was full of shame and embarrassment. The way that Kayla and Whitney had described her, like some sort of predator "lurking" in the back of the room. And what did she mean about the bachelorette? Did Alex say something to Kayla about being uncomfortable? They had flirted a little. Jessica started reviewing all her behavior and trying to figure out if any of it could have been misunderstood.

But that was the problem. Being around people like Kayla made her revert to this shame person, this self-conscious Kafka-esque nightmare of a person, the person who haunted her the years after high school and made her second guess everyone who ever expressed interest in her. These words were just the kind of thing that made Jessica want to be as small and invisible as humanly possible. But, of course Jessica hadn't been predatory. Alex had flirted with her! And the idea that she was looking around that room earlier with anything but boredom was absurd. Even so, the seed of doubt and self-loathing had been planted, that same shame that had blossomed when she was sixteen was close to the surface again.

Looking around her old room, she was reminded of the day she learned that she was outed at school. She was walking through the hallways and she could feel a whisper or two around her, a few people pointing. Then of course it was Kayla who let her know what everyone was talking about. She approached Jessica at her locker and said point-plank, "I heard you were a lesbian. I was just wondering if it was true."

Jessica didn't know what to say. She had barely even come to terms with it herself. The first time she told anyone it had been Tanner alone in the journalism room a week prior. It was scary but at the time, the way Tanner reacted, the way she had hugged her, it had all filled her with such relief. Now she was standing in the middle of her school's hallway, on full display, talking about something so deeply private. And she did the only thing she could think to do, she lied.

"No, I'm not. Who told you that?" The panic was obvious in her voice.

Kayla disregarded it. "I heard you have a huge crush on Tanner." The words slapped her in the face. She hadn't said anything like that to Tanner, but then again, it would have maybe been obvious to her. It struck her then that Tanner must have told, and not only had she told, she'd also deduced the crush and thought it was something to laugh at. Otherwise, why on earth would she have told Kayla?

"Honestly, you should lower your standards. Tanner is clearly out of your league."

She left Jessica there in the hallway, fully gutted. Jessica had never been so embarrassed, so hurt, in her entire life. When she came home that day from school and locked herself in her room, the things that went through her head were not safe. She had a few moments over the course of the following months where she thought it might be better if she just didn't exist. Remembering that thought, that desire to not be alive was the lowest time in her life. Recovering from her insecurities, her fear of her own attraction to others took years. And all of those feelings came back to her in that moment in her room. The power those people downstairs had over her at the time made her angry. How having no one stand up for her, reach out to her, having the only person she trusted betray her and humiliate her, leaving her in that state. The whole thing had her churning in emotions. She was not in a safe place, and she needed to remember who put her there.

And then there was the other thing, what Kayla said about her father, he must own mommy+me. How did that factor into Tanner's story about her mentor having the job? It seemed like there was more to that story, with Tanner actually being some sort of nepotism hire through her good friend Kayla, or her ex-friend. It didn't really matter. This whole "meeting people where they were at" in their blatant homophobia was a crock of shit, and as far as Jessica was concerned, there was no more chance of her continuing that "clean slate" experiment another moment.

She was considering getting an Uber or some other ride home, but she decided instead that she would endure the next hour or so, catch the ride with Tanner she originally planned on, and then put an end to any sort of connection they had been forming. She only had a few more meetings with Tanner to go, and that would be the end of them.

❖

Jessica texted Tanner from her room, letting her know that she was ready to go. The text came back quickly that she was ready too and to meet at the car in ten. There was no pushback about wanting to stay till the end and Jessica didn't indicate that anything was amiss. But first, Jessica wanted to say good-bye to her mom. Even in her upset state, she needed to make sure she was okay without her. She did hear from Bernie that Kayla had set up a cleaning service to come after the shower, which was the least she could do considering her incredible thoughtlessness earlier.

Jessica knocked on her mom's door, then opened it to find her mom sitting in a loveseat in her room reading a book. She had come down a few times during the shower, for Kayla's toast to Bernie and to watch some of the games, but she had returned upstairs pretty quickly. Her mom was usually the life of the party, so Jessica knew she had to be fully exhausted to choose to be up there instead of down at the shower.

"You leaving?"

Jessica could hear the disappointment in her mom's voice. "Yeah, I have to get back. I have work on Monday." It was true, it was a Sunday and it would be better to get some down time during the Sunday Scaries. Her mom pushed her readers down her nose and looked at Jessica straight on.

"What's wrong?" The question was so knowing. Jessica should have known her mom would suss her out easily. Maybe she should have left without saying good-bye.

"Nothing, just…you know how I feel about Bernie's friends."

Jessica's mom put her book down. "Did something happen?"

Jessica was brought back once again to being in high school. After she was outed, her mom had also noticed something was wrong. She wasn't ready to talk about it and her mom became more and more concerned. It was actually her dad who was finally able to reach her. He came in one morning, when she hadn't gotten out of bed the whole weekend and he rubbed her hair and he told her that no matter what was going on with her, he would love her. It was almost like he knew. And looking back, maybe he did.

"Mom, did you and Dad ever talk about the fact that I might be gay?" Her mom softened at the mention of her dad. She didn't avoid talking about him, but it almost always made her mom emotional so Jessica found herself being the one avoiding mentioning him.

"You know, when you have kids, you have all these conversations about who they'll be, all these expectations. I don't know why. I said I always wanted you and your sister to be healthy and happy. But I remember when you were about ten years old and all you wanted to do was ride your skateboard, and I made some comment to your father about how you might be a lesbian. I'm ashamed to say it now, but I wanted to push you into other things, as if riding a skateboard or wearing boys' clothes made any difference. He was adamant that I let you be you. It wasn't a discussion after that."

"So then you weren't surprised when I came out?" Jessica didn't know why she needed to know now, but hearing what her dad said when she was ten felt like a balm on her burns.

"When you came out to me and your father that night, I was surprised. You had been so depressed for months. I don't know what I thought, but those expectations I had for you, they had done a number on me." She seemed to realize how that must have felt for Jessica because she quickly corrected herself. "Honey, I would have loved you no matter what you said that day. But I had to fix something broken in myself. Something your father helped me with. I know I didn't say all the right things that day, but I hope I've done better since."

Jessica could feel the remorse in her mother's voice. "Being here, being with all those people who outed me, it just brings back how lonely I felt."

Jessica's mom her pulled her down into a long warm hug. "You are so special and I wouldn't change anything about you." She let go and put her hands on Jessica's cheeks. "When I pushed you to participate in your sister's wedding, I wasn't thinking about all of this. I just wanted my daughters to show up for each other, to give themselves an opportunity to heal, even if just a little bit. I'm sorry I did that. I should have allowed you to decide how you were going to deal with those girls. Honestly, I can't understand Bernie's taste in friends. And when this day ends, I'm going to tell her exactly that. I've had just about enough of that Kayla Kelly. Just because you share a past doesn't mean you need to share a future."

Jessica was relieved to hear her mom take her side so enthusiastically without even knowing what happened. that showed a change from when Jessica was younger. She wasn't alone. And the truth was, she wasn't doing all of this for the inheritance, not anymore. She was realizing, little by little, that she wanted to know her sister again, and part of that meant being present for the things that were important to her.

"It's okay, mom. I understand why you did it. Listen, I'm going to head out, but I love you, and call me if anything goes wrong with the cleaners."

Her mom gave a tsk and picked her book back up. "Drive safe and say a big thank you to Tanner for me!"

Jessica left without making any promises.

❖

About five minutes into their drive, Tanner seemed well aware that something was off. She had attempted some overly familiar small talk, overly familiar considering the feelings Jessica was having about everything generally and Tanner specifically. Jessica had shut any conversation down with a snarky response or a chilly one-word answer. Tanner seemed to retreat.

As the car ride continued, Jessica could see the way Tanner became more and more like the timid person she had seen at the beginning of the bachelorette. Eventually, they settled on silence. Jessica was still angry and still hurt, and she didn't know what to do with her feelings. Deep down she knew that Tanner wasn't the object of those feelings of anger, but because of her proximity to everything and her relationship to what happened, she was a very safe target for Jessica's ire.

Paired with all of this, Jessica was feeling more and more embarrassed about their almost kiss. It all seemed like a reenactment of when they were young, not that Jessica ever would have made a move. She had been way too insecure for anything like that, but still, Tanner had known she had a crush, as evidenced by Kayla throwing it in her face. Now here Jessica was, a full adult, and she was still in the same dynamic. Tanner would probably tell Bernie about it, another person thinking she was some sort of predator. It was humiliating and it was awkward. Even with all the teamwork she and Tanner had had today, she knew deep down Tanner wasn't a safe person for her. Not as a friend, not as anything.

The ride was excruciatingly long, but they finally pulled up in front of Jessica's house. There was street parking open right in front and Tanner pulled into a spot. Jessica didn't wait for Tanner to say anything. She jumped out quickly and went to the trunk to grab her bag. When she closed it, Tanner was standing outside.

"Did you get everything?" The question sounded so pathetic. Obviously, something was wrong, but Tanner wasn't even willing to ask about it.

"Yeah, I got it all. Thanks for the ride!" Jessica said it with finality. She briskly walked up to her row house. Tanner looked like she was about to say something, but Jessica didn't wait to hear it. She was done with this day. She went in the front door and sprinted up the two flights of stairs. She let herself into her apartment and fell back against the door, hoping the door would protect her from all of the feelings she brought back with her from Maryland. When she finally caught her breath, she started making her way toward her bedroom to put her bag down. Then she heard the buzzer ring. It must have been Tanner. She had one of those talk boxes outside so she spoke into the speaker.

"Did I leave something in your car?" That could be the only reason Tanner would want to continue hanging with someone as fully shut down as Jessica.

"Umm…" She heard Tanner's mumble through the speaker. "No, I just… I… Did I do something wrong?" The question was so hesitant, her voice so small.

Jessica didn't know how to answer. She didn't expect to be confronted over the building speaker.

"No, I'm just tired." It was a lie and completely inadequate, but did she really owe this person anything?

There was no response. Had she left?

"It's just, I thought we were getting along and I just feel like I did something to upset you. Maybe if we could just talk about it, I could—"

Jessica interrupted her. "I don't want to talk about it."

"But maybe, is it because of what happened outside? Because—"

Jessica was not about to have that conversation over her building's call system, so she abruptly pressed the buzzer to let her in. It made a loud noise she could hear from the door to her apartment. She opened her door and shouted down, "Third floor."

Jessica heard Tanner coming up the stairs. Did she want to have this conversation? Not exactly, but at least if she told Tanner off to her face, she wouldn't have to deal with this at the next wedding thing.

Tanner appeared in the frame of the door and looked in with trepidation.

"You can come in," Jessica said as if she didn't care.

Tanner entered, looking around. "Your place is nice."

"Thanks." Jessica went back to her short responses. "What do you need to talk about? I don't need all my neighbors hearing my business."

Tanner looked at her with that lost hurt look she'd had at the airport. "I was just saying that I think you're mad at me or something and I've just really been trying to fix things and I thought we had sort of turned a corner and then outside when we almost...kissed."

"We didn't almost kiss." Jessica was flooded with embarrassment.

"I think… I just, maybe I messed up with whatever that was?"

"There is no fixing things, Tanner. We can't fix what happened."

"What happened with what?" She looked completely confused and how could she not be? Tanner wasn't having some sort of PTSD flashback. She was just dealing with whatever weird thing was happening between them in the past few months, the past few hours.

"I told you, I told only you!" The words caught in Jessica's throat. She could feel the teenager in her speaking the words. "Back in high school. You can't fix that. We can't be friends, do you understand that?"

Tanner looked gobsmacked. She clearly did not expect to be having that conversation at this moment.

"I am so sorry, Jessica." The words were full of emotion. "I've wanted for so long to tell you that. I should have supported you. I should have stuck up for you. I was so immature and self-centered. I don't know how to make you see that I'm not that same person anymore."

"You should have supported me? You outed me! And the worst part is you knew, you knew I had a crush on you. It was humiliating. And Kayla, why did you tell Kayla?" Jessica could feel all the hurt in her chest coming up.

Tanner seemed unable to speak. She just shook her head. "I didn't know you had a crush on me."

"You must have suspected! Enough to spread the rumor!"

"I—I can't explain my choices when I was sixteen, there is no excuse. But I would never do anything like that to anyone, especially not…you."

"Did you know I wanted to die! Did you know that for years, I thought I was unlovable? Did you know that I couldn't trust anyone, not my friends, not even my family? It may seem like everything's just fine, that everything's forgotten, but it isn't."

Jessica was angry, but there was something so incongruent about what she was feeling and the way Tanner was looking at her. Her eyes were glossy, her head was low. She was ashamed. Jessica knew that feeling.

"...Jess, I didn't know. I didn't know that you... I'm so sorry."

She noticed moisture on her own face. Jessica had been crying. She wiped her eyes and lost some of her bravado.

"It doesn't matter anymore." Jessica took a seat on her couch, exhausted.

Tanner sat in the chair across from it. She took a deep breath and then spoke.

"I know I don't deserve your forgiveness, but I have never regretted anything as much as how I acted when we were young, and losing our friendship. Getting to talk to you in Asheville, when you weren't hating me, felt so amazing. And even today, working together, I don't want to lose that again."

The words were honey sweet, and again Jessica found her resolve breaking. She missed their friendship too. Hearing Tanner say those words made her realize just how much. The truth was, she had felt better since the bachelorette, lighter, stronger.

Jessica let out a deep groan and put her face in her hands. Tanner was waiting for some sort of response. When one didn't come, Tanner got up.

"I get it. I'll go." She took a few steps toward the door and Jessica stopped her.

"Wait!" Tanner turned back "I—I can't be your friend just like that. But I think we can be—we can start over again." This starting over thing was getting old. How many times would they do this between now and the wedding?

Tanner let out a sigh of relief. "Okay, that's more than I deserve." She lingered another moment and then said, "I guess I should go."

"I'll see you at the dress fitting," Jessica added, making it clear she didn't want to see her any sooner. The dress fitting was in two months. Enough time for Jessica to figure out how to deal with Tanner in the future.

"At the dress fitting," Tanner repeated with a sad lilt to her voice. She left, closing the door behind her. Jessica sat in the aftermath again, unsure of her feelings about Tanner. She just could not muster that same hate. She didn't get an explanation, but it wasn't like anything could have explained what Tanner had done. She did get an apology, and as much as she didn't want to admit it, hearing that apology mattered a lot.

Chapter Ten

Jessica was sitting at her desk at work on New Year's Eve doing copy for her asshole of a boss. No one was in the office because of course, it was a federal holiday. This was the end of her rope. She didn't want to spend any more of her life wasting away in that awful glass walled overly modern trash can of an office. She was leaving. Even if she didn't get the money for her bookstore. She would freelance if she needed to. She made a promise to herself that night, this would be the last New Year's Eve she would spend working for Tom Wilson, the man who pulled her aside the other week to tell him his ultimate fantasy was a threesome with two women. It had been a new low. She considered going to HR, but she just didn't have any faith that there would be consequences for him, and she was pretty sure he would know it was her. This was the last straw. She got a text from Lisa.

Yo! It's 8, things are already getting crowded. Get your butt over here!

Lisa was referring to the QBar New Year's party. Jessica loved hearing QBar was packed because it meant people were supporting their local queer bar. She wasn't quite done with her work, but since she had made her promise to herself, she decided that she was going to say "fuck it" and leave Tom his own work to fix. What did she care about the blowback if she was leaving?

When Jessica came to the office at four p.m., she'd brought a change of clothes knowing she would most likely not have time to go home. She stole away to the genderless bathroom to change. Luckily, her office was closer to the Eastern Market neighborhood than her apartment was, so she would be there pretty quickly. She texted Bryce to find out his ETA.

Already here babe!

He also sent a picture of himself with his tongue out and making a peace sign, clearly on a jam-packed dance floor. Jessica was out of there.

❖

Inside QBar, New Year's Eve was unfolding in a gritty room adorned with graffiti. Dim neon lights created an underground atmosphere, and the dance floor pulsed to the music. Vintage furniture offered cozy corners for private conversations. The air was thick with the scent of whiskey and the promise of a memorable night.

It was already packed wall to wall with people dancing, flirting, fully making out, all of the above. The small but surprisingly spacious venue had an incredibly fun energy while also keeping that even more rare feeling of intimacy. Jessica was looking for her friends, but it was difficult in the throngs of people. She decided to go to the bar since that was where she was most likely to find Lisa.

Lisa had been MIA for a few weeks because she had recently started dating a new person and was clearly smitten. Usually that meant the "benefits" part of their friendship would go away, something Jessica was happy to notice sort of fit where her mind was lately anyway. She had much more of a need for a friend of late. Lisa was at the bar, completely swamped. She was there along with two other bartenders. Jessica wasn't even able to reach the bar top itself, which was a first in QBar's short history.

Lisa signaled that she saw her but clearly had a queue of people waiting so Jessica moved over to a recently abandoned high top close to the bar to continue to look for Bryce. She saw a few people from the community that she recognized and so many extremely hot people. It felt amazing just being surrounded by her community. She wasn't usually a fan of New Year's just because of all the hype and the expectations, but being in the right place with the right crowd could really set a tone for her next year. As she was gazing around the room, her eyes became caught on a certain hue of blond hair that had become abundantly familiar of late. She was cascaded in strobe light, but it was clear, Tanner Caldwell was also celebrating her New Year's Eve at QBar. This, of course being once again the fate of urban queer women, enbies, and their friends who had a very limited amount of space designated specifically for them.

It had been a month since Jessica saw or spoke to Tanner. Their last meeting was still at the forefront of her mind. Their angsty fight in her apartment after the bridal shower was still fresh in her brain. When Tanner left that day, Jessica had felt so exhausted. The conversation, in retrospect, had been cathartic, and she had felt like she had finally let go of something she had been holding tightly to. She found that her exhaustion persisted a few days after, almost like an emotional hangover, but then she came back to life again. It was sort of similar to how she felt after the bachelorette weekend. She felt lighter.

Bryce had even noticed. He mentioned that she looked rested or happy or something like that. She thought about his inferences later. How much anger had she been holding on to? Were all of her feelings so noticeable? She didn't want that. She wanted her past to be in her past. She wanted to be free. If talking to Tanner had helped in any way to get her to focus more on her present life, then she had come to start thinking of it as a good thing. Not at first, but over the last month she had let go little by little and so seeing Tanner at QBar now felt quite a bit different. There wasn't that feeling of dread or anger. There wasn't an impulse to avoid or hide. There were some of the old feelings, the persistent feelings that those other feelings eclipsed. Interest, attraction, but also new ones like curiosity. Tanner was dancing with very few inhibitions. She was dancing very close to a man Jessica didn't recognize. A very attractive, very scantily clad man.

They were clearly in a small group with some other people, one of whom Jessica did recognize as Keith, the dancer who had been hired to strip at the bachelorette. He was fully dressed this time in a very formal suit that was in an incredibly amazing retro style in pastel blue. Their little group was clearly having a good time because they were all dancing with the same level of enthusiasm as Tanner and laughing. Jessica couldn't help herself, she watched them and thought about how weird it was to see Tanner in this element. Of course Tanner had her own life outside of those people from high school, but Jessica had never seen it with her own eyes. And just looking at her then, it felt like the people she was hanging with could have been Jessica's friends. She was of course going off first observable impressions, but still, that had Jessica at least considering she could have misjudged some things about Tanner's life.

But it wasn't just Tanner's friends, it was Tanner herself. She was getting down and grinding on the man, who looked like a close friend if Jessica were to guess, and all of her conservativeness seemed to be gone. Jessica felt like if she had seen Tanner for the first time that night, she never would have believed she was the same person as the Tanner from high school or even from the bachelorette. The only similarity was that Tanner was still breathtakingly beautiful. Out of everyone in the bar, Jessica would not have been able to help the way her eyes constantly found Tanner. It really wasn't something in her control.

Jessica found that she wanted to say hi, but she didn't know how. They had left things on a weird note. Yes, they had agreed to start over, but they'd also had no contact since then. It felt like the ball was very much in Jessica's court. She initially had no desire to reach out, let alone any reason to, but then as time passed and she started to think more critically, she began to consider contacting her. She could feel her feelings changing about Tanner in general. At one point, she even wrote out a text to send. Something meaningless and unnecessary, but before she could send it, she got in her head about it. She never did send the text. Now, seeing Tanner in person, she was having a whole other debate about how best to deal with her feelings. She wanted to go up to her, but there were butterflies in her stomach.

It was then that Bryce found her. He seemed to somehow sneak up on her, which was pretty shocking since he was coming from a very frontward-facing angle, and he was dressed in the most obnoxiously loud pink mesh onesie. It seemed everyone at the party was either dressed formally, as was typical for New Year's Eve, or some version of queer or naked, as was typical of QBar. The juxtaposition was amazing.

"Yo! Wallflower! Who are you checking out?" The words pulled Jessica out of her dream state.

"I'm not a wallflower," she protested. "I just got here and I have some stretches to do before I get out there." She was ignoring the dig about checking someone out, but her eyes kept darting back to the dance floor,

"The girl being sandwiched by those two hunks?" The sight was pretty hilarious, Jessica had to admit.

"That's Tanner, from the—"

"From your fantasies, I mean, the bachelorette." The stumble was meant to be teasing, but it rung a little too true.

Jessica had told Bryce about some of her thoughts in the past month, but she hadn't told him everything she was feeling. It was obvious from his joke that he had extrapolated enough. It seemed Jessica was brimming with transparency when it came to Tanner.

She was going to respond with some sort of denial, but it was that moment that she accidentally locked eyes with Tanner.

Tanner stopped dancing and said something to a few of her friends.

"Hello!" Bryce was passing his hand in front of Jessica's face. "Earth to Jessica!" Jessica had fully dropped out of the conversation. She then noticed that Tanner's group was heading her way.

"She's coming over, shut up!" Bryce stopped his teasing and greeted Tanner and two of her friends from the dance floor.

"Hey, Jess," Tanner said in a casual tone that Jessica wished she was capable of. Her smile was infectious and it was clear just from Jessica's small amount of time watching Tanner that this was an environment she was comfortable in.

"Umm, hi!" Jessica said, very much on her back foot. There was a slight lull that was quickly filled by Bryce.

"I'm Bryce. You must be Tanner?" He didn't say that he'd heard about her, but the fact that he guessed her name showed Jessica's hand regardless.

"Hi! Bryce, this is my friend Keith and his boyfriend, Sam. They're visiting me from Asheville, so I wanted them to see QBar."

The guy Jessica hadn't met named Sam chimed in. "When we moved a few years ago, there were really only super exclusionary 'gay guy' bars," he said with air quotes. "So we had to come check out this amazing new queer space!"

Jessica knew that this was something she and Bryce often complained about. This was a general issue for Jessica. She preferred a gay or queer space to a straight space, but there was still a tendency to be othering even within the LGBTQ+ community. It was rare to find something like QBar. The fact that Tanner's friends felt the same way said a lot about them.

Keith said hi to Jessica next, saying he remembered her from Asheville. He was way better at covering up anything he might have heard about her, at least in comparison to Bryce.

"So, why aren't you dancing?" Tanner's question was pointed at Jessica. Tanner must have been having a good time because her excitement was contagious.

"I just got off work, so I was sort of getting a lay of the land first." Jessica had forgotten about her shitty day almost instantly upon seeing Tanner.

Bryce pulled Jessica into a side hug and gave her a kiss on the cheek. "Our little queer bar fly here has been MIA for a while 'cause of her shitty boss!" Jessica knew he was much sadder about not seeing her than he was pretending to be by teasing about it.

"Yeah well, I decided tonight, this is the last New Year's I'm going to spend at the Daily Paper. It's decided. I'm not quite ready to give my notice, but that's my resolution." Even saying the words filled Jessica with an overwhelming relief.

"That's amazing!" Tanner placed her hand on Jessica's wrist and squeezed affectionately. "Does this mean the bookstore is happening?" She sounded as excited as Jessica was.

"She told you about the bookstore?" Bryce threw a look at Jessica. Jessica had not told many people about her plan. She had a thing about failing and having everyone know about it. She told her mom, Bryce, and Lisa. Somehow, it slipped her mind that she also told Tanner. It happened so casually that she didn't even register.

Jessica wanted to quickly change the subject, so she asked the group, "What's everyone else's resolution?

Bryce spoke first, clearly supporting Jessica's very blatant wishes not to be publicly investigated for her relationship with Tanner.

"I want to submit my screenplay to the Tribeca Film Festival this year and I want to attempt to pull off a mullet."

"First of all," Keith said, "There's no question you could pull off a mullet." The words were dripping with support. "And second, if you write screenplays, we should talk. When I'm not stripping for lesbians who aren't interested at a bachelorette, I work for Netflix scoping out IP."

Bryce's eyes grew two sizes bigger. "I'm sorry what did you say?"

"I work at Netflix."

"No, about stripping for lesbians."

Keith laughed.

Jessica chimed in. "Keith was one of the strippers at the bachelorette."

"And Jessica and I were the only ones who didn't get a lap dance." Tanner completed Jessica's sentence.

Bryce seemed satisfied by that explanation. "Okay now as far as Netflix goes, let's talk." Bryce gave Keith a flirty smile and he gave one right back.

"Okay, now Tanner, resolution, go!" Sam interjected, very obviously pretending to be jealous.

"I haven't decided yet," she said, seeming to think on it pretty hard.

"You only have a few hours, so you might have to figure something out now."

"I think for my resolution… I think I'd like to be more brave." She let that hang in the air.

Keith responded. "That's pretty cryptic. Do you mean at work or personal life stuff?"

She seemed to think about it. "I think I'll just leave it at that. Brave in all parts of my life."

Sam added in, "I think that's a great one for you, Tan. Maybe that'll get you out of that stupid site."

Jessica remembered that Tanner had said that she and Sam previously worked together at mommy+me, so the fact that he was saying it too said a lot.

"In all parts of my life!" she said, closing the conversation.

"Well," Sam said, "My resolution is to be kinder to myself. It's been a hard few years and I think we all deserve a little more self-compassion." Keith put his arm around Sam and looked at him with eyes that could only be called dreamy. Jessica couldn't help but resonate with Sam. She didn't know what he had been going through, but she felt wholeheartedly that everyone in that room could use a little more self-compassion. This made her think of Tanner and her apology the last time they saw each other. Even she deserved to be kinder to herself, at least that's how Jessica felt right then.

Sam brought them out of their deep thinking. "So, back to the dance floor?" The question was to all of them. Jessica looked at Tanner who seemed to be watching her as well.

"Okay, let's go," Jessica responded, and she could see Tanner smile and gesture them out to where their other friends were. Jessica couldn't help it, the music, the people, she just wanted to dance.

❖

The music was intoxicating. Jessica couldn't help but fully let herself dance. The group that formed between her friends and Tanner's friends was pretty miraculous. Never in her life could she have imagined such an easy fusion. Tanner had two other friends who joined, a couple whose names Jessica learned and then just as quickly forgot since the whole exchange happened through blaring music and everyone singing just as loudly along to all their favorite songs. But everyone was just a perfect gel with her friends. Bryce had basically invited himself to Asheville somehow even with the music blaring, and at one point Lisa's new girlfriend showed up and said hello before parking herself at the bar, obviously hoping to be at the right place for when midnight hit.

Jessica was dancing and enjoying herself so much that she didn't even notice the cohesion she was feeling with Tanner. No matter where they were on the dance floor, they seemed to go together like magnets. It started as just being near each other, but eventually it got closer and it seemed that the group was picking up on something as well because most everyone drifted away, leaving them to whatever connection was building between them. Jessica wasn't thinking, she was just doing what she felt, and being close to Tanner felt good.

Soon the DJ began to speak over the music letting them know they were getting close to the countdown. Everyone seemed to shift with a new energy, clearly looking for whoever they needed to find to have their New Year's kiss. The moment Jessica realized what was going on she started to panic. There was something dangerous happening between her and Tanner, and if she stayed on the dance floor, she felt she couldn't stop what was coming.

Jessica decided to do the only thing that made sense: she left the dance floor. She left and she didn't look back. When she passed the bar, sure enough, she saw Lisa climbing over the bar in what had to be a health code violation to join her new person Laura on the floor. Seeing that didn't make Jessica feel anything but happiness for her friend. Even if she had been looking for Lisa to kiss, their connection wasn't what she craved. The truth was, she hadn't craved anyone, not really, not since Tanner came back into her life. She had even more reason to flee. She decided to get into the bathroom line which was extra long and full of people who were desperate for both the bathroom and a chance to get back out to find whoever they wanted to kiss. Jessica decided not to add to the wait for people, so she went past to the end of the hallway. It was a bit more open and it looked like she was waiting for someone inside versus just taking up space.

The countdown started. ...15, 14, 13... And Jessica was feeling more and more stupid. Why was she spending her last moments of the year hiding from someone? How was that what was best? She was starting to feel like a total loser. All of her friends, everyone in the bar was having fun and she was running from what? ...10, 9... Everyone was chanting together and Jessica couldn't take it. She didn't want to be here. She didn't want to let this control her. She didn't think past that. She left her little hall hiding place and went back out to the bar, hoping to quickly find her friends. The lights were brighter and everyone was chanting. ...5, 4... Jessica spotted Tanner. She wasn't looking around. She was chanting and smiling, holding her friends on each of her arms, and Jessica was hit with a jolt of electricity. Of all the times she had seen Tanner over the years, she had never seen her look so beautiful.

Jessica didn't think. She pushed her way past kissing people, back to where her friends were. When she was close enough, she reached for Tanner's hand. Tanner turned around, her eyes changing from surprise to excitement. Jessica never stopped or hesitated, she kissed Tanner. She kissed her hard. Tanner immediately kissed her back, pulling Jessica's face in closer and deepening the kiss. Jessica put her arms around Tanner and she could feel every beat of her own heart, every molecule of her skin that touched Tanner. The countdown, the cheering, none of it mattered. Jessica was kissing Tanner, and she wasn't stopping. The music started up again and Jessica was sure everyone had started dancing, but for her, time stood still. She did eventually get lightly stepped on, pulling her away, something she allowed with reluctance. She didn't let go and neither did Tanner. Faces finally separated, they looked at each other with shock but also with what could only be called lust.

"Wow." Tanner was the first to speak.

Jessica didn't know what to say. She just knew she wanted to keep kissing her. She was also slowly becoming aware of how public their make-out had been. Not that Bryce or Tanner's friends were paying them any mind. The fact that Jessica didn't even think about it was just astonishing. Jessica did finally let go of Tanner. Without the hype of the countdown, she couldn't justify continuing to make out in the middle of the dance floor.

When they separated, Jessica could see the deepest blush on Tanner's face, so dark that it was visible in the dance floor lights.

Jessica couldn't help but feel the desire to continue kissing her. She held back. She didn't regret the kiss, but she didn't know exactly how it was going to feel later and she wanted to keep her good feeling going. She wanted to feel better this year, and if that meant kissing who she wanted to, then okay. But it also meant checking in with herself before doing anything more. And the truth was, she wanted to do more. She could feel it all over her body. She wanted to kiss her, she wanted to touch her, she wanted to say fuck it—invite her back to her apartment and fuck Tanner Caldwell.

And that was something she couldn't allow herself to do, as much as she wanted to. So she danced. She danced like she had before. She danced close to Tanner, but then she danced with her friends. And when she started to feel her heart calm down, she decided she needed to go home. She said good-bye to her friends, she said good-bye to Tanner's friends, and when she said good-bye to Tanner, she gave her a hug. The hug felt weird, but it also felt good. It felt like their connection was still there, still simmering, but that maybe Tanner was also struggling to understand what was happening between them.

She left and caught the Metro home. Even with all the drunk people screaming, playing music, passed out on the train, she noticed none of it. All she could think about was how it felt kissing Tanner and how it took everything in her power not to text her to say come over.

Chapter Eleven

Jessica didn't text Tanner that night, and she didn't the next day. She did find that the fact that Tanner didn't text either genuinely hurt her feelings. She wasn't hoping for anything, but she was sort of feeling weird. But then her head got involved again, and when she replayed what happened, she was reminded that she was the initiator. Tanner was just hanging with her friends. Before she could go down a bad spiral, she remembered the feeling of Tanner kissing her back. That was unmistakable. But there was still that old feeling, the anxiety when it came to Tanner. Last time she thought there was something between them, when she told Tanner she thought she was gay, she had misread the situation. A lot had changed, but as much as she was attracted to Tanner, she didn't trust her and that's what kept her from texting.

The next time she heard anything from or about Tanner, it was when her sister called a few weeks later. She wanted to iron out details for the dress fitting in New York. Jessica was planning to take the train up and meet everyone on the day of the fitting in Manhattan, and then stay with her ex Riley in Brooklyn. They were still friends, and the breakup was now over a year ago, but she hadn't yet stayed with her in New York. Ultimately, it was an economic decision. One night in a hotel in New York was not in Jessica's budget, especially if she was quitting her job before the wedding, which was becoming something she was considering more and more.

Riley was great, and in many ways, she had been a great partner to Jessica, but ultimately, they both just didn't seem to want to move to be together. After two years of going back and forth, Jessica decided that the reason she wouldn't move to Brooklyn was not because she couldn't compromise for a partner she loved, but because the love she felt for Riley wasn't enough for her to want to do that. This revelation was finally how it ended. It hurt both of them, and they got some space from each other, but they had been on texting and even phone call terms for the last six months, so Jessica figured it was just about time to test out the next step on their journey to being "just friends."

Bernie called on a Sunday afternoon, just as Jessica was coming in the door. They had been having weekly calls, but they skipped a few. Jessica assumed it was because she had so much planning to do.

"Hey, Bern. What's up?"

"Hey, Jess, just finalizing some stuff with the caterer. I have to say, I'm definitely agreeing more and more with your anti-wedding thing!" It was obviously a joke, but nevertheless, Jessica felt bad for expressing that view so strongly.

"You know, Bern, I've also been more open to the idea that a big party with all your friends isn't the worst thing in the world." Jessica realized after saying it that she meant it. She had thought a few times that if she really loved someone, it might be nice to have the people she considered family and friends celebrate it. She hadn't changed her mind about "marriage" or the institution, but just about that. Just the love and community part, she was open.

"Look at that! I guess what Tanner said on the trail really stuck with you. I basically forgot everything once that mountain lion almost killed us."

The mention of Tanner's name made Jessica's stomach jump. She was nervous but she was also excited just hearing her name—something that was completely new to her.

"Yeah, maybe…. Have you heard from Tanner?" She wanted to hear more.

"Umm, yeah, I basically text her every day. She's good! Oh yeah, she said she ran into you on New Year's Eve! How was that?" The question was innocent enough. It seemed to Jessica that Bernie didn't know. She had never seen her sister be very good at lying or being evasive.

"Yeah, it was good, I think." Jessica was just starting to feel comfortable with her sister, and they had never been able to talk about Tanner. In the past few months, there had been some mention, but there was an unspoken rule about Tanner—don't say too much.

When Jessica was younger and they were in high school together, Tanner was over a lot and that wasn't too weird, except for Jessica's crush. When Tanner and Jessica worked together on the paper, the friendship was separate from Tanner's friendship with Bernie, but there was a moment, a brief one, where it almost seemed like the three of them could have hung out all together. Before that could solidify, Jessica was outed, ending any comfort she could possibly feel with Tanner.

After that, Tanner came over less, and when she did, Jessica made herself as scarce as possible. Any hallway crossover was basically Jessica pretending Tanner didn't exist, which was probably why Tanner seemed to avoid their house. Bernie and Jessica's relationship suffered as well. It wasn't exactly that Jessica held her responsible for the outing just by being friends with Tanner and Kayla, but it felt like when everything happened, Bernie had said nothing.

And although she was doing well enough in her life now, Jessica shuddered to think of what could have happened if her dad hadn't showed up to support her when he did. She knew there was a chance that if things had continued on the trajectory she was on—isolated, self-hating—she very well could have been a teen suicide statistic. Jessica was sure that Bernie didn't know the extent of what she went through, but Bernie had seen the way her friends treated Jessica. And as far as Jessica could tell, Bernie's friendship with Tanner at least never wavered a moment. This just fed into her anxiety that Bernie would have rather had someone like Tanner as a sister. Someone cooler and more popular. Someone who liked girly things and was conventionally pretty, and instead she got this emo lesbian sibling who didn't fit in with her.

Jessica remembered the day she was outed so vividly and the way her sister seemed to distance herself, almost as if association with her would hurt her reputation as well. Jessica couldn't be sure that was why, but that's what she decided in her head. After that, she avoided Bernie and Bernie seemed to accept that. A few times, Bernie tried to connect or invite her somewhere, but Jessica just couldn't recover from what she felt was an abandonment. Then she left for college shortly after everything and it seemed things just stayed as they were. She could remember her dad noticing and asking her about it. In some ways he understood, but he would always say, "Your sister loves you and I hope someday you forgive her."

When he passed away, she was too consumed with her own grief to truly ask herself if it was time to reconnect with Bernie. She remembered seeing Bernie at the funeral, and she heard from her mom sometimes that Bernie was struggling, but weren't they all? It didn't occur to her that they could have helped each other. They both lost someone they loved. The wounds were still too fresh, and only now after so much careful work between the both of them, but mostly Bernie, were they coming to a place where there weren't as many landmines and Jessica was able to see her sister had grown into a kind and beautiful person. So when Tanner came up this time, she decided not to be so evasive.

"Actually, it was interesting. I got to meet some of her friends and we danced..."

Jessica could hear a pause on the line, clearly a double take from Bernie. "Wow, so you guys like, really hung out?" It was clear from Bernie's tone that she was pretending not to be excited, but Jessica could tell.

"Yeah, it was interesting and actually, something kind of, um, surprising happened." Jessica paused. "We kind of kissed..." She said it in such a way that even Jessica wasn't sure if she was serious.

"I'm sorry, I must have misheard you. Did you say you and Tanner kissed?"

"Yeah, at midnight, you know how people do..." Jessica was already trying to downplay it.

Bernie was silent on the other end.

"Hello?"

Then she heard a loud scream on the other end followed by, "Oh my God oh my God, that's amazing!!" Bernie's excitement was a total one-eighty and Jessica was genuinely shocked, but she also couldn't help but laugh herself. She didn't know why, but part of her had been afraid that Bernie would be upset. It was sort of an awkward situation, her sister hooking up with her best friend.

"It wasn't a big deal!" Jessica again tried to downplay. "It was seriously just a thing that happened."

"Of course, not a big deal." Bernie was clearly trying now to be faux nonchalant. "So, like...how was it? Actually, you know what, I don't want to know. I feel like I'm too close. But also, I'm just now realizing, Tanner didn't even tell me!"

Jessica thought about that as well. What did it mean? "Maybe she was embarrassed or something?" The old fears crept up.

"I don't think it was that," Bernie said confidently. "Maybe she just wanted to keep it private. But now I can't wait to tease her about this!"

Jessica realized in that moment that if Bernie teased Tanner, she would know Jessica told. What would Tanner read into that? "Maybe it's better if it's just between us," Jessica said, already feeling insecure.

"Why? It's not like there's anything to hide, right? I mean unless there is…" Bernie said in an especially playful way. But the subject was starting to get closer to the actual fear.

"I'm not super comfortable with her yet, just with everything that happened when we were younger. I'm telling you this kiss thing in confidence, but I still don't really know her anymore."

"Yeah, I guess there's a lot of history there." Something changed in Bernie's tone and she seemed to no longer have that same exuberant excitement that she was showing earlier.

"Maybe, if it's okay, can you just wait till she tells you, if she tells you?" Jessica could hear the child like tone in her own voice. It was almost like she and her sister were kids again.

"Okay, I won't say anything," Bernie said with such sincerity and seriousness that Jessica couldn't help but laugh.

"I mean, it's not that serious, Bern. I'm just saying I'd prefer you wait."

"I know, but I just want you to know how seriously I take our relationship." The words were laced with emotion and Jessica couldn't help but feel grateful to be able to get this connection back with her sister.

"So tell me about your awful day of wedding food planning!"

Bernie went into all the things that were giving her a headache. Jessica listened and only suggested they call off the wedding once, which was a record for her.

❖

Tanner did end up texting. A couple of weeks later, when the dress fitting was about a week out. Jessica was just leaving a meeting with a commercial real estate firm that was renting a property that had the perfect location for her shop. The owners were retiring and the building was going to become available in about six months. It was both very soon and very far away. Jessica was feeling excited and nervous. She stopped for some coffee at a place across from the location and she was sitting looking at her building from the outside when she received the text from Tanner.

Hey, was thinking about you, how are you?

She was thinking about her? Jessica had never received anything like that from Tanner. There was a moment after New Year's Eve when she almost texted Tanner in a more than friends way, and she felt like it was possible Tanner might do the same thing. When it didn't happen, she decided that things would just go back to how they were. But now, with this text, she found herself trying to interpret every word. "Thinking about you," that had to be a more than friends thing to say. But then again, who knew? Maybe that was just the kind of thing Tanner would send to a friend. Still, the last time they saw each other, they kissed. No, they fully made out. There was no way that this wasn't a charged text interaction, Tanner had to know that.

Jessica: *Hey, I'm good, just checking out a potential site for my store!*

Tanner's response came quickly.

Tanner: *What!! That's amazing! It seems like maybe you're ready to make your move?*

Jessica: *Just about a couple more months and then I'm done. Hbu, work getting any better?*

Tanner: *sigh, I think I might be closer than you are to giving notice*

Jessica: *I'm sorry it hasn't gotten better*

Tanner: *No you aren't, you think I'm a sellout!*

Jessica was taken off guard by the accusation. It was hard to read tone by text, but it felt like Tanner was teasing.

Jessica: *No I don't. I do however think your book will be amazing and I can't wait to read it.*

Jessica could see a pause then the three dots then another long pause. She was done with her coffee, but she didn't want to stop texting Tanner. It felt nice even just getting to talk so casually about their jobs and their future. It felt like maybe the kiss would just go undiscussed. Maybe that was for the best.

Tanner: *Maybe someday I'll let you read it. I'm sure your notes could only make it better :)*

It wasn't that the texts were overtly flirty, they were almost borderline friendly, but still, this was not how their relationship was before. Possibly back when they were kids, but Jessica could barely remember that now.

Tanner: *So how are you getting to NYC?*

This was interesting, was she trying to carpool again?

Jessica: *I was thinking the train but I'm not sure yet.*

Could Jessica handle another car ride with Tanner?

Tanner: *I was thinking the same thing*

Okay, that was a relief. It was still confusing trying to figure out why Tanner was asking if she wasn't trying to carpool.

Tanner: *I was thinking if we are going the same way, rather than running into each other like last time, maybe we could ride up together on the same train?*

The request was interesting. It wasn't trying to make the trip easier, it was wanting to ride together, like almost to hang out. Jessica couldn't help but feel her chest flutter. She didn't know what to say. She was still deeply conflicted about her relationship with Tanner, and she knew she didn't want to have anything happen between them, or at least she thought that's what she wanted. But she also couldn't see the harm in taking the train together. It was perfect in a way, she could hang with Tanner but it wasn't in any sort of formal or especially intentional way. It was just a bit more planned than a coincidence. She had left Tanner waiting awhile when she saw another message.

Tanner: *obviously it's fine if not. I'm sure our schedules wouldn't line up anyway.*

The inferring lack of confidence by Tanner made the decision for her.

Jessica: *I'm thinking a Friday morning train, does that work for you?*

The reply came quickly again.

Tanner: *perfect :)*

Jessica could feel her heart beating, she had been fully derailed from her bookstore excitement to her Tanner excitement. The idea of seeing her again after their kiss had her palms sweaty. As much as she didn't want to admit it, she knew deep down that something was happening between them. She didn't know how much longer she wanted to be good.

❖

The Acela Train was on time and fully packed. The only available seats were in the quiet car. At first, Jessica was beyond nervous, and then she was disappointed that they wouldn't be able to talk without seriously violating some long established social norms. Even with her hidden agenda to get some time alone with Tanner without it being clear to Tanner, or herself what she was doing. So they sat next to each other, quietly. Jessica read a book and Tanner worked on her laptop. Every so often, Jessica would look over at Tanner with her horn-rimmed glasses and her scrunched up scowly concentration face and she would be completely transfixed. Sometimes she'd catch Tanner doing the same, which created a flutter of nerves. But what stood out most to Jessica was how nice it was to just be next to Tanner. It was strangely intimate being silent together, intimate and somehow comfortable.

Jessica was certain at this point that the kiss wasn't going to come up, but she didn't know what that meant. On one hand, she definitely didn't want to talk about it. But it didn't sit well with her that Tanner seemed to not want to as well. They exited the train together, and as they both stepped off the train, Jessica accidentally ran into Tanner, bringing their bodies together in a clash, the first time she had touched her since that night. She could feel the electricity where her hands held Tanner's shoulders steadying her. She let go and they continued on their way off the platform, but Jessica couldn't stop being aware of having touched her. The electricity came alive again, and their comfortable silence became something else.

They moved through the train station with an awkward awareness. Jessica was thinking about how much of the last few months their relationship was built inside limbic spaces. They were always coming and going and meeting in-between. Except this time, for the first time, being on the train together was intentional.

They grabbed a cab to midtown to meet the other bridesmaids at the dress shop. They got out at a small but clearly expensive boutique that reminded Jessica not only had she never been in a wedding dress store, she couldn't remember the last store she'd been in that sold dresses. It had to have been at least high school when her mom was still trying to persuade her to add a little more femme to her look.

Jessica and Tanner entered the shop and were greeted by a woman in a sleek pencil skirt and the air of that shop owner from *Pretty Woman*—"big mistake!" When Tanner gave Bernie's name, the woman's whole demeanor changed.

"Oh, of course, they are in our best room. Would you ladies like some champagne?"

Jessica was still reeling from the whiplash, but she was definitely not going to turn down free champagne. Especially as she tried to survive the gender dysphoria that had already hit her when she looked at all the lace and frills. Tanner and Jessica were led into a room where Bernie, Alex, and Kayla were already seated. Both Chris's mother and Jessica's mom had been invited, but because they hadn't gotten a lot of time to meet solo, Bernie set up a special lunch for just the two of them instead. Something Jessica was able to hear about on her weekly call with Bernie.

"Jess! Tanner!" Bernie exclaimed as she hugged each of them. Jessica couldn't help but notice the extra excitement she had saying both of their names, and the underlying knowing tone. Jessica was already regretting telling Bernie about the kiss.

"Look at you two, walking in together. After the bachelorette airport trip, I never thought I'd see you both looking so chummy," Alex said, adding insult to injury as she also gave them both a hug. Jessica didn't have a quick response. She thought it was unlikely Alex knew about the kiss, but even just saying something like that was drawing a lot of extra attention to the two of them. Tanner rescued them.

"Well. Jessica still owes me for saving her life from the mountain lion." That was a simple enough redirect.

Kayla raised her champagne to them in a perfunctory cheers from across the room, an obvious indicator once again of how little she cared how she came off. The only difference was now Tanner was explicitly and visibly receiving the same treatment.

The shop associate brought them each a glass of champagne.

"So, a dress fitting," Jessica said, taking a spot on the dangerously white couch next to Alex. "You already have a dress, and now we just have to see if it fits? What if it doesn't? Do you get your money back?" Jessica was mostly joking. Again, she had become very good at googling over the past few months.

Tanner took a seat in a solo chair not too far from Jessica. The electricity from earlier still hadn't fully died down.

Bernie laughed. "I guess I don't know? I think it's more likely they would rush fix it or get me a new one, but I think the main point is to have my closest friends get to see me first? Or something…"

Tanner added, "I know I want to see how it all came out. I'm also just relieved you weren't one of those people getting a smaller size and then crash-dieting to fit."

Bernie groaned. "Listen, I can't imagine doing all that while working, and while planning this. Besides, Chris asked me to marry him looking like this, why would I need to change?"

Jessica was proud to hear her sister speak so confidently about herself. She had read that a lot of people tried to lose a certain amount of weight before their wedding for the dress or for the wedding photos, and just knowing her sister's history with body issues in high school, that could have been a very dangerous thing.

"Chris has absolutely nothing to complain about!" Alex added with a flirtatious pinch on Bernie's butt.

Bernie shouted from the pinch but blushed adorably. Jessica looked at her phone and saw a missed text from Riley.

Hey, hope you got in okay. I have a break in a bit from work, want to meet in midtown?

Riley lived in Brooklyn, where Jessica was planning on staying, but she had planned to just go over that direction whenever they were done. Riley worked at a law firm in midtown and she almost never got any "breaks," so Jessica had assumed they wouldn't be able to hang out earlier. She didn't know how to say it, but really, she didn't want to meet up earlier. Leaving after the dress shop would take away from some of the time she was planning to accidently have to spend with Tanner. She didn't want to seem ungrateful to Riley, and this was their first time officially hanging out in person as "just friends" so she was torn.

"Hey, Bernie, would it be okay if a friend met up with us in a bit? My friend Riley, I'm staying with her and she works right around here."

"Of course!" Bernie responded with that amazing openness that was characteristic of her. Jessica did notice the face Kayla made. She was probably scared of having to hang out with another lesbian.

"Who's this friend?" Alex asked. Jessica was dreading the question. She hadn't been consciously thinking about it, but she had said "friend" very intentionally in front of Tanner. Why was still not clear to her. With a direct question from Alex, it was hard for Jessica to omit the reality.

"She's actually my ex, Riley. She lives in Brooklyn and she's letting me stay with her." Tanner seemed to be paying a little more attention suddenly. "It's just more economical that way," Jessica added, hoping that clarified the reason for staying with an ex.

"Well, that's interesting," Alex said. "How long ago did you break up?"

"A while ago—" she said, but Kayla interrupted.

"Okay, enough about other people's relationships. This is about Bernie!" Her homophobia was perfectly hidden in what would have been the first selfless thing she had ever said.

"Fine, let's get this dress show on the road!" Bernie said. She went into the changing room while the rest of them continued to sip their champagne and catch up on things.

Alex seemed genuinely disappointed that she missed the bridal shower, and Jessica deduced from the conversation that she and Tanner had been keeping up with each other a bit by text. Jessica could understand very easily why someone would want to be friends with Alex. Kayla, on the other hand, was not so easy for her to understand. She stayed relatively quiet, which wasn't unexpected since judging by Tanner's body language, they had not made up in any way since the bridal shower. And the way she continued to treat Jessica was evidence of their unthawed relationship.

With some help from the attendant, Bernie was able to get into her dress and do a very dramatic unveiling which led to gasping and all the things people did when they saw someone in a wedding dress. Jessica didn't love all that, and she didn't particularly like a white dress, but she did find it special seeing her sister in that moment. She seemed so much older suddenly. Not like the little nine-year-old sidekick she remembered following her around, trying on her clothes, annoying her with stories that had no direction. Bernie looked like someone else. And that struck her, that whatever she felt about weddings, they marked a change or a growth in someone's life and being there to witness it for her sister, it turned out, meant a lot to Jessica.

Jessica looked over to Tanner and noticed her eyes were glossy. She must have been having some sort of reaction as well. She was struck again by how it filled her with affection to see someone loving her sister in that way. And knowing that someone had loved her even when Jessica couldn't be there.

❖

The dress store tailor was taking measurements and making adjustments, so the rest of them were basically all just sitting around. Tanner was a bit more reserved in front of the other bridesmaids, or at least more reserved than she had been on the cab ride over, but as time went by she did seem to be opening up more, especially to Jessica. That didn't go unnoticed by Bernie, who was pretending not to care but was clearly moony-eyed at both of them.

"Hey, is this Jessica's sister's group?" Jessica turned to see Riley looking around, clearly confused about where she was. That description couldn't have been easy for the store attendant to interpret either.

"Hey!" Jessica said when she saw her. She got up off the couch and moved to show Riley she was there and to give her a hug. She looked great as usual. She was clearly coming from work, since she was wearing a very expensive looking lawyerly suit and she looked absolutely gorgeous. Jessica wasn't blind, she knew her ex was hot. That was never the problem. And although she looked beautiful, the attraction wasn't there, or at least not like before. It was hard to feel pulled to anyone when she was feeling so much gravity toward Tanner. She did, however, like seeing the face of someone she once loved, and when she hugged her, she felt a comfort there. It had been almost a year since they had been close enough to touch.

"Hi!" Jessica said again. "This is my sister." Bernie gave Riley a little wave since she was a bit wrapped up in the measurement process. Jessica proceeded to introduce Riley to everyone else in the room. They were all kind and welcoming except for Kayla, who was just exactly what you would expect— bare minimum, barely paying attention.

"Are you okay hanging a little bit?" Jessica asked.

"Yeah, I actually took off early, so I thought we could get dinner later?"

This was a surprise since, again, Jessica knew how much Riley worked and how hard it always seemed to be for her to get time off. Especially when Jessica most needed attention. But here she was leaving early to go to dinner with her, and all she wanted was to think of some excuse to not go on the off chance that Tanner was free too. But given Riley had already taken the afternoon off, and she was hosting her, Jessica would have to let go of her plan to "accidentally" hang with Tanner.

"Yeah, of course."

Riley sat down next to Jessica, closer than she needed to based on the size of the couch. She also put her arm on the back of the couch, in that way that showed a level of intimacy. Jessica wasn't sure how she felt about it. It wasn't weird, exactly, but it was something she was aware of and she wasn't really sure where they stood as far as physical intimacy since last time they saw each other they were still together. She decided it was fine and went back to getting Riley caught up on who everyone was and how they all knew Bernie.

Jessica did notice a shift in Tanner. She seemed to be very aware of Riley's proximity to Jessica and it felt like some of that comfort they had established was seeping out. She was back to the quiet enigma she had been months ago.

Kayla seemed to perk up a bit when Riley explained that she worked at a very prestigious law firm. Kayla name-dropped a few people who worked for her dad that used to be at the firm, all of which was very confusing since she was definitely not treating this "queer person" with her usual animosity.

"Yeah, I don't really know those two lawyers. I know them from the firm, but we don't really hang in the same circles, you know. They're pretty conservative and I'm an out lesbian, so." That explained the irritation in Riley's voice at being asked about some random men.

Riley very elegantly changed the subject. "Jessica, a wedding gown store was the last place I expected to meet up with you. Do they all know you're the opposite of a romantic?"

That stung a bit. Jessica knew what she meant, but still. Not only did it feel untrue, she was struggling to feel like it could possibly be a compliment, and was she saying something about their relationship?

"Yeah, well, I love my sister, so I'm leaving my jaded hat at home." Jessica didn't love the oversimplification she was being forced into, but she didn't exactly want to go into all of it.

"It's weird to imagine you two dating." The comment came from Kayla. The last person Jessica expected to want to discuss their relationship. Everyone went silent.

"Why is that?" Riley asked.

"Well, you're so accomplished and sophisticated. I mean... look at your job."

"And so?" Riley was clearly lost.

"And Jessica is just, you know, a bit more, like, average." Kayla was truly an idiot. "I mean you're pretty and feminine, I mean, I'm just saying it's hard to imagine."

"Are you hitting on me?" Riley asked, causing Kayla to turn as red as a beet. It was the perfect response, and Jessica was just so relieved to have Riley so easily understand what was happening there.

"I don't know if I'd call Jessica average." The comment came from Tanner who wasn't feeling quite so quiet anymore.

"Yeah, well, you wouldn't, would you?" Kayla said, getting her footing.

What did that mean? Jessica wasn't really following.

"I mean, Jessica is smart, kind, and damn hot, and I'm pretty sure everyone who matters knows it," Riley said, making sure it was clear how wrong Kayla was.

Kayla seemed to retreat into herself, and Tanner went back to giving Riley a look that wasn't quite decipherable. Jessica was so proud to be defended by Riley. She had always been a strong supporter of Jessica, and seeing it relative to Tanner's attempt to defend her, she could see what she always wanted from Tanner, and from Bernie. But Tanner *had* defended her. That was something wasn't it?

"How did y'all meet?" Alex asked, changing the subject.

Jessica went to respond, but Riley got there first. "I went to law school in DC and we met in my 3L year." Riley laughed. "Jessica was like this 'thing' in DC. Everyone was into her and she was just totally unaware. I would see her at this monthly party sometimes and I would psych myself up to go and talk to her and then whenever I would get up the courage, she'd move spots, or she'd be talking to someone else, and basically, I would just chicken out. I'd go home and just be so mad at myself. So I found out her name and all that and I sent her a message on whatever the app was then, maybe Facebook. I just said hey, I think you are the hottest person I've ever seen. Can I take you out for a drink sometime?"

"Wow, that's so bold," Alex said, sounding impressed.

"Yeah, well, I didn't want to miss my chance again. I felt like if I didn't tell her, I'd always wonder. And you know what she did?" By this time everyone was riveted.

"What?" Bernie asked.

"She left me on read for a WEEK! Can you believe that?" There was a collective gasp.

"I did not! Or at least I didn't mean to!" Jessica could feel herself falling into her old dynamic with Riley. They had told this story many times, but as a couple. She knew what really happened was she saw the message, but she didn't realize she'd turned on read receipts, so she was just trying to formulate something cool to say to someone so out of her league messaging her. Or that's how it felt at the time. But Riley already knew that. She just liked the story.

Riley's arm came a little closer to Jessica's shoulder. It could have been unconscious, but she wasn't the only person who noticed. Tanner was looking more and more white-faced.

"It seems like y'all had a great thing going," Alex said, somehow not picking up on the dynamics, or more like picking up on half of the dynamics in the room. "Seems like you two were a good match. It's cool you can still be friends." The comment was a reminder that they were friends, not a couple. Jessica could almost feel the way that registered with Riley.

"Yeah well, that's a different regret." The disclosure was charged. This was becoming a bit too public. She hadn't heard anything like that from Riley in their phone calls and texts over the past year. This was starting to get a little sticky.

"She still is 'a thing' in DC," Tanner chimed in finally. "I mean I know I'm not the only one who notices her. On New Year's, I had to fight two other admirers just to get to dance with her." This was the first time Tanner had acknowledged that night, and here she was doing it in front of everyone. Riley seemed to be confused by the remark.

"Oh, are you queer too?" The question was harmless, but Jessica knew Riley long enough to know that there was something off about it.

"Yeah, I am."

Riley turned toward Jessica "Are you two?" She gestured between them, and the awkwardness was palpable in the room as Jessica tried to think of how to respond.

"No, we're…sort of friends." The line was harsh, but what was she supposed to say?

Riley was still looking between them suspiciously. "Okay, 'cause I was kind of hoping we could talk later and I don't want to step on any toes."

This was starting to sound like a conversation Jessica did not want to have, not in the middle of whatever was going on between her and Tanner, and definitely not in front of the rest of the group.

"I don't know if—" Jessica began, but Tanner interrupted.

"You know, if I was ever lucky enough to get to be with Jessica, I wouldn't choose my job over her. I'd do anything to keep her." The proclamation was completely staggering. Jessica would have said something, but she was completely slack-jawed, and so was Bernie. Kayla and Alex were clearly still trying to catch up.

The silence was heavy. Riley responded, "Okay well, then let me just say this." She turned to Jessica, and seemed to be entirely missing how incredibly awkward this was and how much Jessica didn't want to be having this conversation at all.

"Jessica, she's totally right. I fucked up. I know that. I regret staying here and taking you for granted. I just couldn't see how much my life was consumed by work and how rare it is to meet someone like you. I've been interviewing at this firm in DC and I wasn't really"—she looked at Tanner with what could only be described as irritation—"planning to spring this on you, but I wanted to see if maybe we could see each other when I get to DC? Or if that would even be something you would want…."

The words were something Jessica would have loved to have heard a year ago, but now they were so extremely not what she wanted to hear. She didn't know what to say. She didn't want to reject Riley in front of everyone, but she was definitely not interested in Riley moving for her and she definitely did not want to start dating again. She had ended that relationship for more reasons than the distance and Riley's work. She didn't have strong enough feelings, especially not anymore, and not when she so clearly was starting to have stronger feelings for Tanner.

Tanner's face was completely red. Jessica was tongue-tied yet again.

"If you'll excuse me, I'm going to get some air." Tanner got up and left the show room.

Riley's words still hung in the air. "I did that wrong didn't I." The question was rhetorical. She already knew it was not going well for her.

"Ry, that is sweet and I want to talk about this, but no, I don't think this is the best idea for us right now." She could feel herself being pulled to leave and chase after Tanner, but she couldn't fully leave her friend. "Let's go and we can talk about this, okay?"

Riley definitely looked embarrassed, but more than that she seemed sad. Riley wasn't a bad person. The decision to profess her feelings in such a public situation was not a great one, but clearly there were a lot of confusing dynamics at play.

Jessica said good-bye to everyone, giving an extra-long hug to Bernie. Bernie whispered in her ear, "Don't be too mad at Tanner."

Jessica gave her an extra squeeze and left with Riley. She didn't see Tanner when she left. But first, she had to deal with her friend, then she'd talk to Tanner.

Chapter Twelve

Jessica didn't go to dinner with Riley. They went to a park nearby and they talked. They talked for a long time. At first, it felt like Riley still didn't understand. She thought she had bad timing and that if she could just try again, she could show Jessica how much she meant to her and how well they could work together. But the truth was no matter how perfect their dinner was or which words she put in which order, Jessica didn't want to be with Riley. Yes, because of their history and how much she had changed since their breakup, but mostly because with every second she became more and more sure of who it was making it so she couldn't think about anyone else.

"So I guess I missed my chance." They were still sitting on a bench in the park as the sun started to go down. "I should have made the move a year ago when you asked me to."

"No," Jessica responded firmly, putting her arm around Riley in a very different way than Riley had in the dress shop. "I don't think any of it would have made a difference. I think we were meant to be friends." Jessica didn't mean this as some sort of platitude. "When you stood up for me in there, I was reminded how much love you showed me and how little I showed myself when we were together. You taught me what it's like to be with someone who chases all the ghosts away. I want you in my life, but I don't feel those feelings for you anymore. Do you understand?"

Riley took a moment, considering. "I recognized her name, Tanner."

Jessica could feel her chest squeeze. She wasn't sure if Riley would remember the stories she told her about her first crush and her outing. But of course, she had to tell her girlfriend at the time. "She's the girl you liked when you were younger, right? The one who told everyone."

Jessica could feel herself deflate. "Yeah, that's her." It all felt like shame.

Riley searched Jessica's face. "It seems like she's gotten better since high school, but she had a long way to go if my memory is right. Do you have feelings for her?"

Jessica could finally admit it to herself, so she thought she might as well be honest.

"I have feelings. I don't know if I want to have feelings, but I have them."

Riley nodded. "Be careful." She hadn't meant to undercut Tanner. It was just her friend, the person she appreciated so much, looking out for her. Riley let out an audible sigh. "I'm not really sure I can be friends right now, I'm sorry."

Jessica understood. One year might not have been too soon for her, but everyone was different, and Riley was definitely not yet in a place to move on.

"I understand. I hope someday though."

"Of course, I'll get there." Riley let out a laugh. "Let me just get over some of my embarrassment and I'm sure we can get back on track." She smiled her open, gracious smile and Jessica couldn't help but hug this person who was so beautiful and was an amazing partner for someone else.

"I do want my sweater back," Riley added pointedly.

Jessica laughed. "I was hoping you wouldn't say that!"

Riley got up. "You should stay with me still of course."

As much as Jessica knew Riley was genuine, she didn't think this was the best plan after what all had happened between them.

She still wanted to talk to Tanner, and she figured if she couldn't find a place to stay between Tanner, Bernie, or Alex she'd spring for a hotel. It would be better for their friendship to give them both some air. "I have somewhere else to stay, but thank you. Let's talk soon, okay?"

Riley gave her a genuine smile, one more hug, and then she headed toward the subway. Jessica sat back on the bench and let the last few hours pass over her.

As she went over the argument in the bridal shop, she could pick out the most important parts. First, Tanner was jealous. That was the only explanation for her outburst. She was jealous because she openly and explicitly had some sort of feelings for Jessica. Maybe it was just attraction, but Jessica would never know, not unless she talked to her. She also knew that she did not want to let Tanner leave. She wanted to stop her, she wanted to fix things, she wanted to…. *Tell her how she felt.* How did she feel?

Yes, she was attracted to Tanner. That was a given. Even just thinking of her smile, her eyes, her body, had Jessica's heart racing. But it was more than that. She felt their connection as strongly as when she was a teenager. That was what was so scary. She had started to realize that maybe she hadn't felt something that strong since the last time she felt that way about Tanner, and look how that ended.

She wanted to trust Tanner, she was almost there, but there was still something in her that was holding her back. As she sat on the bench, feeling fully paralyzed, she came to a realization. It didn't matter if she was sure of Tanner. The truth was she was never going to be able to move on until she took that step with her. She had tried resisting, she had tried avoiding, but the reality was her feelings were not decreasing. It was the opposite and she needed to take this risk. With the confidence of a person who had barely come to the realization of what she wanted, she texted Tanner.

Where are you? Can we talk?

The response came quickly.

I'm at my hotel.

She didn't answer the second question, but Jessica didn't care. She wanted to go to wherever Tanner was and just say the things that she needed to say.

Can I come to you?

The dots came and left, came and left, and then eventually an address appeared.

163 Orchard St, Room 606

The hotel was in the Lower East Side. As much as she wanted to be a good New Yorker, she decided to take a cab. She didn't want any more time to pass without saying what she needed to say to Tanner.

❖

Jessica knocked on the door to Tanner's room at the Orchard Street Hotel and waited for the locks to be undone. The door opened and Tanner was there, looking exhausted. She must have been festering over whatever she had been feeling since she left the bridal store because Jessica had never seen her look so sad. And over the last few months, she had seen Tanner look sad many times. Tanner let her in. The room was not big enough for a couch, but there was a small chair across from the bed and basically no space to stand, so Jessica took the chair, not knowing where else to be. Tanner sat across from her on the bed, way too close for the conversation.

"We need to talk about what happened in the store," Jessica said. It came off harshly, but she didn't know how else to get to what she wanted to say.

"I'm so sorry. I shouldn't have put Riley on the spot like that. I don't know why I did it. I'm just so embarrassed." Tanner looked down. Part of Jessica heard Riley's words and her fear creeped in. They weren't on the same page. But she pushed through. She had to say what she had to say.

"I'm not."

"You're not what?"

"Embarrassed. Or at least not about what you said. It wasn't the perfect time to say it, but I'm not embarrassed."

"Umm, I don't understand. Riley was lovely and kind and beautiful, and she clearly wants you back and I'm sitting there getting in the way because I was feeling..."

"You were feeling what?"

"It doesn't matter. The point is, you deserve to be with someone great and..."

"You were jealous. You were jealous because you want me." The words were matter-of-fact. There was no way Tanner could avoid it.

She began to speak, but then stopped. "I was jealous... because I want you."

Jessica took a moment to feel the words. Words she had needed to hear, words she had wanted to hear so many times over the years. In that moment, there was no part of her that didn't trust Tanner's words. She knew it was true because she felt it too.

"I'm not staying with Riley." Jessica wanted to make her intentions clear.

"So does that mean you didn't get back together with her? 'Cause I just thought..." Tanner trailed off again.

"How could I be with anyone else when it is taking everything in me not to grab you right now and kiss you?"

Shock flashed across Tanner's face. Jessica liked the way Tanner looked, visibly stunned yet unwilling to let herself register what was happening. But then, a flicker of understanding sparked in Tanner's eyes and Jessica could see her breath quicken. She began to grip the bed sheets, almost as if trying to keep her in place. Jessica watched her, holding herself back too, allowing Tanner's reaction to fuel her anticipation, fully aware that once their lips met, there would be no turning back for either of them. This time, Jessica had no intention of stopping herself.

Jessica rose from her chair and closed the distance between them in a single step. She stood over Tanner and caressed her cheek with one hand while combing through Tanner's hair with the other. Tanner opened her legs to allow Jessica to come in closer, the movement seeming almost unconscious. She looked up at Jessica and Jessica could feel Tanner's desire. They were both holding back.

Jessica leaned down and her lips touched Tanner's, igniting a palpable wave of hunger between them. The initial softness of their touch intensified, and Jessica let the months, or maybe years, of pent-up frustration, anger, and raw lust seep into her kiss, hardening it with urgency and need. She could feel Tanner's tongue, the way her mouth seemed to pull her in deeper. Tanner's hands were all over Jessica, on her lower back, on her butt, on her thighs. There was no hesitation in their movements. They were the movements of two people who, whether Jessica would admit it or not, had probably imagined this moment a million times.

Jessica couldn't feel enough of Tanner. It was hard to stop kissing her, so when she began to take off Tanner's white button-down, the process went very slowly. She couldn't pull away; she had to feel the buttons, and at a certain point she couldn't take it anymore so she ripped the shirt. If she had any hesitation about how Tanner might feel, she was assuaged by the fact that Tanner ripped the final button.

Once the shirt was gone, Jessica was able to pull her lips away, if only because she had to look at Tanner's breasts. Her bra was barely holding her in, and Jessica could feel herself moving to lick and bite her breasts through the fabric on one side all while pulling the other side down. She touched her nipple delicately and then put her mouth over it, hearing a moan from Tanner who had put her hand in Jessica's hair and was pulling her in. If she wasn't so turned on, Jessica would have felt the pain of having her hair pulled like that. Instead, the sensation just made her feel how wet she was.

She moved her hands to the back of Tanner's bra and unclasped it. Her breasts fell slightly and the curve below her breasts looked so sexy that Jessica had to drag her tongue from the bottom to the top of her right breast just to be everywhere but still wanting to be in more places. Tanner was panting and Jessica looked up into Tanner's eyes. She could see the way Tanner was looking at her. That look that said that she was turned on just by the sight of it. Jessica knew the look because she was looking up at her just the same way. She stopped kissing Tanner, and a moment of clarity passed between them. This was not a normal attraction. Jessica was out of control of how she was feeling. Was there a word for more than turned on?

Tanner pulled her up to a standing position and pushed her back a little. She got on her knees in front of Jessica. Jessica was stunned by the turning of the tables. Tanner was looking up at her from the floor. As she undid her jeans. She wasn't going slow. She pulled Jessica's jeans to her ankles and then brought her mouth up to Jessica's underwear. She kissed her softly right where her clit was covered by the fabric of her underwear, and then she slowly pulled her underwear down her legs, shackling her with her jeans. Jessica already knew how wet she was, she didn't need to be told, but Tanner told her. She brought her finger to Jessica's pussy lips and touched her softly, still hard enough for Jessica to feel it like lightning through her body, but still quite delicately. She could see when Tanner pulled her finger away that she was dripping. Tanner was the one who moaned as she brought her finger to her tongue. The sight of Tanner on her knees, fully enthralled just from that one taste, made her pussy clench. She was not going to last long. Not if Tanner continued to tease her.

"You are so fucking hot," Tanner said, and her words came out with such exasperated frustration.

"Show me," Jessica demanded. She didn't want to wait any longer.

Tanner clearly didn't either because she put her mouth on Jessica's pussy and licked and sucked and moaned so intensely that the contact nearly made Jessica fall. She got control of herself and she put her hand in Tanner's hair, not quite as hard as Tanner had earlier, but she pushed her closer, and Tanner moaned louder. Which was nothing compared to how loud Jessica was. She was so close, and they had barely gotten started, but it was clear that Tanner understood because she didn't waste time. She took two fingers, put them in her own mouth and then went back to licking and sucking Jessica only to enter her hard. The sensation was so intense that Jessica came immediately. She could feel her skin exploding and Tanner was fucking her through every contraction until she finally collapsed onto the floor.

Tanner tried to continue, but Jessica pushed her away, already feeling the sensation was too sensitive after she came. She fell to her knees and then she let herself lie down on her back panting, her legs still shackled at her knees. She reached for Tanner, pulling her down with her to lie next to her on the floor. Tanner came down still breathing hard, clearly still deeply turned on, but she put her arms around Jessica and held her while she came down.

"Fuck." It was the first word that Jessica could think to say. Tanner was lying close to her, still slightly out of breath. Feeling them tangled together was almost as intense as the orgasm Jessica had just had.

Tanner was lightly kissing her neck, but Jessica could tell that she was holding herself back. She could feel herself already bouncing back, which was pretty shocking after how intense she just came.

"Can you help me get my legs free?" Jessica motioned to the fabric that had her fully bound on the floor.

"Are you sure? I was kind of enjoying having you tied up like that." Tanner's voice was raspy and sexy, and Jessica could still hear the desire in her timbre.

"If anyone is going to be tied up next, it's you," Jessica said, kissing Tanner, delaying being freed from her pants. Tanner pushed her back onto her back and moved to sit on top of her. They kissed slowly and sensually until it turned frantic again. Tanner pulled herself away and sat up. Jessica was reluctant to have her pull away, but then she was able to get a better view of Tanner's breasts and stomach and the way her eyes were devouring her, and even just the sight of her like that brought another surge through her body.

Tanner grabbed both of her arms and placed them over her head, taking away yet another avenue of control for Jessica.

"I don't want you to touch me until I've fucked you in every single way I want to."

How could Jessica refuse her? It wasn't actually a request, it was more of a warning.

"Is this what you've been fantasizing about?" Jessica asked. Both because it was turning her on and because she wanted to hear how much Tanner wanted her and for how long.

"I've fantasized about you in so many ways. You are so.... Frustrating!" It was meant to be sexy, but Jessica couldn't help laughing.

"I know exactly what you mean." Jessica reached her head up still fully incapacitated from her ankles to her wrist, but Tanner met her halfway and kissed her letting out another moan.

"I'm going to release you, but only because I want you naked, so remember what I said…"

Jessica didn't imagine Tanner would be so commanding. It wasn't a readily available aspect of her personality. But in bed, it was beyond hot.

"Okay, you can do what you want first." Tanner kissed her softly and then let her out of her body cage. She worked on getting her pants off as quickly as she could from the floor while Tanner did the same. They were past any sort of slow reveal. By the time Jessica was done Tanner was already on top of the bed, making it very clear where Jessica needed to be next.

Jessica crawled toward Tanner already thinking about how it was going to be a struggle not to be the person in control. She was about to test her luck, when Tanner got ahead of it by moving quickly and rolling Jessica over, very much topped for the second time.

"I promise, you'll get your chance." Tanner's skin was all over her. It was so intense just considering how much had happened with just a portion of their skin touching. They were making out slowly, taking time to touch every inch of each other's bodies. When Tanner began to touch her pussy, she wasn't soft, and she wasn't delicate.

"You are so fucking wet," Tanner said through a moan.

But Jessica couldn't reply, she was already unable to think or talk because Tanner was fucking her so deeply. Again, she wasn't far from orgasming, something that never happened this quickly with anyone. It was clear that Tanner knew how close she was because she took her to the edge only to stop, watching Jessica squirm. It wasn't till she begged that Tanner allowed her to come, and again she found herself fully destroyed on Tanner's bed unable to speak or think. Tanner moved to lie next to her entangling herself as close as humanly possible. Jessica didn't know how it happened, but she fell asleep.

She didn't end up getting a chance to do things she wanted to Tanner, just another promise broken.

❖

Jessica woke from what was the best and worst sleep of her life. After coming to Tanner's hotel room, having sex on the floor and then the bed, she passed out only to wake up at two a.m. to

Tanner kissing her neck while she spooned her leading inevitably to more sex and basically a repeat of being so incredibly satiated that she passed out. She woke up tired but feeling that cloud-like nice flowy feeling of being so completely satisfied that she felt she could stay in that same spot in Tanner's bed forever.

She moved slightly, making Tanner let out a sleepy sound indicating she was waking up too. She held Jessica tighter, and Jessica could already feel her body coming back to life. Once she was sure Tanner was awake, she turned herself around and their sleepy eyes met. It was odd, to already feel a comfort between them. Maybe it was knowing someone for such a long time. Even when Jessica hated Tanner, she felt she knew her. Her name, her face, had been in her life for such a long time.

For a moment, Jessica was nervous one of them might feel weird in the morning, but all of her fears were assuaged when Tanner kissed her, through both of their morning breaths and smiled that same contented smile that could not be as satisfied as Jessica's smile since their interlude had been fully focused on her.

"Last night was…" Tanner began. "Amazing?" The question in her voice made it seem like she was still not sure Jessica was on the same page.

"Last night was amazing," Jessica reiterated, wanting to give the reassurance that she so clearly needed. They kissed some more, but before things got too heavy, Tanner proposed an idea.

"What do you think about going to breakfast? I know a place near here with amazing beignets and I just need to take a quick shower, but then we can go. What do you think?"

Jessica's mouth was watering just thinking about the sweet breakfast pastries.

"I would love to, but I need to look up a shop in Alphabet City for my mom so I might force you to go on an errand after."

"As long as we can come back here after. I'm pretty sure I can request a late check out."

Wanting to have more sex wasn't a difficult thing for Jessica to agree to. She felt the exact same way. She was more concerned about all the things that they hadn't talked about. She needed to get some more understanding about what was happening between them. What was the plan when they got back to DC?

"Okay, I'm going to take a shower. Feel free to use my laptop if you don't want to use your phone." Tanner took her computer from the bedside table and unlocked it for Jessica with a browser open.

"Thanks!" She did prefer a bigger screen than her phone.

Tanner gave her a long sultry kiss and then headed to the bathroom to shower. Jessica could hear the water as she googled the store her mom gave her, making sure they had this natural soap that she had promised she would bring back. She usually got it shipped, but she wanted to take advantage of Jessica's trip to stock up.

While she was googling, a message popped up on the screen from Bernie. She tried to ignore it, but the preview had her own name. She didn't think, she just selected it, opening up an entire iMessage chat between Bernie and Tanner.

Bernie: *I know it isn't fair to you, but she can't know.*

Tanner: *I just think Jess would understand*

Bernie: *I just got her back, she'd never forgive me. She's already forgiven* you

Tanner: *I don't think she'll ever forgive me*

Bernie: *What about the kiss?*

Tanner: *I think if Jess finds out that I've been lying to her, she'll never talk to me again*

Bernie: *I'm sorry, Tan, I know I'm asking a lot but please, I don't want to lose my sister*

Tanner: *Okay*

The last text from that conversation was sent just minutes before Jessica came over to Tanner's hotel room. Then there was another text from that morning. The text that brought her to the conversation.

Bernie: *Have you heard from Jess?*

Jessica felt like she had been struck. Her body was rigid and she was suddenly acutely aware of how naked she was. A vigilance took over her body and she was transported back to that day in high school when she could feel everyone in the school looking at her, talking about her, knowing something about her that even she wasn't ready to fully look at for herself. She didn't need to know what the secret was that Bernie and Tanner were keeping from her, she just knew she never wanted to feel this feeling again. The lack of control, the feeling that there was no one around her she could trust. She woke up feeling so good, feeling so close to Tanner only to be drenched in a bucket of cold water. This person, this person who had again felt so close to her, was lying to her. She knew better, Tanner had proven in the worst way that she couldn't be trusted. It didn't matter what the secret was, it could have been something small, but the fact that Tanner was talking about her behind her back, keeping something from her, choosing to protect others first, even her sister was enough to bring on the flood of shame and fear that she had worked so very hard not to feel ever again. Jessica knew what she needed to do. She needed to leave. Jessica left the bed scrambling under the bed and to all the places their sex had left her clothes. Each item reminding her how much she had lost her head last night. She put on her tarnished clothes and grabbed her bag, hearing the shower stop just as she was opening the door. She didn't owe an explanation to Tanner. If Tanner could keep things from her after everything they had been through, she didn't deserve closure.

Jessica let the door close softly only to lock eyes with the last person on earth she wanted to run into, Kayla. Jessica didn't realize, but Kayla must have had the room across the hall and Jessica just had the world's most awful timing. They both barely acknowledged each other but simultaneously headed toward the one elevator. Jessica pressed the button furiously and

Kayla seemed to be eyeing her with curiosity. Once they both awkwardly entered the elevator Kayla broke the silence.

"I guess you finally bagged the prom queen."

The words were so cheesy and so insulting that Jessica was fully seeing red.

"Excuse me?"

"Come on, I saw whose room you were slinking out of. You guys are both gross."

Jessica could have reacted. She wanted to tell her off, but the truth was, she was so upset about Tanner and Bernie that she really couldn't even keep straight what she was feeling. When the elevator opened, Jessica left first almost at a sprint. She left the hotel and turned down Orchard Street heading toward anywhere. She couldn't breathe. The icing on the cake was once again having Kayla Kelly see her right then. It was just like that day at her locker. Why did it always have to be Kayla who saw how desperate she was for just an ounce of attention from Tanner? That's what she was, desperate. She felt so small and so pathetic for letting them all treat her like nothing. After she walked and fumed, she looked at her phone to get an Uber to the train station. Luckily, the Amtrak tickets were transferable so she could get an earlier train easily and be saved from having to see Tanner again. When she looked at her phone she saw four unanswered texts from Tanner, two from Bernie, and two missed calls from Tanner. She looked at the Tanner texts first.

Tanner: *Hey, where'd you go?*

Jessica had to make a decision. Did she want to tell her what she saw? Did she want to get into all this? In the end it felt like all of that just brought out more reminders, more shame, more just more. She needed to find a way to close this chapter. She knew this would hurt Tanner, but to be honest, at this point, that wasn't far from what she wanted.

Jessica: *Hey I'm sorry I couldn't say good-by. I had an emergency come up for work and I had to catch an earlier train*

The lie was so ridiculous and obvious that she was honestly almost embarrassed.

Tanner: *I don't understand, is everything okay? You've gone back to DC?*

Jessica was imagining how confusing it must feel for Tanner. A moment ago, everything was fine.

Jessica: *Yeah it's fine I just didn't want to interrupt your shower.*

Jessica's phone rang. Obviously, none of this was making sense.

"Hey," Jessica answered.

"Hey." Tanner's voice was weird and small. She clearly already knew something was very wrong. "So you left..."

"Yeah, sorry, it was just a super time sensitive thing." Fuck, this wasn't working.

Tanner didn't respond right away.

"So I feel like something must have happened because I'm not really buying a work emergency. I mean maybe you got freaked out or need a second?"

That would explain things, wouldn't it? Maybe she could go with that.

"Umm, I don't know, yeah, maybe I got a little freaked out."

Tanner's voice started to sound normal again. "I think that's fair. I wish you didn't leave, but I know we've been through a lot and if you need a minute to think about things I can understand that."

Tanner was being so kind and accepting on what must have felt like a total sucker punch to the face.

"Yeah, I think I do need some time. I think maybe I got caught up last night."

The silence was back.

"Umm, I guess I'm wondering now if maybe you are feeling like you regret last night?" This was the pain point.

"Tanner I... I think maybe we should take some steps back here. I don't regret last night. I just, I think we're really different people and I'm not sure we make a lot of sense together." All lies. An hour ago, she was definitely thinking they made the most sense possible together.

"Okay, so, I'm just really confused because last night and even this morning it felt like we were...I guess I must have misunderstood."

It was hard for Jessica to explain what changed without saying what she saw, and she decided she didn't want to go into that.

"I think maybe last night was just a one-time thing. I think we have a lot of history and I think it just isn't what I want."

Jessica couldn't find an elegant way to say it. She was muddling through the conversation, desperate for it to be over.

"Okay...if that's what you want, I guess I don't know what to say."

"I'm sorry, it's just how I feel."

Again, that awful painful silence.

"I guess I'm going to go." Jessica could hear the emotion welling in Tanner just as it was welling in herself. "I hope you get what you want, Jessica." It was kind, even at the end.

"You too, Tanner." And even after everything, she felt like she meant it. At least in this moment. They both hung up and a heaviness set in. When she got off the train, she didn't go home. She didn't know where to go to feel better so she just kept walking. She walked until it was dark and until she could no longer feel the burn of Tanner's eyes on her, until she couldn't smell her on her clothes, the same clothes Tanner had peeled off of her. She walked until she could breathe again.

Chapter Thirteen

It was a couple of weeks later, and a lot had changed for Jessica. The biggest thing was that she had given notice at work. After her tumultuous weekend in New York, she came back feeling like absolute garbage. She went to work that Monday and her boss had assigned her to do a profile on the gay penguins at the zoo and their upcoming nuptials, and for whatever reason that was the last straw. She quit. Maybe it was having to write about gay penguins or just another ridiculous marriage conversation she didn't want to have, but she was done. Her boss was fully shocked but mostly because he realized he would have to spell-check his own articles again.

Jessica had spoken to her mom earlier in the week and she was assured that she would be able to access her trust as long as she promised she was going to follow through on going to Bernie's wedding. The truth was, even with the unknown secret Bernie was keeping from her, she wasn't going to miss Bernie's wedding. They had come such a long way. The healing she had experienced those last months, the connection she had gone without for so long was just not something she was going to give up. That did not mean that she wasn't extremely upset with Bernie, but she was putting that aside for now. She could deal with Bernie after the wedding. They had time.

After Jessica quit, she could feel a weight lift from her shoulders. She was tying up some loose ends, but mostly she was checked out from work. She decided she needed to spend some time alone getting her feelings back in check. The Tanner incident had brought up a lot of old feelings, a lot of pain, and she wanted to get back in her body, get back to her life. She made sure to see her friends, especially Bryce and Lisa. Her relationship with Lisa had fully transitioned to friends only since Lisa was seeing someone and Lisa was obsessed with her girlfriend. Jessica was happy for her. Lisa did note at one point that Jessica hadn't been her usual self. And the truth was she wasn't herself. She was feeling better knowing she was free from her job and starting this new business, which excited her, but as the weeks went by, it was clear her heart was broken. And as hurt as she was by discovering that Tanner was lying to her, she was also unable to get Tanner out of her mind.

At first, their night together had been blocked from her mind, a clear self-defense mechanism to get over the hump of the first few days, but slowly, the memories were seeping in. She could remember her smell, she could see flashes of Tanner's smile or the face she made when she came, and all of that just mixed to such a painful and exhausting space. And to make it worse, she really wasn't attracted to anyone else. It was so obvious and so out of her control. This had always been the issue with Tanner. Even when she hated her, she was still attracted to her. This was all made one thousand times worse by having had sex with her.

She told Lisa and Bryce what happened, and they were supportive. They knew all the extra baggage that came with Tanner just from hearing the whole saga over the last few months, and it was clear they were both disappointed in Tanner, especially Bryce.

Jessica met up with Bryce for a walk in Rock Creek Park. He recently adopted an elderly dog so he had gotten in the habit having slow park walks at least once a day. The subject of Tanner came up again because Bryce had stayed in touch with Sam and Keith. It seemed that wasn't just a New Year's miracle, they had some mutual friends and were now in some sort of movie sharing group chat.

"I did hear something about 'she-who-shall-not-be-named' in my group chat."

Jessica couldn't even pretend she wasn't interested. It sucked that Tanner had infected her life in such a way that she couldn't even talk to her best friend without being tempted.

"What did you hear?"

"Apparently, she quit her job at the fucked up site."

Jessica stopped in her tracks. "When was this?"

"Basically, right around when you quit. No notice, just some exposing post on her column that they took down. She also said something about being gay on her fan page and all hell broke loose. It was actually pretty cool."

Jessica fought the urge to google to figure out exactly what happened. She wouldn't be able to help it later.

"That's good, I guess. I mean for the people who were being brainwashed by her column."

Bryce looked at her with a look that said he did not buy what she was saying at all.

"I know you're hurt, but I've been thinking about what happened, and I don't know, I feel like there is more to this story with Tanner."

"What do you mean?" Jessica was not liking where this was going.

"Listen, don't shoot me for saying this, but I just think maybe her keeping a secret from you might not be the end of the world, you know?"

Jessica was getting angry. "Maybe it wouldn't be, if not for our history. I don't know if she's necessarily the worst person in the world, but I know that I don't want to feel like this anymore."

Bryce was thoughtful before he responded.

"Maybe it's worth considering that the way you're feeling has less to do with Tanner, and more to do with you. I mean, you really have a hard time trusting anyone, not just her. I don't know if avoiding this person, this person that you clearly have big feelings for, is going to truly heal this hurt."

Jessica wasn't in the mood to be analyzed. "Let's not talk about Tanner."

Bryce didn't need to be told twice. He had already gone over the line.

"Okay, I'll leave it alone." He kindly changed the subject. "I am excited to be your date for the wedding next week."

Jessica decided last minute that she didn't want to go up to New York alone. Not with how she was feeling about Tanner and Bernie, who she still hadn't spoken to in any way but text since New York. It was definitely looking suspicious to Bernie, but it was also so close to the wedding that Bernie was distracted. Jessica was going to confront her, but she wanted to wait till after the wedding. So going up to New York in a week for the rehearsal dinner was starting to feel like it had before the bachelorette, like going into a snake den. She asked Bernie for a plus-one last-minute and she was extremely obliging. Apparently, someone had un-RSVPed so it worked out as far as place settings, and even if it didn't, Jessica had a feeling Bernie would have made it work.

"I'm so relieved you could come. I just have to get through this and then I can focus fully on my bookstore."

"You know I love weddings! I just wish I had known sooner so we could have coordinated more wardrobe-wise."

Jessica looked at him with fake exasperation. "I guess we will just have to clash."

A few weeks ago, Jessica was starting to turn a corner on weddings and marriage and everything. Not that all of that was for her, and not that all her political issues weren't just as important as they had been, but she was more open to the idea that a wedding could have something redeemable. But now, it was back to being the final ring of hell again. All she had to do was go to the rehearsal dinner, then the ceremony, then the reception and she was done, she would never have to see Tanner again.

❖

The rehearsal dinner was at Greenwich Grille & Lounge in the village. Jessica didn't make the mistake of staying with Riley again. They had spoken on the phone so she knew they were on the right track toward a friendship, but Jessica really didn't want to ruin any of the progress they had made so she got an Airbnb. She wasn't in the group rate hotel because she was booking so late, but she was able to get into the neighborhood of the wedding, at a pretty expensive price, but not staying in the hotel was a good way to reduce the amount of time she would spend running into Tanner. Bryce was planning to stay with her at her Airbnb, but knowing him, he would most likely end up somewhere else. He had someone he usually hooked up with in New York, as well as a very active life on the apps that would most likely lead him to some sort of after-hours something. Either way, Jessica was just relieved to have a friend.

Bryce and Jessica arrived at the restaurant slightly late. She was instructed to be early just based on her bridesmaid duties, but she had decided that she wasn't going to do this at the sacrifice of her own mental health. Not after everything and not after she hadn't really worked things out with her sister. So she was late, but she was earlier than most guests. One thing that was a relief was her outfit. Bernie did not have a matching dress mandate. The only requirement was that they all had to wear a certain shade of blue and that it had to be semi-formal. Jessica double checked, and wearing a dress wasn't a requirement.

Instead she opted for a black silk shirt for the rehearsal and a blue suit for the wedding. Bryce, on the other hand, was in a light pink lace shirt and semi-matching slightly heeled boots. He looked amazing as always. A few months ago, Jessica would have assumed they both would have looked odd at the wedding, but after meeting Chris's family and spending some time with Bernie, Jessica was really starting to feel like maybe everyone was a little cooler than she gave them credit for. With the only exception being Kayla, and at this point she was barely even a presence to Jessica.

Jessica's mom was there and she and Bryce went over to say hi.

"Bryce, you look gorgeous! I could never pull off pink lace with this complexion," Jessica's mom said.

"You know the thing about pulling things off is you don't really have to look good, you just have to commit!"

Jessica was just a totally different kind of person. She mostly wore things to feel comfortable, not to stand out. But he was probably right, even though he looked good and committed fully to everything he wore, so who knew what was true.

Jessica hadn't filled her mom in on everything with Tanner. It was all just a little embarrassing and a little painful.

"Bernie's in the back with the wedding planner, but Tanner is over near the tables with Alex if you want to go check in."

Jessica looked over to where the tables were and could see Tanner talking to Alex. Seeing Tanner felt like an out-of-body experience. She was wearing a black dress that made her look so incredibly gorgeous that Jessica could barely stand it. It was somehow worse now, after being with her that night. She could feel herself coming alive just at the sight of her. It was clear Tanner and Alex were doing some sort of coordinating, maybe another thing that bridesmaids did that Jessica missed the memo on.

Or more likely, Tanner was just helping like she always did. Tanner hadn't seen her, or at least it seemed that way so Jessica was able to take her in. She looked beautiful as always, but she also looked stressed. The last time Jessica saw her they were both tangled up in bed and every single possible stress in the world was a million miles away. Now, it was almost as if, emotionally, time had spun back six months. Jessica didn't want to go over, but she also felt like there was some type of checking in she should do. She knew there were some sort of assigned seats based on families that she needed to find out about. So she decided to bite the bullet and talk to Tanner. Bryce was more than happy to continue to mingle with her mom, so Jessica slowly made her way over to the long rehearsal dinner table.

Alex saw her first and came over to give her a hug.

"Where have you been? I wanted to get some time to catch up before we have to be on Bernie support mode." The idea that Alex felt close enough to Jessica that she would want to "catch up" was still a surprise to Jessica, a nice surprise.

"Yeah, sorry, just bad planning. How are things going?"

Tanner was looking at her now. Instead of the awkwardness or the timidness she expected, or that she had become accustomed to, Tanner was giving her what could only be called a withering stare. There was no hello, there was no fake hug or even a nod. Tanner was angry.

This possibility hadn't occurred to Jessica, but of course she would be. Tanner had put herself out there, she had been fully in, and Jessica basically ghosted her the next morning. Their phone call barely counted as closure, and so from her perspective, Jessica was a total asshole. Jessica wished she didn't care, but she was starting to feel ashamed. A lot of her anger and her justification for leaving without a word had faded and she was starting to think it was possible that Tanner wasn't the only one who handled things badly.

"Tanner, do you need any help with anything?"

The answer came quickly and with ice. "No, the wedding planner is handling it."

Alex looked between them, finally picking up on the tension between them.

"Umm…okay…I think I'll go get a drink from the bar," Alex said, clearly trying to angle out of an awkward situation.

"Me too," Tanner chimed in and they both left Jessica alone reassessing her role as victim of the story.

People started to arrive and mingle, and Jessica was able to rejoin Bryce who was meeting Chris and making five *Fifty Shades of Grey* jokes a minute. Before Jessica could interject and let Bryce know he hated them, Chris was already laughing with an openness that still surprised her. Maybe it was just when the frat guys joked that he didn't like it. Or maybe he was just a sweetheart. Tanner was nowhere to be seen. Jessica wanted to avoid her, but some part of her was feeling a different way. Knowing she was angry was making her feel sort of different suddenly. Finally, Jessica saw Bernie emerge from the back room and she came around saying hi to her guests. Once she saw Jessica, she came over and gave her the biggest hug.

"Jess, I'm so happy you're here." Jessica was still upset with Bernie, but she really couldn't help feeling happy for her sister.

"Me too," she said earnestly.

Bernie looked at her conspiratorially. "You and Tanner need to come with me. I have something for you both in the back room."

Before Jessica could respond with a request to come later or whatever it was she was going to say, Bernie was dragging her over to where Tanner was chatting with their mom.

"Excuse me, Mom, I need to borrow Tanner," she said in that way that only a bride could pull off. No one really needed you to explain yourself when it was your rehearsal dinner. Tanner came along just as reluctantly as Bernie led them into a smaller party room off their room where the restaurant was storing some of the food and some of the extra chairs. Bernie led them to the back corner where there was a small bar and she began rummaging on a shelf. Jessica looked at Tanner, but she was fully not acknowledging Jessica.

Bernie brought out two small boxes and presented them to both Tanner and Jessica. Jessica didn't know what to say. Was it normal to give gifts when you were the bride?

"What's this?" Tanner asked. She seemed to find this unexpected as well.

"Go ahead and open it."

Tanner opened hers first. Inside was a part of a heart necklace. It was corny and it was kitschy, but it was also kind of adorable.

"Open yours too," Bernie insisted.

Jessica did the same and found another part of a heart necklace. She realized after getting a closer look that the two parts of the heart weren't complete. This was her first fear upon seeing it, that Bernie had gotten Tanner and Jessica some sort of relationship necklace. But then Bernie showed her that she had the third part, the way less beautiful middle part.

"It's for us three."

They both looked at Bernie at a loss. Yes, it was awkward, and it was also kind of out of the blue.

"Tanner, you're my best friend, and I am so grateful for everything you've done for me these past few months. To say you've gone above and beyond is an understatement. You are the best and I love you!"

Tanner blushed at the words.

"Jessica, I know you aren't my maid of honor and that might be kind of weird just 'cause you're my sister and all, but the truth is…I just wasn't sure if you would want to be. We've been so close these last few months and I just finally feel like I have you back. Usually people give a gift to their maid of honor, and I just felt like in this situation, I want the maid of honor role to be a little bit you as well. I love you."

Jessica was completely taken aback. What Bernie said was so sweet, and of course Jessica had no idea that Bernie would want her to be maid of honor, I mean she literally was shocked to be a bridesmaid. There was so much she didn't understand about how Bernie felt about her. But Bernie wasn't done. She grabbed both of their hands and held them.

"Both of you are the most important people in my life. Well, you two and Chris," she said with a laugh. "Seeing you both getting along so well lately has reminded of something I always wanted when we were younger. I know you two have your own thing going on," she said with a wink, and Jessica could already feel her stomach drop. "But I just want us all to have something to remember this time we had together. And maybe we could stay in each other's life. I want you both in my life, and I want you both in each other's lives, friend or otherwise."

What started as something very sweet had turned into something that was piercing Jessica's heart. Clearly, Tanner hadn't shared what had happened. Last Bernie knew, they were becoming friends and kissed on New Year's. How could they explain how incredibly incongruent this entire conversation and the gifts were. Bernie pulled them both into a hug, and Jessica couldn't help but hold Tanner as well. The whole thing made her feel so empty and sad she couldn't bear it.

When they pulled away, Jessica could see how incredibly white-faced Tanner looked. She could imagine that's how she looked as well.

There were so many things that Jessica could have said, things that could have let Bernie in on what was really going on, but instead she decided not to.

"Bern…thank you. I love you too." Jessica looked over at Tanner and she could see she was crying. Jessica felt the same way.

"Thank you," she said through her tears.

Bernie was also choked up, but she finally gave a settling sigh.

"Okay, I guess we have to get out there and get this dinner started." They all agreed and started to leave.

"Jessica, can I talk to you for a minute?" Tanner said softly.

Bernie gave them both a not understanding knowing look.

Jessica didn't respond, but she hung back as Bernie left them alone.

Tanner was holding her necklace in her hand while Jessica kept hers closed in its box. Then Tanner spoke.

"I didn't know what to say to Bernie. Partially because I didn't want to disappoint her, as you can see, and partially because I don't understand myself what happened." Tanner's eyes were still watery, but some of that anger and frustration she saw in her earlier was in her voice.

"I get out of the shower and you were gone. I talked myself into thinking you just left to get coffee or something, but I knew in my gut something was wrong. I thought we… I thought we both wanted…what happened?" Her voice was so tentative, she was so unsure of herself.

"I saw your texts with Bernie, on your computer."

Tanner looked confused.

"You were both lying to me about something. After that, I just had to leave."

Tanner didn't look confused anymore. She seemed almost resolved.

"That makes more sense."

She sounded so defeated. She wasn't even trying to explain or excuse.

"Now that we're talking about it, what is it you haven't told me?"

Tanner closed her eyes and shook her head. Almost as if it hurt to hear the question.

"You aren't going to tell me, are you?"

Her eyes began to water again and she shook her head.

"Because Bernie asked you not to."

"Because it's not my secret to tell."

Jessica listened. The explanation was inadequate, but she could see just from the way Tanner was acting that she wanted to say it. Ultimately, it didn't matter.

"Reading that text brought it all back. I don't think you understand what it was like for me, how alone I was. There were days when I wasn't sure I wanted to be alive. And I know all of that isn't on you, but when I think about what I felt when I told you, how much I trusted you and then hearing those same words coming out of Kayla's mouth…"

Tanner wiped at her cheeks. "I know that you don't trust me, and I get why, but that night in New York it could have been a new start." Tanner hesitated. "It still could be."

Jessica understood Tanner. She could see it all too. She could see how well they worked together, how intense their feelings were, but ultimately it wouldn't work.

"Tanner, I can't build a relationship on a faulty foundation. There is too much baggage here."

Tanner nodded, seeming to be coming to terms with the reality.

They stood there not saying anything, not leaving. Perhaps they both didn't want to leave knowing whatever there was between them would be over.

Tanner finally spoke. "I don't want to go another ten years not saying this, and I know it's too little too late, but I want you to know how much I've missed you. Not just these last weeks, but all these years. I know that what happened when we were young. I know that I fell short, that I continually fall short with you." She seemed to get some energy. "I know you've already decided and it doesn't matter, but I don't want to miss my chance. My chance to say how I feel. You are the bravest, most magical person I've ever known. Just being around you gives me courage, and I don't know how long ago or when it started, but I think that maybe I've always been in love with you." The words were heavy and Jessica couldn't breathe. "I know you feel something too, I know because I felt it the night we spent together." Tanner took a step closer and reached for Jessica's hand. "If there is any chance, any way I can fix things any way you could give me another shot. I think we could make each other happy."

Jessica wanted to fall into Tanner's words. She had longed to hear them for so long, she knew deep down some part of her loved Tanner too. But the truth was, she loved herself more. She wasn't going to sacrifice the progress she had made. She wanted to be someone who wasn't a fun mirror. She wanted someone real and strong, and ultimately, Tanner was just too triggering and too inconsistent to build anything with. She had to deny the beating of her heart. She had to take care of herself.

"I can't." The words were short and didn't encapsulate all that she was rejecting in Tanner, but she could see by the way Tanner deflated that the point had been received. There was more she wanted to say, but she just couldn't trust herself to get through the conversation without folding.

Tanner nodded in acceptance. "I understand." She wiped her cheek again. "What about Bernie, are you going to disappear from her life again?"

Jessica had thought about that. She felt betrayed by Bernie, but there had been so much rebuilding between them. She knew she needed to talk to her and maybe she would take some space, but the truth was it just wasn't the same. She had healed so much from getting that family bond back that she felt, depending on Bernie, that there was something salvageable.

"I'm going to talk to her, but she's also my sister. I can't really kick her out of my life."

Tanner seemed relieved by that.

"Good, I know she couldn't lose you again." Tanner's voice broke. Jessica didn't want to be near her anymore. It was too hard.

"I'm going to go back out there." Jessica's voice was breaking too.

"Okay." Tanner clearly didn't have any fight left. Jessica began to walk away.

"I'm sorry, Jess."

"I'm sorry too."

Once she left the room the heaviness came back. The dinner was starting so she found her seat next to Bryce on the right side of Bernie. She saw that her place was next to Tanner so she asked Bryce to change seats. He did while whispering under his breath,

"Did something happen?" She told him she'd tell him after and focused on the mask she needed to put up since all she wanted was to fall apart.

❖

Jessica was ready for the rehearsal dinner to be over, but she still had a long way to go. She resolved that if she could just get through the speeches, she'd be able to sneak out and go fall apart in private. But everyone else seemed to be having a wonderful time, including Bryce. The only person who seemed completely on her page was of course Tanner. She couldn't see her very clearly, but sometimes she would catch a snippet of her conversation or get a look at her profile, and it was clear she was suffering just as much or more than Jessica. The speeches began and Chris's parents thanked everyone for coming. They were very sweet, and they talked about how wonderful Bernie was and what Chris said the first time he came home and told them about her. Jessica's mom was next. She talked about how beautiful Bernie was inside and she talked about their dad and how proud he would have been of her. She talked about how she wished he could have met Chris, and by the end there wasn't a dry eye in the crowd. Next was Chris's brother who totally changed the tone with a very *The Hangover* story about their bachelor party that made everyone laugh and once again reminded Jessica why she hated weddings. Then Tanner spoke. It was impossible for her not to hang off every word Tanner said.

"Bernie, when I met you I was thirteen years old. I couldn't find my classroom on the first day of school and you stopped to help me. Even at the sacrifice of your own lateness. But that's just Bernie. You are always the kind of person who helps your friends. I remember that year I had just moved to Maryland and I didn't know anyone. I was nervous people wouldn't like me, or think I was too different because I was gay, but you immediately showed up for me. You were always ride or die, Bern. When I was eighteen and I had to defer going to college to help my sister, you called me every day. You flew down from school as often as you could and you never once let me feel alone. I don't think anyone could be there for anyone the way you've been there for me. When you told me about meeting Chris, I was scared. First, I was scared that he wouldn't deserve you." People laughed. "But also I was scared I would lose you. But neither was true. Chris shows up for you in exactly the same way you show up for others. I can't believe you both found each other because I thought it was impossible for anyone to deserve you, Bern. And as far as me losing you? You have never let a minute pass where I didn't feel your love and support."

Tanner took a pause seeming to switch gears.

"Falling in love is scary, and it takes courage. I haven't always been brave. But watching you both make this promise to each other, in front of everyone you love, that's brave. And the decision to stay, even when it's hard, even when it hurts, that's brave. I wish you both so much bravery. Thank you."

Jessica listened to the speech and she could hear the sadness from before, but also the joy that Tanner felt for Bernie. She wasn't able to be there for her when their dad died, but knowing there was someone like Tanner there, was something special.

Bryce gave her a look but didn't say anything more. He knew the Tanner issue was not something Jessica wanted to talk about further.

The dinner was wrapping up and Jessica was trying to not stay later then she needed to. She gave her sister, her mom, and Alex a hug good-bye but decided she didn't need to belabor all of the feelings that were swirling around when it came to Tanner. Tanner was talking to Chris and one of his friends, and although she looked normal enough, Jessica knew Tanner was upset. In the same way she knew Tanner knew she was upset. She and Bryce left and walked toward their Airbnb

"So that was very classy and sweet. Your sister's husband-to-be is wonderful!"

"Yeah, I'm kind of shocked to say it, but I kind of like him."

Bryce hesitated before asking, "So I did notice you were sort of in a weird mood after Bernie pulled you to the back with Tanner."

Jessica didn't reply. She was thinking about all the different things that were said and what she was feeling.

"So it seems like maybe, y'all talked?"

"Yeah, Bernie had this necklace for us and it was all very sweet but also sad. I mean, she knows about us kissing at New Year's but not about everything after."

"So what happened?"

"I told Tanner about the texts I saw."

"Did she explain?"

"No, and I didn't expect her to."

"That sucks. I thought it might be something absolving. Don't you want to know?"

Jessica thought about it. "I guess I do, but I still don't think it would change anything."

"Well, what did she say to you?

"She asked me if we could start over again...again."

"And so I guess that's it."

Jessica was hit again with that heaviness. "Yeah, I guess that's it."

It still didn't feel like it was over, but it had to be.

Chapter Fourteen

Jessica went back to her Airbnb with Bryce, and although he offered to hang out with her, she insisted he go meet one of his friends in Bushwick for a drag show. She wasn't up for anything like that. She just wanted to curl up on the couch and watch HGTV or *Great British Bake Off*. If she really had it her way, she'd be going to sleep, but her thoughts were all over the place. She was just about to try to lie in her bed when she heard her phone ring. It was Bernie. Part of her wanted not to answer, just because she was still unsure how to explain everything that had changed over the last few weeks. She decided she had to answer just based on the fact that she was getting married the next day and it could be anything.

"Hey, Bern."

"Hey, Jess, did I wake you?" She sounded nervous.

"I was up. What's up? You okay?" Now Jessica was feeling nervous. Was she getting cold feet? Looking for someone to talk her off the cliff? If she was calling Jessica, maybe she wanted to be talked out of it. Jessica wasn't likely to do that, not after everything.

"Yeah, yeah, I'm fine. I just needed to talk to you."

"Okay. What's up?" It was hard for Jessica to imagine what could be this important.

"I'm actually in your neighborhood. Can I come over?"

This was even more weird. Jessica shared her Airbnb info with her sister, but she couldn't imagine what was so important it needed to be said in person.

"Okay, sure, um, come on over."

A silence on the other end.

"Actually, I'm outside."

Jessica was shocked again. "I'll buzz you in."

She went to the door and she could see in the apartment camera that Bernie was at the walk-up entrance. She buzzed her up and waited, fully thrown off by her.

Bernie climbed the stairs and came to the doorway looking extremely stressed. Usually she would have hugged Jessica, so it was notable that she didn't. It felt pretty clear that something was wrong.

Jessica let her in, but she seemed to stay on the periphery of the room, almost as if she wasn't sure if she should really be there. This was not the way they had been recently. So much progress had been made and now she was acting like a stranger.

"I need to talk to you," Bernie said.

"Okay, sure. Why don't you sit down. Do you want anything to drink?"

She didn't sit. "I'm okay." She fidgeted nervously.

"What is it, Bern?"

"I spoke to Tanner tonight. She told me what happened and I'm just so... I'm so sorry, Jess. I've fucked everything up."

Jessica knew Bernie would feel bad about the texts, but "fucking everything up" seemed a bit intense.

"Look, Bern, I wasn't going to say anything till after the wedding, but yeah it hurt me that you've been keeping something from me."

"It's not just that," she said. "I fucked up a lot more than that. And I just can't let this happen again. And listen, Jess, you might hate me for what I'm going to say, but I want you to know I love you and I have been just so extremely happy that you've come back into my life and I was so scared to lose you. So just remember that when I tell you this."

Jessica felt like the floor was moving under her. "Okay, tell me."

Bernie took a deep breath. "I'm the reason everyone at school found out you were gay. I'm the person who told Kayla and she told enough people for it to spread."

Jessica tried to take in what her sister was saying. "I don't understand."

"It wasn't Tanner who outed you, it was me."

Jessica didn't believe that for a second. "Bern, that's impossible. I never told you. I only told her. She must have told you."

Bernie shook her head. "She didn't tell me. You were so withdrawn and you wouldn't talk to me. I knew you two were hanging out and I felt like I was losing you or something. So I read your journal. I was trying to figure out what I did or why you didn't like talking to me as much anymore. It was wrong on so many levels, but it's what I did. And then I saw in your journal that you had a crush on Tanner and that you thought you might be gay. I wanted to talk to you about it or something, but I couldn't tell Tanner because I didn't want to tell her that you were into her or anything. So I made the huge mistake of talking about what I read with Kayla."

Jessica couldn't believe what she was hearing. This was such a different situation.

"And then you know what happened next. Kayla told everyone."

"Why didn't you tell me the truth? Why didn't Tanner tell me it wasn't her?"

If possible, Bernie shrunk even smaller. "When it all happened, I was so scared you would hate me. I didn't know what to do. Then you just assumed it was Tanner, and she insisted she didn't do it, but you were so sure you didn't tell anyone else. I think she was just really confused by everything. I know now, from talking to her that she felt really guilty about not defending you more. She had so much anxiety back then about what people thought about her. She didn't think she could convince you and I think she just gave up. I didn't tell her it was me till years later. It was actually after Dad died. She was mad, but eventually she forgave me. I think at the time you weren't in her life, so she didn't say anything about telling you the truth. But when you both started being friends again, she asked and I begged her not to tell you. I wanted us to be close again and I just felt like if you knew you wouldn't connect with me. Then when she and you started getting closer, I felt like maybe it didn't matter anymore. When she texted me about telling you, I was just being a coward. Tanner has been such an amazing friend and she has taken this on for me for too long. The fact that all of this has totally ruined what you two have, I just can't live with it anymore."

Jessica listened to her sister with a thousand feelings running through her head.

"Jess, I'm so sorry for lying to you. I'm so sorry for telling Kayla. I can't even begin to tell you how ashamed I am for how I treated you. I wish I could give you some reason, something that explains what I did, but the truth was I was young and stupid and I just didn't think. And then when everyone was talking about you and you were withdrawing even more, all I was thinking about was myself and my reputation, and the pain I was causing you felt like something I couldn't fix."

Jessica didn't know what to say. There were so many things she was feeling. There were different parts of her that were having different reactions. The teen in her was hurt and betrayed by her sister. The adult in her was sad about all that was lost. There was another part of her that was hearing her sister and understanding. The truth was they weren't the same people anymore. There were so many things that were confusing when they were younger and she knew deep down that her sister was a good person who did a bad thing. She knew this wouldn't be something she'd get over easily, but she knew they were going to get through this. They were going to survive this.

"Bernie, I appreciate you telling me the truth."

Bernie looked at her with what was obvious embarrassment and shame. "I know this is selfish for me to ask, but do you think someday, maybe, you could forgive me? I would do anything to have you in my life."

Jessica made the decision in that moment. She reached for Bernie and hugged her. She could feel the tension in her shoulders. She squeezed her as hard as she could and she felt Bernie release the tension. She almost collapsed in Jessica's arms.

Once Jessica could sense that her sister had calmed down a bit, she pulled away and looked her in the eye.

"I'm sorry I made you feel like there was something you could do that I wouldn't forgive you for. I love you, and this really hurts, but you will always be my sister."

Bernie wiped her cheek. "I will spend my life making this up to you, Jess."

Jessica had more questions, but she was too emotionally spent from the whole situation. She needed to let this all settle in. What Bernie did and what this changed about Tanner. She initially was sure she couldn't forgive Tanner for lying to her, but she didn't expect this. She didn't expect the source of all her hatred for Tanner to be a misunderstanding.

It seemed Bernie was reading her mind because she said, "I know you ended things with Tanner, but I was hoping you would reconsider."

Jessica wasn't ready to figure out what this meant. Did she want to change her mind? Could she trust someone after years of resentment? There was so much to consider, to reconsider.

"I don't know, Bern. There's just so much that's happened."

Bernie nodded. "I know what you went through at school was hard. I mean, I've learned from the things you've opened up about in the last few months, and I think one of the worst things I did was ruin your friendship with Tanner. The truth is, when you two were getting closer, I was jealous. I wanted it to be me you wanted to talk to. I wanted it to be all of us. I didn't understand that there were things she might get that I didn't, and even when I read your journal I just wasn't able to see how different it is for you two. Seeing you together these past few months, it just made me so happy, like maybe something could be repaired."

This part was hard for Jessica to hear.

"And it wasn't just you, I don't think you know everything she's been through. Her anxiety in high school, her delaying going to college to help her sister raise her niece, then that site. I think she's been struggling for a long time and she could have used a different friend. She could have used you. Someone strong and decisive, but I got in the way of it. I think you both could have used each other in your lives."

"I don't know, Bern," Jessica said again. "High school was a long time ago. Who knows if we would have been friends at this point."

Bernie looked at her knowingly. "I know Tanner, and she wouldn't have let you go. Look at how long she stayed friends with Kayla, to her own detriment. She doesn't leave people behind unless they make it impossible. Honestly, I think both of us needed to be more intentional about who we hold on to. More like you."

Jessica sat on the couch, letting herself sink into it, hoping it would swallow her whole.

"I don't know how I feel about her. It's hard to just flip a switch and undo everything."

Bernie sat down next to her.

"Well, what about after the dress fitting? She told something happened between you two. I don't mean to be too explicit, and I definitely didn't want to hear the details, but based on what she said it seemed like there might have been a chance you two were going to get together?"

Jessica thought about that night. This was the first time she allowed herself to hope since that morning. "I think it's just really complicated."

"Do you have feelings for her?"

Jessica didn't have to consider her answer. "Yes."

"So then now that you know the truth, what's in your way?"

Jessica wasn't sure how to explain.

"I think I spent a long time not trusting Tanner. I don't know if I can switch my paranoia off just like that. And then there's her feelings. I rejected her pretty hard. Who knows if she even wants anything with me anymore."

Bernie looked at her with exasperation. "Please. That girl has been into you forever. She would not change her mind after twenty-four hours. Trust me, if you even blinked, she'd be outside your window with a boombox."

Jessica blushed at the thought.

"Just think about it, okay? She's amazing and so are you. It's kind of a no-brainer."

"I'll think about it," she responded.

Bernie held her hand. "I guess I should go. I'm getting married tomorrow!"

"Yes!" Jessica said. "Get out of here, you have to look good for Chris!"

They hugged and Bernie added "Thank you for not giving up on me."

"I love you," Jessica said as her sister left.

Jessica was left in what could only be described as a puddle of emotion.

❖

Jessica arrived at the Gotham Hall with Bryce on her arm having exactly zero hours of sleep the night before. After Bernie left, Jessica felt as if a bomb had gone off. Every feeling she had was suspect. At first, she was stunned. She decided the information didn't change anything. The fear remained, this time not of Tanner. The fear was that she couldn't trust herself in a relationship with Tanner. She was constantly triggered and reliving everything, it had been a roller coaster since Tanner came back in her life and she thought the best way to deal with it was still to shut it all down. But then she went through it all again, this time from the beginning. She considered what Bryce said to her the other day on their walk. Maybe she wasn't trusting of others anywhere in her life. Was Tanner being in her life such a bad thing? Maybe she hadn't been doing so well long before she came back in her life. Then she thought about what Bernie said. When Bernie said the part about how they both could have helped each other, how she felt she robbed them of someone they needed and maybe still needed.

There was something special about her chemistry with Tanner. She brought up new and different sides to her. And that's something Tanner said to her the day before, that Jessica made her brave. But they also hurt each other. They also hadn't been able to communicate easily basically ever. But then she thought about the times they worked together. The times they shared their lives, their dreams. New Year's when she got to see who Tanner really was, who her friends were. Their lives seemed to really match.

Jessica couldn't make sense of it. Was she scared? What was she so afraid of? There was the obvious—she was scared of being hurt. But it was more than that. That day when she told Tanner that she thought she might like girls, she had made a leap of faith. She was trying to let someone in, let someone close. From that day onward it felt like everyone was a disappointment. Everyone was going to leave or let her down and she would have to keep moving and never fully let herself settle her heart.

Even with Riley. Looking back, she wondered how much her fear played a role in the end of their relationship. Was it simply that Riley wasn't available and that Jessica didn't love her enough to move for her? Or was it that Jessica wasn't available in the way she needed to be to love like that? And then there was the issue with Tanner and the way she didn't always stick up for Jessica. Looking at the last six months, Jessica could see that the Tanner she knew when she was sixteen had changed. She was brave in so many ways. She stuck up for Jessica in her own way, and even more importantly, she stuck up for herself. But there was also a part of Jessica that felt like maybe it wasn't the most important thing anymore. Jessica wasn't a lonely, insecure kid anymore. She could take care of herself. Having someone who had a different temperament but who showed up in so many ways, who saw her, who knew her, was maybe more important at this point.

So by the time the sun came up, Jessica had made up her mind. Bryce came home eventually, and she told him what had happened with Bernie.

"I told you it was something! That girl didn't seem like the type, you know?"

Bryce was so easily converted to team Tanner that Jessica began to question if he ever really was suspicious of her. The wedding ceremony began in the afternoon. Jessica was so nervous by the time four p.m. came around. She knew that her focus needed to be on her sister, but she was having a hard time just knowing Tanner would be there and there was so much she wanted to say to her. There was another fear—was it too late? How many ways had Jessica, to use Tanner's words, fallen short? The way she treated her, the way she ignored her, the way she hazed her the last few months, and finally leaving her in that hotel room. Jessica could see now, even with the things she didn't understand, she had treated Tanner awfully. Tanner had worn her heart on her sleeve for a long time and Jessica had basically kicked her in the teeth. She knew that if Tanner changed her mind, she would be well within her rights.

Jessica came into the hall with Bryce trying not to look like she was frantically searching for someone. Bryce let her know very quickly that she had not been successful. The wedding planner approached her at about four thirty p.m.—fifteen minutes before the ceremony was going to start—to get her to the back with the other bridesmaids. Of course, she learned her role in the wedding via email a few weeks ago. She was going to walk down the aisle with one of Chris's groomspeople and stand next to Tanner, who would be next to her sister during the ceremony.

Jessica followed the planner to the back room. The moment she spotted Tanner she was hit with the most intense experience of nerves she had ever had in her life. And over the months she had been nervous so many times around Tanner. Tanner watched her approach and gave her a small smile. She didn't look like she had slept much either. Jessica wanted to talk to her, but it wasn't the right time. The wedding planner was going back over the instructions and Jessica, Tanner, Alex, and Kayla all had specific directives. Once they were done, they got some time to chat with the person they were walking down the aisle with. Jessica was matched with Chris's best friend while Tanner was matched with one of his brothers. Jessica tried to find an excuse to leave her small talk and interrupt Tanner, but there wasn't a lot of time and she had so much she needed to say. They all assembled in a line, knowing the ceremony was going to start.

Jessica was behind Tanner, close in a way that made her heart jump. Tanner didn't look back, but she could see the tension in her shoulders, the nervousness she was clearly experiencing. It could have been the ceremony, but it also could have been having Jessica be so close.

The music started, a piano version of "Yellow" by Coldplay. The doors opened and Tanner walked down the aisle. Jessica wasn't able to see her face. She was next. She successfully navigated the footing she'd been instructed on and followed Tanner to the front of the room, passing all of the guests. When she got to the front, her eyes locked with Tanner and she literally stopped walking. She didn't know how long she froze like that, but Tanner was staring back at her, looking at her with feelings she could only guess. Finally, Tanner indicated to her that she froze. Embarrassed, Jessica moved to her spot next to Tanner. She couldn't help stealing glances as the other members of the wedding party came down the aisle. Then the music changed to "Canon in D."

Bernie came through the doors and walked toward Chris, who was waiting with the rest of them. Bernie looked gorgeous and most of all, she looked happy. Then, to Jessica's surprise, she noticed that Chris was wiping his eyes. He was crying. This was not something Jessica expected. He was clearly floored by how beautiful his wife looked. Once Bernie got to him, she reached for his hand, and Jessica saw that even just that touch had put him at ease. Jessica looked at Tanner again. She was watching Bernie with tears in her eyes as well. All Jessica could think was how much she wanted to be the person who could bring comfort to Tanner just by holding her hand.

The ceremony was simple and although they did their own vows, they were short and sweet. Chris kissed Bernie and everyone stood up and clapped as they went back down the aisle together. Tanner hadn't moved. Alex and Kayla were heading toward the back to do a quick wardrobe adjustment before the reception, but Tanner seemed like she wasn't ready. Jessica didn't leave either. She was so touched by what had just happened. Not the procession or the rituals, she could have done without all the weird rules that she didn't understand. She was touched by watching her sister and Chris look at each other and promise to take care of each other. Who knows how long things last, she thought, but promising to take care of each other was a pretty special thing.

"It was beautiful, wasn't it?" Jessica asked Tanner when they were the only two left.

Tanner wiped her tears again. "Yeah, it was. Kind of overwhelming."

Jessica was searching for the words, but Tanner began to move toward the room Alex and Kayla went back to. "Excuse me."

It made sense that she didn't want to chat. How much rejection could one person endure? Jessica let her go, not because she wanted to, but because she couldn't find the words. She needed to find a way to say what she needed to say. Instead of going back with the other bridesmaids, she went out to the reception. She wanted to talk to Bryce. She felt like she really only had one chance to get this right.

❖

The bride and groom joined the reception, and everyone clapped. Jessica hadn't seen Tanner since the ceremony, but she had to be somewhere. Bernie was walking around, greeting all her guests and she and Chris were smiling from ear to ear, looking moony at each other. When Bernie got to her, she gave her the biggest hug. Jessica knew that the hug communicated so much more than just a greeting. They had been through a lot in the last twenty-four hours. Jessica wasn't fully healed, but she loved her sister, and she needed her to know that.

"You look beautiful, Bern."

"So do you!" she said, and Jessica could already see her misty eyes.

"I love you."

"I love you too, Jess." They held hands for a moment and just took in all that they had been through.

"I wish Dad was here." Jessica didn't know where the sentiment came from, but it was the truth, and she wanted to start talking about him with Bernie.

"I wish he was too. Wait till you hear the DJ. It's like fifty percent Celine Dion. He would have loved it."

Jessica laughed. That sounded completely awful.

"I don't know if this is helpful, but," Bernie said, "Tanner is out front. She said she needed some air. Seemed like something you might want to know." Bernie gave her a wink and then headed toward their mom and their other guests. Jessica was very interested in that information. She made sure to hug Chris and tell him how excited she was to have him in her life. She also made sure Bryce was occupied, and then she headed to the front to find Tanner.

❖

Jessica found Tanner on the sprawling steps of Gotham Hall. She looked serene. Jessica couldn't think of a better opportunity. They were alone and she had the time to say what she needed to say.

Tanner turned when she heard Jessica approach.

"I'm sorry, I didn't know you'd be out here," Tanner said. It was so ridiculous that she would think she needed to apologize for disturbing Jessica. Jessica was clearly the one doing the disturbing.

"Bernie told me you were out here. I was hoping we could talk."

Tanner looked at her with exhaustion. "Jessica, I'm barely holding it together. I'm not sure how many more of these talks I can take."

That was fair.

"How about this, I'll talk. All you have to do is listen."

Tanner nodded. She obviously didn't quite have the energy to keep her spirits up, but she was listening and that was something.

"Tanner, I have spent my whole life feeling so alone. I push everything good away, and even when things are good for me, I protect myself first. These past six months are a perfect example. Every feeling I had, every good thing you brought into my life,

I pushed away. You asked me yesterday if we could start over again, and I said I couldn't. But the truth was, even when I tried multiple times over the last few months, I never really succeeded. I wanted so much to be seen as a stronger person than I was when I was younger, but I never considered for a second that you could change too. When I think about how stubborn I've been, how closed off I've been, I just can't imagine what that did to you. Tanner, I made a mistake. I've made so many mistakes with you. You said I made you brave, well you make me brave. And kind and loyal. You make me accept the complexities of people. You helped me reconnect with my sister, you challenged my judginess, and the truth is I have been in love with you for a very long time. Even when I thought I hated you, it's hard to know what was hate and what was just the inside out love I couldn't let go of."

Tanner was looking at Jessica now with what could only be shock. She definitely thought this conversation was going to go the opposite way.

"Bernie explained that she was who told Kayla and told the school. I'm so sorry I didn't believe you when you said you didn't tell. I wasn't in a place then to understand everything that I was going through, but I'm older now and I think that we were meant to take care of each other. I think the way you kept Bernie's secret once you found out it was her was you taking care of her. You cared more about her being able to have a relationship with me than about absolving yourself. I'm still upset I wasn't told the truth, but I can see what kind of person you are, and she is lucky to have you. I would be lucky to have you in my life, if you would still have me."

Tanner let out a relieved laugh. She was smiling in a way Jessica hadn't seen since their night together in New York.

"Of course I still want you in my life."

Jessica also smiled. She was feeling the tight coil of anxiety in her chest loosening as well.

"Okay, so maybe we could start over again again again? What do you think?" It was a joke, and Tanner responded by shoving Jessica lightly. But once Tanner was close enough, Jessica took her face in her hands and kissed her. The feeling was staggering. They fell into each other so easily, as if they had been holding themselves back the whole time, which they probably were. Jessica pulled away and looked into Tanner's eyes.

Tanner asked next, "So just to be clear, you want to be friends now?"

Jessica laughed. "I do, I want to be friends. Friends plus everything else..."

"Define everything else?" she said playfully.

"Well, I know there were some promises made at the Orchard Hotel that I still need to cash in on, but first, I want to go back into the wedding and I want to dance with you all night. Then after dancing and whatever else the night holds, I want to hang with you in DC. Maybe go to dinner? Maybe go to a hundred dinners? How does that sound?"

Tanner kissed her, showing her exactly how it sounded.

"I think that sounds perfect." Tanner laced her hand in Jessica's and they both headed back inside. Jessica decided as she watched Bernie leave at the end of the night, that she kind of liked weddings after all.

About the Author

Spencer Greene is a fiction writer who lives in Washington, DC. When she's not writing, she's making music or riding her bike around the city. She is an avid reader and loves queer media, especially the bad stuff.

Books Available from Bold Strokes Books

Blood Rage by Illeandra Young. A stolen artifact, a family in the dark, an entire city on edge. Can SPEAR agent Danika Karson juggle all three over a weekend with the "in-laws," while an unknown, malevolent entity lies in wait upon her very skin? (978-1-63679-539-3)

Ghost Town by R.E. Ward. Blair Wyndon and Leif Henderson are set to prove ghosts exist when the mystery suddenly turns deadly. Someone or something else is in Masonville, and if they don't find a way to escape, they might never leave. (978-1-63679-523-2)

Good Christian Girls by Elizabeth Bradshaw. In this heartfelt coming of age lesbian romance, Lacey and Jo help each other untangle who they are from who everyone says they're supposed to be. (978-1-63679-555-3)

Guide Us Home by CF Frizzell and Jesse J. Thoma. When acquisition of an abandoned lighthouse pits ambitious competitors Nancy and Sam against each other, it takes a WWII tale of two brave women to make them see the light. (978-1-63679-533-1)

Lost Harbor by Kimberly Cooper Griffin. For Alice and Bridget's love to survive, they must find a way to reconcile the most important passions in their lives—devotion to the church and each other. (978-1-63679-463-1)

Never a Bridesmaid by Spencer Greene. As her sister's wedding gets closer, Jessica finds that her hatred for the maid of honor is a bit more complicated than she thought. Could it be something more than hatred? (978-1-63679-559-1)

The Rewind by Nicole Stiling. For police detective Cami Lyons and crime reporter Alicia Flynn, some choices break hearts. Others leave a body count. (978-1-63679-572-0)

Turning Point by Cathy Dunnell. When Asha and her former high school bully Jody struggle to deny their growing attraction, can they move forward without going back? (978-1-63679-549-2)

When Tomorrow Comes by D. Jackson Leigh. Teague Maxwell, convinced she will die before she turns 41, hires animal rescue owner Baye Cobb to rehome her extensive menagerie. (978-1-63679-557-7)

You Had Me at Merlot by Melissa Brayden. Leighton and Jamie have all the ingredients to turn their attraction into love, but it's a recipe for disaster. (978-1-63679-543-0)

All Things Beautiful by Alaina Erdell. Casey Norford only planned to learn to paint like her mentor, Leighton Vaughn, not sleep with her. (978-1-63679-479-2)

Appalachian Awakening by Nance Sparks. The more Amber's and Leslie's paths cross, the more this hike of a lifetime begins to look like a love of a lifetime. (978-1-63679-527-0)

Dreamer by Kris Bryant. When life seems to be too good to be true and love is within reach, Sawyer and Macey discover the truth about the town of Ladybug Junction, and the cold light of reality tests the hearts of these dreamers. (978-1-63679-378-8)

Eyes on Her by Eden Darry. When increasingly violent acts of sabotage threaten to derail the opening of her glamping business, Callie Pope is sure her ex, Jules, has something to do with it. But Jules is dead...isn't she? (978-1-63679-214-9)

Head Over Heelflip by Sander Santiago. To secure the biggest prizes at the Colorado Amateur Street Sports Tour, Thomas Jefferson will do almost anything, even marrying his best friend and crush—Arturo "Uno" Ortiz. (978-1-63679-489-1)

Letters from Sarah by Joy Argento. A simple mistake brought them together, but Sarah must release past love to create a future with Lindsey she never dreamed possible. (978-1-63679-509-6)

Lost in the Wild by Kadyan. When their plane crash-lands, Allison and Mike face hunger, cold, a terrifying encounter with a bear, and feelings for each other neither expects. (978-1-63679-545-4)

Not Just Friends by Jordan Meadows. A tragedy leaves Jen struggling to figure out who she is and what is important to her. (978-1-63679-517-1)

Of Auras and Shadows by Jennifer Karter. Eryn and Rina's unexpected love may be exactly what the Community needs to heal the rot that comes not from the fetid Dark Lands that surround the Community but from within. (978-1-63679-541-6)

The Secret Duchess by Jane Walsh. A determined widow defies a duke and falls in love with a fashionable spinster in a fight for her rightful home. (978-1-63679-519-5)

Winter's Spell by Ursula Klein. When former college roommates reunite at a wedding in Provincetown, sparks fly, but can they find true love when evil sirens and trickster mermaids get in the way? (978-1-63679-503-4)

Coasting and Crashing by Ana Hartnett Reichardt. Life comes easy to Emma Wilson until Lake Palmer shows up at Alder University and derails her every plan. (978-1-63679-511-9)

Every Beat of Her Heart by KC Richardson. Piper and Gillian have their own fears about falling in love, but will they be able to overcome those feelings once they learn each other's secrets? (978-1-63679-515-7)

Grave Consequences by Sandra Barret. A decade after necromancy became licensed and legalized, can Tamar and Maddy overcome the lingering prejudice against their kind and their growing attraction to each other to uncover a plot that threatens both their lives? (978-1-63679-467-9)

Haunted by Myth by Barbara Ann Wright. When ghost-hunter Chloe seeks an answer to the current spectral epidemic, all clues point to one very famous face: Helen of Troy, whose motives are more complicated than history suggests and whose charms few can resist. (978-1-63679-461-7)

Invisible by Anna Larner. When medical school dropout Phoebe Frink falls for the shy costume shop assistant Violet Unwin, everything about their love feels certain, but can the same be said about their future? (978-1-63679-469-3)

Like They Do in the Movies by Nan Campbell. Celebrity gossip writer Fran Underhill becomes Chelsea Cartwright's personal assistant with the aim of taking the popular actress down, but neither of them anticipates the clash of their attraction. (978-1-63679-525-6)

Limelight by Gun Brooke. Liberty Bell and Palmer Elliston loathe each other. They clash every week on the hottest new TV show, until Liberty starts to sing and the impossible happens. (978-1-63679-192-0)

Playing with Matches by Georgia Beers. To help save Cori's store and help Liz survive her ex's wedding they strike a deal: a fake relationship, but just for one week. There's no way this will turn into the real deal. (978-1-63679-507-2)

The Memories of Marlie Rose by Morgan Lee Miller. Broadway legend Marlie Rose undergoes a procedure to erase all of her unwanted memories, but as she starts regretting her decision, she discovers that the only person who could help is the love she's trying to forget. (978-1-63679-347-4)

The Murders at Sugar Mill Farm by Ronica Black. A serial killer is on the loose in southern Louisiana and it's up to three women to solve the case while carefully dancing around feelings for each other. (978-1-63679-455-6)

Fire in the Sky by Radclyffe and Julie Cannon. Two women from different worlds have nothing in common and every reason to wish they'd never met—except for the attraction neither can deny. (978-1-63679-573-7)

A Talent Ignited by Suzanne Lenoir. When Evelyne is abducted and Annika believes she has been abandoned, they must risk everything to find each other again. (978-1-63679-483-9)

An Atlas to Forever by Krystina Rivers. Can Atlas, a difficult dog Ellie inherits after the death of her best friend, help the busy hopeless romantic find forever love with commitment-phobic animal behaviorist Hayden Brandt? (978-1-63679-451-8)

Bait and Witch by Clifford Mae Henderson. When Zeddi gets an unexpected inheritance from her client Mags, she discovers that Mags served as high priestess to a dwindling coven of old witches—who are positive that Mags was murdered. Zeddi owes it to her to uncover the truth. (978-1-63679-535-5)

Buried Secrets by Sheri Lewis Wohl. Tuesday and Addie, along with Tuesday's dog, Tripper, struggle to solve a twenty-five-year-old mystery while searching for love and redemption along the way. (978-1-63679-396-2)

Come Find Me in the Midnight Sun by Bailey Bridgewater. In Alaska, disappearing is the easy part. When two men go missing, state trooper Louisa Linebach must solve the case, and when she thinks she's coming close, she's wrong. (978-1-63679-566-9)

Death on the Water by CJ Birch. The Ocean Summit's authorities have ruled a death on board its inaugural cruise as a suicide, but Claire suspects murder and with the help of Assistant Cruise Director Moira, Claire conducts her own investigation. (978-1-63679-497-6)

Living For You by Jenny Frame. Can Sera Debrek face real and personal demons to help save the world from darkness and open her heart to love? (978-1-63679-491-4)

Mississippi River Mischief by Greg Herren. When a politician turns up dead and Scotty's client is the most obvious suspect, Scotty and his friends set out to prove his client's innocence. (978-1-63679-353-5)

Ride with Me by Jenna Jarvis. When Lucy's vacation to find herself becomes Emma's chance to remember herself, they realize that everything they're looking for might already be sitting right next to them—if they're willing to reach for it. (978-1-63679-499-0)

Whiskey and Wine by Kelly and Tana Fireside. Winemaker Tessa Williams and sex toy shop owner Lace Reynolds are both used to taking risks, but will they be willing to put their friendship on the line if it gives them a shot at finding forever love? (978-1-63679-531-7)